I0784666

Will Lillibridge

Where the Trail Divides

OK Publishing 2021

Will Lillibridge
Where the Trail Divides

The Original Book Behind the Hollywood Movie: An Unusual and Powerful Tale of Friendship between a Native Indian Boy and a Rancher

Published by
MUSAICUM
Books

- Advanced Digital Solutions & High-Quality book Formatting -

musaicumbooks@okpublishing.info

2021 OK Publishing

ISBN 978-80-272-7575-5

Contents

Chapter I
Presentiment

The man was short and fat, and greasy above the dark beard line. In addition, he was bowlegged as a greyhound, and just now he moved with a limp as though very footsore. His coarse blue flannel shirt, open at the throat, exposed a broad hairy chest that rose and fell mightily with the effort he was making. And therein lay the mystery. The sun was hot-with the heat of a cloudless August sun at one o'clock of the afternoon. The country he was traversing was wild, unbroken-uninhabited apparently of man or of beast. Far to his left, just visible through the dancing heat rays, indistinct as a mirage, was a curling fringe of green trees. To his right, behind him, ahead of him was not a tree nor a shrub nor a rock the height of a man's head; only ungrazed, yellowish-green sun-dried prairie grass. The silence was complete. Not even a breath of wind rustled the grass; yet ever and anon the man paused glanced back the way he had come, listened, his throat throbbing with the effort of repressed breathing, in obvious expectation of a sound he did not hear; then, for the time relieved, forged ahead afresh, one hand gripping the butt of an old Springfield rifle slung over his shoulder, the other, big, unclean, sunbrowned, swinging like a pendulum at his side.

Ludicrous, unqualifiedly, the figure would have been in civilisation, humorous as a clown in a circus; but seeing it here, solitary, exotic, no observer would have laughed. Fear, mortal dogging fear, impersonate, supreme, was in every look, every action. Somewhere back of that curved line where met the earth and sky, lurked death. Nothing else would have been adequate to arouse this phlegmatic human as he was now aroused. The sweat oozed from his thick neck in streams and dripped drop by drop from the month-old stubble which covered his chin, but apparently he never noticed it. Now and then he attempted to moisten his lips; but his tongue was dry as powder, and they closed again, parched as before.

No road nor trail, nor the semblance of a trail, marked the way he was going; the hazy green fringe far to the east was his only landmark; yet as hour after hour went by and the sun sank lower and lower he never halted, never seemed in doubt as to his destination. The country was growing more rolling now, almost hilly, and he approached each rise cautiously, vigilantly. Once, almost at his feet a covey of frightened prairie chickens sprang a-wing, and at the unexpected sound he dropped like a stone in his tracks, all but concealing himself in the tall grass; then, reassured, he was up again, plodding doggedly, ceaselessly on.

It was after sundown when he paused; and then only from absolute physical inability to go farther. Outraged nature had at last rebelled, and not even fear could suffice longer to stimulate him. The grass was wet with dew, and prone on his knees he moistened his lips therefrom as drinks many another of the fauna of the prairie. Then, flat on his back, not sleeping, but very wide awake, very watchful, he lay awaiting the return of strength. Upon the fringe of hair beneath the brim of his hat the sweat slowly dried; then, as the dew gathered thicker and thicker, dampened afresh. Far to the east, where during the day had appeared the fringe of green, the sky lightened, almost brightened; until at last, like a curious face, the full moon, peeping above the horizon, lit up the surface of prairie.

At last-and ere this the moon was well in the sky-the man arose, stretched his stiffened muscles profanely-before he had not spoken a syllable-listened a moment almost involuntarily, sent a swift, searching glance all about; then moved ahead, straight south, at the old relentless pace.

The lone ambassador from the tiny settlement of Sioux Falls vacillated between vexation and solicitude.

"For the last time I tell you; we're going whether you do or not," he announced in ultimatum.

Samuel Rowland, large, double-chinned, distinctly florid, folded his arms across his chest with an air of finality.

"And I repeat, I'm not going. I'm much obliged to you for the warning. I know your intentions are good, but you people are afraid of your own shadows. I know as well as you do that there are Indians in this part of the world, some odd thousands of them between here and the Hills, but they were here when I came and when you came, and we knew they were here. You expect to hear from a Dane when you buy tickets to 'Hamlet,' don't you?"

The other made a motion of annoyance.

"If you imagine this is a time for juggling similes," he returned swiftly, "you're making the mistake of your life. If you were alone, Rowland, I'd leave you here to take your medicine without another word; but I've a wife, too, and I thank the Lord she's down in Sioux City where Mrs. Rowland and the kid should be, and for her sake —"

"I beg your pardon."

The visitor started swiftly to leave, then as suddenly turned back.

"Good God, man!" he blazed; "are you plumb daft to stickle for little niceties now? I tell you I just helped to pick up Judge Amidon and his son, murdered in their own hayfield not three miles from here, the boy as full of arrows as a cushion of pins. This isn't ancient history, man, but took place this very day. It's Indian massacre, and at our own throats. The boys are down below the falls getting ready to go right now. By night there won't be another white man or woman within twenty-five miles of you. It's deliberate suicide to stand here arguing. If you will stay yourself, at least send away Mrs. Rowland and the girl. I'll take care of them myself and bring them back when the government sends some soldiers here, as it's bound to do soon. Listen to reason, man. Your claim won't run away; and if someone should jump it there's another just as good alongside. Pack up and come on."

Of a sudden, rough pioneer as he was, his hat came off and the tone of vexation left his voice. Another actor, a woman, had appeared upon the scene.

"You know what I'm talking about, Mrs. Rowland," he digressed. "Take my advice and come along. I'll never forgive myself if we leave you behind."

"You really think there's danger, Mr. Brown?" she asked unemotionally.

"Danger!" In pure impotence of language the other stared. "Danger, with Heaven knows how many hostile Sioux on the trail! Is it possible you two don't realise things as they are?"

"Yes, I think we realise all right," tolerantly. "I know the Tetons are hostile; they couldn't well be otherwise. Any of us would rebel if we were hustled away into a corner like naughty little boys, as they are; but actual danger —" The woman threw a comprehensive, almost amused glance at the big man, her husband. "We've been here almost two years now; long before you and the others came. Half the hunters who pass this way stop here. It wasn't a month ago that a party of Yanktons left a whole antelope. You ought to see Baby Bess shake hands with some of those wrinkled old bucks. Danger! We're safer here than we would be in Sioux City."

"But there's been massacre already, I tell you," exploded the other. "I don't merely surmise it. I saw it with my own eyes."

"There must have been some personal reason then." Mrs. Rowland glanced at the restless, excited speaker analytically, almost superciliously. "Indians are like white people. They have their loves and hates the same as all the rest of us. Sam and I ran once before when everyone was going, and when we got back not a thing had been touched; but the weeds had choked our corn and the rabbits eaten up our garden. We've been good to the Indians, and they appreciate it."

A moment Brown hesitated impotently; then of a sudden he came forward swiftly and extended his hand, first to one and then to the other.

"Good-bye, then," he halted. "I can't take you by force, and it's pure madness to stay here longer." Baby Elizabeth, a big-eyed, solemn-faced mite of humanity, had come up now and stood staring the stranger silently from the side of her mother's skirts. "I hope for the best, but before God I never expect to see any of you again."

"Oh, we'll see you in the fall all right-when you return," commented Rowland easily; but the other made no reply, and without a backward glance started at a rapid jog trot for the tiny settlement on the river two miles away.

Behind him, impassive-faced Rowland stood watching the departing frontiersman steadily, the pouches beneath his eyes accentuated by the tightened lids.

"I don't believe there's a bit more danger here now than there ever was," he commented; "but there's certainly an unusual disturbance somewhere. I don't take any stock in the people down at the settlement leaving-they'd go if they heard a coyote whistle; but Brown tells me there've been three different trappers from Big Stone gone through south in the last week, and when they leave it means something. If you say the word we'll leave everything and go yet." "If we do we'll never come back."

"Not necessarily."

"Yes. I'm either afraid of these red people or else I'm not. We went before because the others went. If we left now it would be different. We'd be tortured day and night if we really feared-what happens now and then to some. We came here with our eyes wide open. We can't start again in civilisation. We're too old, and there's the past —"

"You still blame me?"

"No; but we've chosen. Whatever comes, we'll stay." She turned toward the rough log shanty unemotionally.

"Come, let's forget it. Dinner's waiting and baby's hungry."

A moment Rowland hesitated, then he, too, followed.

"Yes, let's forget it," he echoed slowly.

"Well, in Heaven's name!" Rowland's great bulk was upon its feet, one hand upon the ever-ready revolver at his hip, the dishes on the rough pine dining table clattering with the suddenness of his withdrawal. "Who are you, man, and what's the trouble? Speak up —"

The dishevelled intruder within the narrow doorway glanced about the interior of the single room with bloodshot eyes.

His great mouth was a bit open and his swollen tongue all but protruded.

"Water!" The word was scarce above a whisper.

"But who are you?"

"Water!" fiercely, insistently.

Of a sudden he spied a wooden pail upon a shelf in the corner, and without invitation, almost as a wild beast springs, he made for it,

grasped the big tin dipper in both hands; drank measure after measure, the overflow trickling down his bare throat and dripping onto the sanded floor.

"God, that's good!" he voiced. "Good, good!"

After that first involuntary movement Rowland did not stir; but at his side the woman had risen, and behind her, peering around the fortress of her skirts as when before she had argued with Frontiersman Brown, stood the little wide-eyed girl, type of the repressed frontier child.

Back to them came the stranger, his great jowl working unconsciously.

"You are Sam Rowland?" he enunciated thickly,

"Yes."

"The settlement hasn't broken up then?"

"Why do you ask?"

"Is it possible that you don't know, that they don't know?" Involuntarily he seized his host by the arm. "I've heard of you; you live two miles out. We've no time to lose. Come, don't stop to save anything."

Rowland straightened. The other smelled evilly of perspiration.

"Come where? Who are you anyway, and what's the matter? Talk so I can understand you."

"You don't know that the Santees are on the 'big trail'? of the massacre along the Minnesota River?"

"I know nothing. Once more, who are you?"

"Who am I? What does it matter? My name is Hans Mueller. I'm a trapper." Of a sudden he drew back, inspecting his impassive questioner doubtfully, almost unbelievingly. "But come. I'll tell you along the way. You mustn't be here an hour longer. I saw their signal smokes this very morning. They're murdering everyone-men, women, and children. It's Little Crow who started it, and God knows how many settlers they've killed. They chased me for hours, but I had a good horse. It only gave out yesterday; and since then-But come. It's suicide to chatter like this." He turned insistently toward the door. "They may be here any minute."

Rowland and his wife looked at each other. Neither spoke a word; but at last the woman shook her head slowly.

Hans Mueller shifted restlessly.

"Hurry, I tell you," he insisted.

Rowland sat down again deliberately, his heavy double chin folding over his soft flannel shirt.

"Where are you going?" he temporised with almost a shade of amusement.

"Going!" In his unbelief the German's protruding eyes seemed almost to roll from his face. "To the settlement, of course."

"There is no settlement."

"What?"

Rowland repeated his statement impassively.

"They've-gone?" The tongue had grown suddenly thick again.

"I said so." The look of pity had altered, become almost of scorn.

For a half minute there was silence, inactivity, while despite tan and dirt and perspiration the cheeks of Hans Mueller whitened. The same expression of terror, hopeless, dominant, all but insane, that had been with him alone out on the prairie returned, augmented. Heedless of appearances, all but unconscious of the presence of spectators, he glanced about the single room like a beaten rabbit with the hounds close on its trail. No avenue of hiding suggested itself, no possible hope of protection. The cold perspiration broke out afresh on his forehead, at the roots of his hair, and in absent impotency he mopped it away with the back of a fat, grimy hand.

In pity motherly Mrs. Rowland returned to her seat, indicated another vacant beside the board.

"You'd best sit down and eat a bit," she invited. "You must be hungry as a coyote."

"Eat, now?" Swiftly, almost fiercely, the old terror-restless mood returned. "God Almighty couldn't keep me here longer." He started shuffling for the door. "Stay here and be scalped, if you think I lie. We're corpses, all of us, but I'll not be caught like a beaver in a trap." Again he halted jerkily. "Which way did they go!"

Lower and lower sank Rowland's great chin onto his breast.

"They separated," impassively. "Part went south to Sioux City; part west toward Yankton." Involuntarily his lips pursed in the inevitable contempt of a strong man for one hopelessly weak. "You'd better take a lunch along. It's something of a journey to either place."

Swift as the suggestion, Mrs. Rowland, with the spontaneous hospitality of the frontier, was upon her feet. Into a quaint Indian basket of coloured rushes went a roast grouse, barely touched, from the table. A loaf of bread followed: a bottle of water from the wooden pail in the corner. "You're welcome, friend," she proffered.

Hans Mueller hesitated, accepted. A swift moisture dimmed his eyes.

"Thanks, lady," he halted. "You're good people, anyway. I'm sorry —" He lifted his battered hat, shuffled anew toward the doorway. "Good-bye."

Impassive as before, Rowland returned to his neglected dinner.

"No wonder the Sioux play us whites for cowards, and think we'll run at sight of them," he commented.

Mrs. Rowland, standing motionless in the single exit through which Mueller had gone, did not answer.

"Better come and finish, Margaret," suggested her husband.

Again there was no answer, and Rowland, after eating a few mouthfuls, pushed back his chair. Even then she did not speak, and, rising, the man made his way across the room to put an arm with rough affection around his wife's waist.

"Are you, too, scared at last?" he voiced gently.

The woman turned swiftly and, in action almost unbelievable after her former unemotional certainty, dropped her head to his shoulder.

"Yes, I think I am a bit, Sam. For baby's sake I wish we'd gone too; but now," —her arms crept around his neck, closed, —"but now-now it's too late!"

For a long minute, and another, the man did not stir but involuntarily his arms had tightened until, had she wished, the woman could not have turned. He had been looking absently out the door, south over the rolling country leading to the deserted settlement.

In the distance, perhaps a quarter of a mile away, Hans Mueller was still in sight, skirting the base of a sharp incline. Through the trembling heat waves he seemed a mere moving dark spot; like an ant or a spider on its zigzag journey. The grass at the base of the rise was rank and heavy, reaching almost to the waist of the moving figure. Rowland watched it all absently, meditatively; as he would have watched the movement of a coyote or a prairie owl, for the simple reason that it was the only visible object endowed with life, and instinctively life responds to life. The words of his wife just spoken, "It is too late," with the revelation they bore, were echoing in his brain. For the first time, to his mind came a vague unformed suggestion, not of fear, but near akin, as to this lonely prairie wilderness, and the red man its child. In a hazy way came the question whether after all it were not foolhardy to remain here now, to dare that invisible, intangible something before which, almost in panic, the others had fled. To be sure, precedent was with him, logic; but-of a sudden-but a minute had passed-his arms tightened; involuntarily he held his breath. Hans Mueller had been moving on and on; another half minute and he would have been behind the base of the hill out of sight; when, as from the turf at one's feet there springs a-wing a covey of prairie grouse, from the tall grass about the retreating figure there leaped forth a swarm of other similar dark figures: a dozen, a score-in front, behind, all about. Apparently from mother earth herself they had come, autochthonous. Almost unbelieving, the spectator blinked his eyes; then, as came swift understanding, instinctively he shielded the woman in his arms from the sight, from the knowledge. Not a sound came to his ears from over the prairie: not a single call for help. That black swarm simply arose, there was a brief, sharp struggle, almost fantastic through the curling heat waves; then one and all, the original dark figure, the score of others, disappeare d —as suddenly as though the earth from which they came had swallowed them up. Look as he might, the spectator could catch no glimpse of a moving object, except the green-brown grass carpet glistening under the afternoon sun.

Yet a moment longer the man stood so; then, his own face as pale as had been that of coward Hans Mueller, he leaned against the lintel of the door.

"Yes, we're too late now, Margaret," he echoed.

Chapter II
Fulfilment

The log cabin of Settler Rowland, as a landmark, stood forth. Barred it was-the white of barked cotton-wood timber alternating with the brown of earth that filled the spaces between-like the longitudinal stripes of a prairie gopher or on the back of a bob-white. Long wiry slough grass, razor-sharp as to blades, pungent under rain, weighted by squares of tough, native sod, thatched the roof. Sole example of the handiwork of man, it crowned one of the innumerable rises, too low to be dignified by the name of hill, that stretched from sky to sky like the miniature waves on the surface of a shallow lake. Back of it, stretching northward, a vivid green blot, lay a field of sod corn: the ears already formed, the ground whitened from the lavishly scattered pollen of the frayed tassels. In the dooryard itself was a dug well with a mound of weed-covered clay by its side and a bucket hanging from a pulley over its mouth. It was deep, for on this upland water was far beneath the surface, and midway of its depth, a frontier refrigerator reached by a rope ladder, was a narrow chamber in which Margaret Rowland kept her meats fresh, often for a week at a time. For another purpose as well it was used: a big basket with a patchwork quilt and a pillow marking the spot where Baby Rowland, with the summer heat all about, slept away the long, sultry afternoons.

Otherwise not an excrescence marred the face of nature. The single horse Rowland owned, useless now while his crop matured, was breaking sod far to the west on the bank of the Jim River. Not a live thing other than human moved about the place. With them into this land of silence had come a mongrel collie. For a solitary month he had stood guard; then one night, somewhere in the distance, in the east where flowed the Big Sioux, had sounded the long-drawn-out cry of a timber wolf, alternately nearer and more remote, again and again. With the coming of morning the collie was gone. Whether dead or answering the call of the wild they never knew, nor ever filled his place.

Lonely, isolated as the place itself, was Sam Rowland that afternoon of late August. Silent as a mute was he as to what he had seen; elaborately careful likewise to carry out the family programme as usual.

"Sleepy, kid?" he queried when dinner was over.

Baby Bess, taciturn, sun-browned autocrat, nodded silent corroboration.

"Come, then," and, willing horse, the big man got clumsily to all fours and, prancing ponderously, drew up at her side.

"Hang tight," he admonished and, his wife smiling from the doorway as only a mother can smile, ambled away through the sun and the dust; climbed slowly, the tiny brown arms clasped tightly about his neck, down the ladder to the retreat, adjusted the pillow and the patchwork quilt with a deftness born of experience.

"Go to sleepy, kid," he directed.

"Sing me to sleep, daddy," commanded the autocrat.

"Sing! I can't sing, kid."

"Yes, you can. Sing 'Nellie Gray.'"

"Too hot, girlie. My breath's all gone. Go to sleep."

"Please, papa; pretty please!"

The man succumbed, as he knew from the first he would do, braced himself in the aperture, and sang the one verse that he knew of the song again and again-his voice rough and unmusical as that of a crow, echoing and re-echoing in the narrow space-bent over at last, touched his bearded lips softly to the winsome, motionless brown face, climbed, an irresistible catch in his breath, silently to the surface, sent one swift glance sweeping the bare earth around him, and returned to the cabin.

Very carefully that sultry afternoon he cleaned his old hammer shotgun, and, loading both barrels with buckshot, set it handy beside the door.

"Antelope," he explained laconically; but when likewise he overhauled the revolver hanging at his hip, Margaret was not deceived. This done, notwithstanding the fact that the sun still beat scorchingly hot thereon, he returned to the doorstep, lit his pipe, drew his weather-stained sombrero low over his face, through half-closed eyes inspected the lower lands all about, impassively silent awaited the coming of the inevitable. Of a sudden there was a touch on his shoulder, and, involuntarily starting, he looked up, into the face of Margaret Rowland.

The woman sat down beside him, her hand on his knee.

"Don't keep it from me," she requested steadily. "You've seen something."

In the brier bowl before his face the tobacco glowed more brightly as Rowland drew hard.

"Tell me, please," repeated Margaret. "Are they here?"

The pipe left the man's mouth. The great bushy head nodded reluctant corroboration.

"Yes," he said.

"You-saw them?"

Again the man's head spoke an affirmative. "It's perhaps as well, after all, for you to know." One hand indicated the foot of the rise before them. "They waylaid Mueller there."

"And you —"

"It was all over in a second." Puff, puff. "After all he-Margaret!"

"Don't mind me. I was thinking of baby. The hideous suggestion!"

"Margaret!" He held her tight, so tight he could feel the quiver of her body against his, the involuntary catch of her breath. "Forgive me, Margaret."

"You're not to blame. Perhaps-Oh, Sam, Sam, our baby!"

Hotter and hotter beat down the sun. Thicker and thicker above the scorching earth vibrated the curling heat waves. The very breath of prairie seemed dormant, stifled. Not the leaf of a sunflower stirred, or a blade of grass. In the tiny patch of Indian corn each individual plant drooped, almost like a sensate thing, beneath the rays, each broad leaf contracted, like a roll of parchment, tight upon the parent stalk. In sympathy the colour scheme of the whole lightened from the appearance of the paler green under-surface. Though silently, yet as plainly as had done Hans Mueller when fighting for life, they lifted the single plea: 'Water! Water! Give us drink!"

Silent now, the storm over, side by side sat the man and the woman; like children awed by the sudden realisation of their helplessness, their hands clasped in mute sympathy, mute understanding. Usually at this time of day with nothing to do they slept; but neither thought of sleep now. As passed the slow time and the sun sank lower and lower, came the hour of supper; but likewise hunger passed them by. Something very like fascination held them there on the doorstep, gazing out, out at motionless impassive nature, at the seemingly innocent earth that nevertheless concealed so certain a menace, at the patch of sod corn again in cycle growing darker as the broad leaves unfolded in preparation for the dew of evening. Out, out they looked, out, out —.

"Sam!"

"Yes,"

"You saw, too?"

An answering pressure of the hand.

"The eyes of him, only the eyes-out there at the edge of the corn!"

"It's the third time, Margaret." Despite the man's effort his breath tightened. "They're all about: a score at least —I don't know how many. The tall grass there to the east is alive —"

"Sam! They're there again-the eyes! Oh, I'm afraid-Sam-baby!"

"Hush! Leave her where she is. Don't seem afraid. It's our only chance. Let them make the first move." Again the hand pressure so tight that, although she made no sound, the blood left the woman's fingers. "Tell me you forgive me, Margaret; before anything happens. I'm a criminal to have stayed here, —I see it now, a criminal!"

"Don't!"

"But I must. Tell me you forgive me. Tell me."

"I love you, Sam."

Again in the expanse of grass to the east there was motion; not in a single spot but in a dozen places. No living being was visible, not a sound broke the stillness of evening; simply here and there it stirred, and became motionless, and stirred again.

"And-Margaret. If worst comes to worst they mustn't take either of us alive. The last one —I can't say it. You understand."

"Yes, I understand. The last load-But maybe —"

"It's useless to deceive ourselves. They wouldn't come this way if-Margaret, in God's name —"

"But baby, Sam!" Of a sudden she was struggling fiercely beneath the grip that kept her back. "I must have her, must see her again; must, must —"

"Margaret!"

"I must, I say!"

"You must not. They'll never find her there. She's safe unless we show the way. Think-as you love her."

"But if anything should happen to us-She'll starve!"

"No. There are soldiers at Yankton, and they'll come-now; and Landor knows."

"Oh, Sam, Sam!"

There was silence. No human being could give answer to that mother wail.

Again time passed; seconds that seemed minutes, minutes that were a hell of suspense. Below the horizon of prairie the sun sank from sight. In the hot air a bank of cumulus clouds glowed red as from a distant conflagration. For and eternity previous it seemed to the silent watchers there had been no move; now again at last the grass stirred; a corn plant rustled where there was no breeze; out into the small open plat surrounding the house sprang a frightened rabbit, scurried across the clearing, headed for the protecting grass, halted at the edge irresolute-scurried back again at something it saw.

"You had best go in, Margaret." The man's voice was strained, unnatural. "They'll come very soon now. It's almost dark."

"And you?" Wonder of wonders, it was the woman's natural tone!

"I'll stay here. I can at least show them how a white man dies."

"Sam Rowland-my husband!"

"Margaret-my wife!" Regardless of watchful savage eyes, regardless of everything, the man sprang to his feet. "Oh, how can you forgive me, can God forgive me!" Tight in his arms he kissed her again and again; passionately, in abandon. "I've always loved you, Margaret; always, always!"

"And I you, man; and I you!"

It came. As from the darkness above drops the horned owl on the field mouse, as meet the tiger and the deer at the water hole, so it came. Upon the silence of night sounded the hoarse call of a catbird where no bird was, and again, and again. In front of the maize patch, always in front, a dark form, a mere shadow in the dusk of evening, stood out clear against the light of sky. To right and left appeared others, as motionless as boulders, or as giant cacti on the desert. Had Settler Rowland been other than the exotic he was, he would have understood. No Indian exposes himself save for a purpose; but he did not understand. Erect now, his finger on the trigger of the old smoothbore, he waited passive before the darkened doorway of the cabin, looking straight before him, God alone knows what thoughts whirling in his brain. Again in front of him sounded and resounded the alien call. The dark figures against the sky took life, moved forward. Simultaneously, on the thatch of the cabin roof, appeared two other figures identical with those in front. Foot by foot, silent as death, they climbed up, reached the ridge pole, crossed to the other side. On, on advanced the figures in front. Down the easy incline of the roof came the two in the rear, reached the edge, paused waiting. Of a sudden, out of the maize patch, out of the grass, seemingly out of space itself, came a new cry-the trilling call of the prairie owl. It was the signal. Like twin drops of rain from a cloudless sky fell the two figures on Rowland's head; ere he could utter a sound, could offer resistance, bore him to earth. From somewhere, everywhere, swarmed others. The very earth seemed to open and give them forth in legion. In the multitude of hands he was as a child. Within the space of seconds, ere waiting Margaret realised that anything had happened, he had disappeared, all had disappeared. In the clearing before the door not a human being was visible, not a live thing; only on the thatched roof, silent as before, patient as fate, awaited two other s hadows, darker but by contrast with the weather-coloured grass.

Minutes passed. Not even the call of the catbird, broke the silence. Within the darkness of the cabin the suspense was a thing of which insanity is made.

"Sam!" called a voice softly.

No answer.

"Sam!" repeated more loudly.

Again no answer of voice or of action.

In the doorway appeared a woman's figure; breathless, blindly fearful.

"Sam!" for the third time, tremulous, wailing; and she stepped outside.

A second, and it was over. A second, and the revel was on. The earth was not silent now. There was no warning trill of prairie owl. As dropped the figures from above there broke forth the Sioux war-cry: long drawn out, demoniac, indescribable. Blood curdling, more savage infinitely than the cry of any wild beast, the others took it up, augmented it by a score, a hundred throats. Again the earth vomited the demons forth. Naked, breech-clouted, garbed in fragments of white men's dress, they swarmed into the clearing, into the cabin, about the two prisoners in their midst. Passively, patiently waiting for hours, of a sudden they seemed possessed of a frenzy of haste, of savage abandon, of drunken exhilaration in the cunning that had won the game without a shot from the white man's gun, without the injury of a single warrior. They were in haste, and yet they were not in haste. They looted the cabin like fire and then fought among themselves for the plunder. They applied the torch to the shanty's roof as though pressed by the Great Spirit; then capered fiendishly in its illumination, oblivious of time until, tinder

dry, it had burned level with the earth. Last of all, purposely reserved as a climax, they gave their attention to the pair of half-naked, bound and gagged figures in their midst. Then it was the scene became an orgy indeed. The havoc preceding had but whetted their appetite for the finale. Savagery personified, cruelty unqualified, deadly hate, primitive lust-every black passion lurking in the recesses of the human mind stalked brazenly into the open, stood forth defiant, sinister, unashamed. But let it pass. It was but a repetition of a thousand similar scenes enacted on the swiftly narrowing frontier, a fraction of the price civilisation ever pays to savagery, inevitable as a nation's expansion, as its progression.

It was eight of the clock when came that final warning whistle of prairie owl. It was not yet ten when, silent as they had come, unbelievably impassive when but an hour before they had been irresponsible madmen, temporarily cruelty-surfeited, they resumed their journey. Single file, each footstep of those who followed fair in the print of the leader, a long, long line of ghostly, undulatory shadows, forming the most treacherous deadly serpent that ever inhabited earth, they moved eastward until they reached the bank of the swift little river; then turned north, leaving the abandoned, desolated settlement, the ruined cornfields, as tokens of their handiwork, as a message to other predatory bands who might follow, as a challenge to the white man who they knew would return. As passed the slow hours toward morning they moved swiftly and more swiftly. The gliding walk became a dog trot, almost a lope; their arms swung back and forth in unison, the pat, pat of their moccasined feet was like the steady drip of eaves from a summer rain, the rustle of their passing bodies against the dense vegetation a soft accompaniment. Autochthonous as they had appeared they disappeared. Night and distance swallowed them up. But for a trampled, ruined grainfield, the smouldering ruins of what had once been a house, the glaring white of two naked bodies in the starlight against the background of dark earth, it was as though they had not come. But for this, and one other thing —a single sound, repeated again and again, dulled, muffled as though coming from the earth itself.

"Daddy! Daddy! I want you." Then repeated with a throb in its depths that spoke louder than words. "Daddy, come! I'm afraid!"

More than a mere name was Fort Yankton. Original in construction, as necessity ever induces the unusual, it was nevertheless formidable. To the north was a typical entrenchment with a ditch, and a parapet eight feet high. To the east was a double board wall with earth tamped between: a solid curb higher than the head of a tall man. Completing the square, to the south and west stretched a chain of oak posts set close together and pierced, as were the other walls of the stockade, by numerous portholes. Within the enclosure, ark of refuge for settlers

near and afar, was a large blockhouse wherein congregated, mingled and intermingled, ate, slept, and had their being, as diverse a gathering of humans as ever graced a single structure even in this land of myriad types. Virtually the entire population of frontier Yankton was there. Likewise the settlers from near-by Bon Homme. An adventurer from the far-away country of the Wahpetons and a trapper from the hunting ground of the Sissetons drifted in together, together awaited the signal of the peace pipe ere returning to their own. Likewise from the wild west of the great river, from the domain of the Uncpapas, the Blackfeet, the Minneconjous, the Ogallalas, came others; for the alarm of rapine and of massacre had spread afar. Very late to arrive, doggedly holding their own until rumour became reality unmistakable, was the colony from the Jim River valley to the east; but even they had finally surrendered, the dogging grip of fear, that makes high and low brothers, at their throats, had fled precipitately before the conquering onslaught of the Santees. Last of all, boldest of all, most foolhardy of all, as you please, came the tiny delegation from the settlement of Sioux Falls. Hungry, thirsty, footsore, all but panic-stricken, for with the actual retreat apprehension had augmented with each slow mile, thanking the Providence which had permitted them to arrive unmolested, a sorry-looking band of refugees, they faced the old smoothbore cannon before the big south gate and craved admittance. Out to them went Colonel William Landor, colonel by courtesy, scion of many generations of Landors, rancher at present, cattle king of the future. The conversation that followed there with the east reddening in the morning sun was very brief, very swift to the point.

"Who are you, friends?" The shrewd grey eyes were observing them collectively, compellingly.

"My name is McPherson."

"Mine is Horton."

"Never mind the names," shortly. "I can learn them later."

"We're homesteaders." Again it was stubby, sandy-whiskered McPherson who took the lead.

"From where?"

"Sioux Falls."

"Any news?"

Curt as the question came the answer, the tale of massacre now a day old.

"And the rest of your settlement-where are they?"

McPherson told him.

"They all went, you say?"

For the first time the Scotchman hesitated. "All except one family," he qualified.

"There was but one family there." Landor was not observing the company collectively now. "You mean to tell me Sam Rowland did not go?"

"Yes."

"That you-men here went off and left him and his wife and little girl alone at this time?" The questioner's eyelids were closing ominously. "You come here with that story and ask me to let you inside?"

McPherson was no coward. His short legs spread belligerently, his shoulders squared.

"We're here," he announced laconically.

"I observe." Just a shade closer came the tightened eyelids. "Moreover, strange to say, I'm glad to see you." He leaned forward involuntarily; his breath came quick. "It gives me the opportunity, sir, to tell you to your face that you're a damned coward." In spite of an obvious effort at repression, the great veins of the speaker's throat swelled visibly. "A damned coward, sir!"

"What! You call me —"

"Men! Gentlemen!"

"Don't worry." Swift as had come the burst of passion, Landor was himself again; curt, all-seeing, self-sufficient, "There'll be no blood shed." Early as it was, a crowd had collected now, and, as he had done with the newcomers, he addressed them collectively, authoratively. "When I fight it will not be with one who abandons a woman and a child at a time like this.... God! it makes a man's blood boil. I've known the Rowlands for ten years, long before the kid came." Cold as before he had been flaming, he faced anew the travel-stained group. "Out of my sight, every one of you, and thank your coward stars I'm not in command here. If I were, not a man of you would ever get inside this stockade-not if the Santees scalped you before my eyes."

For a second there was silence, inaction.

"But Rowland wouldn't come," protested a voice. "We tried —"

"Not a word. If you were too afraid of your skin to bring them in, there are others who are not." Vital, magnetic, born leader of men, he turned to the waiting spectators. "It may be too late now, —I'm afraid it is; but if Sam Rowland is alive, I'm going to bring him here. Who's with me? Who's willing to make the ride back to Sioux Falls?"

"Who?" It was another rancher, surnamed Crosby, hatchet-faced, slow of speech, who spoke, "Ain't that question a bit superfluous, pard? We're all with you-that is, as many as you want, I reckon. None of us ain't cats, so we can't croak but once-and that might as well be now as ten years from now."

"All right." Hardened frontiersman, Landor took the grammar and the motive alike for granted. "Get your horses and report here. The first twenty to return, go."

From out the group of newcomers one man emerged. It was McPherson.

"Who'll lend me a horse?" he queried.

No man gave answer. Already the group had separated.

For a moment the Scotchman halted, grim-jawed, his legs an inverted V; then silent as they, equally swiftly, he followed.

Very soon, almost unbelievably soon, they began to trickle back. Not in ignorance of possibilities in store did they come. They had no delusions concerning the red brother, these frontiersmen. Nor in the hot adventurous blood of youth did they respond. One and all were middle-aged men; many had families. All save Landor were strangers to the man they went to seek. Yet at a moment's call they responded; as they took it for granted others would respond were they in need. Had they been conscious of the fact, the action was magnificent; but of it they were not conscious. They but answered an instinct: the eternal brotherhood of the frontier. Far away in his well-policed, steam-heated abode urban man listens to the tale of unselfishness, and, supercilious, smiles. We believe what we have ourselves felt, we humans. First of all to come was lean-faced Crosby, one cheek swelled round with a giant quid. Close at his heels followed Trapper Conway: grizzled, parchment-faced veteran, who alone had followed the Missouri to its source and, stranger to relate, had alone returned with his scalp. Then came Landor himself, the wiry little mustang he rode all but blanketed under the big army saddle. Following him, impassive, noncommittal as though an event of the recent past had not occurred, came McPherson, drew up in place beside the leader. All-seeing, Crosby spat appreciatively, but Landor gave never a glance. Following came not one but many riders; a half dozen, a score, —enough to make up the allotment, and again. In silence they came, grim-faced, more grimly accoutred. All manner of horseflesh was represented: the broncho, the mustang, the frontier scrub, the thoroughbred; all manner of apparel, from chaperajos to weather-beaten denim; but, saddled or saddleless, across the neck of every beast stretched the barrel of a long rifle, at the hip of every rider hung a holster, from every belt peeped the hilt of a great knife.

Long ere this word of the unusual had passed about, and now, on the rise of ground at the back of the stockade, a goodly group had gathered. Silent as the prairies, as the morning itself, they watched the scene below, awaited the *dénouement*. Not without influence was the taciturn example of the red man in this land from which he was slowly being crowded. From over the uplands to the east the red face of the morning sun was just peeping when Landor separated himself from the waiting group, led the way to the big gate and paused. "Twenty only, men," he repeated. "All ready."

First through the opening went Crosby.

"One."

Close as before, at his horse's heels followed Conway.

"Two."

From out the motley, looking neither to right nor left, came Scotchman McPherson; but though he passed fair before the leader's eyes and not a yard away, no number was spoken; no hint of recognition, of cognisance, crossed the latter's face. Implacable, relentless as time, he awaited the next in line, then voiced the one word: "Three."

On filed the line; close formed as convicts, as convicts silent-halting at a lifted hand. A moment they paused, one and twenty men who counted but as a score, started into motion, halted again; as by common consent every head save one of a sudden going bare. Hitherto silent as they, the watching group back in the stockade had that instant found voice. All but to the ground swept twenty sombreros as out over the prairies, cut where no human ear could hear, rolled a cheer, and repeated, and again; tribute of Fort Yankton to those who went. At the rear of the column one rider alone did not respond, apparently did not hear. Implacable as Landor himself, he looked straight before him, awaited the silence that would bring with it renewed activity.

And it came. With a single motion as before, every hat returned to its place, was drawn low over its owner's eyes. From his position by the gate Landor advanced, took the lead. Behind him, impassive again as figures in a spectacle, the others fell in line. At first a mere walk, the pace gradually quickened, became a canter, a trot. By this time the confines of the tiny frontier town were passed. Before them on the one hand, bordering on the river, stretched a range of low hills, dun-brown from its coat of sun-dried grass. On the other, greener by contrast, glittering now in the level rays of the early morning sun on myriad dew-drops, and seemingly endless, unrolled the open prairie. Straight into this Landor led the way, and as he did so the cavalcade for the first time broke into a gallop; not the fierce, short-lived pace of civilisation, but the long-strided, full-lunged lope of the frontier, which accurately and as tirelessly as a clock measures time, counts off the passing miles. Hitherto a preliminary, at last the play was on.

Sixty-odd miles as migrates the sandhill crane, separated the settlements of Yankton and Sioux Falls. Trackless as a desert was the prairie, minus even the buffalo trails of a quarter century before; yet with the sun only as guide, they forged ahead, straight as a line drawn taut from point to point. Nothing stopped their advance, nothing made them turn aside. Seemingly destitute of animal life, the country fairly teemed at their approach. Grouse, typical of the prairie as the blue-faced anemone, were everywhere; singly, in coveys, in flocks. Troops of antelope, startled in their morning feeding, scurried away from the path of the invaders; curious as children, paused on the safety of the nearest rise, to watch the horsemen out of sight. Every marshy spot, every prairie pond, had its setting of ducks. The teal, the mallard, the widgeon, the shoveller, the canvasback-all mingled in the loud-voiced throng that arose before the leader's approach, then, like smoke, vanished with almost unbelievable swiftness into the hazy distance. Prairie dog towns, populous as cities of man a minute before their approach, went lifeless, desolate, as they passed through. In the infrequent draws and creek beds between the low, rolling hills, great-eyed cotton tails scampered to cover or, like the antelope, just out of harm's way, watched the passage of this strange being, man. Wonder of wonders that display of life would have been to another generation; but of it these grim-faced riders were apparently unconscious, oblivious. Their eyes were not for things near at hand, but for the distance, for the possibility that lurked just beyond that far-away rise which formed their horizon, when they had reached that for the next beyond, and the next.

Hour by hour the morning wore away. Hotter and hotter rose the sun above them. Instead of drops of dew, tiny particles of sun-dried grass flew away from beneath the leaders' feet, mingled with the dust of prairie, became a cloud shutting the leaders from the sight of those in the rear. From being a mere breath, the south wind augmented, became positive, insistent. Hot with the latent heat of many days, it sang in their ears as they went, bit all but scorching, at their unprotected hands and throats. Under its touch the horses' necks, dark before with sweat, became normal again: between their legs, under the, edges of the great saddles where it had churned into foam, dried into white powder, like frostwork amid the hair. Gradually with the change, their breathing became audible, louder and louder, until in unison it mingled with the dull impact of their feet on the heavy sod like the exhaust of many engines. No horseman who values the life of the beast between his legs, fails to heed that warning. Landor did not, but at the first dawdling prairie creek that offered water and, with its struggling fringe of willows, a suggestion of shade, he gave the word to halt, and for four mortal, blistering hours while, man and beast alike, the others slept, kept watch over them from the nearest rise. Relentless to others this man might be, but not even his dearest enemy could accuse him of sparing himself.

It was three by the clock when again they took up the trail. It was 3.45 when they swam what is now the Vermilion River, the last water-course of

any size on their way. The dew was again beginning to gather when, well to the south, they approached the bordering hills that concealed the site of Sioux Falls settlement. Then for the first time since they began that last relay Landor gave an order.

"It'll be a miracle if we don't find Sioux there in the bottom, men," he prophesied. "Perhaps there are a whole band, perhaps it'll only be stragglers; but no matter how many or how few there may be, charge them. If they run you know what to do-this is no holiday outing. If they stand, charge them all the harder." He faced his horse to the north and gave the word to go. "It's our only chance," he completed.

What followed belongs to history. Over that last intervening rise they went like demons. The first to gain the crown, to look down into the valley beyond, was Landor. As he did so, grim Anglo-Saxon as he was, his whole attitude underwent a transformation. Back to the others he turned his face, and, plain as on canvas thereon was portrayed war, carnage, and the lust of battle.

"They're there; a hundred, if a single red!" he shouted. "Come on!" and the rowels of his great spurs dug deep at his horse's flanks, dug until the blood spurted.

But a few minutes it took to make the run, yet only a fraction of the time that mounted swarm in the valley held their ground. Outnumbering those who charged many times, it was not in savage nature to face that unformed oncoming motley of howling, bloodthirsty maniacs. Slowly at first began the retreat; then as, with great swiftness, the others shortened the distance intervening, it became a contagion, a mania, a stampede. Every brave for himself, stumbling, crowding through the dismantled ruins of what had the day before been a settlement, howling like their pursuers, seeking but one thing, escape, they headed for the thicket surrounding the river bank; the whistle of bullets in their ears, cutting at the vegetation about them. Into its friendly cover they plunged, as a fish disappears beneath the surface of a lake, and were swallowed from sight. That is, all but one. That one, unhorsed by accident, was left to face that oncoming flood. . . . But why linger. Like the charge itself, his fate is history. These men were but human, and thick about them were the ashes from the roof-trees of their friends.

Summer night, dreamy with caress of softest south wind, musical with the drone of myriad crickets, with the boom of frogs from the low land adjoining the river, melancholy with the call of the catbird, with the infrequent note of the whip-poor-will, was upon the land of the Mandans when the score and one, their dripping ponies once more dry, took up the last relay of their journey. Night had caught them there in the deserted settlement, and Landor had given the word to halt, to wait. Now, far to the east, apparently from the breast of Mother Earth herself, the face of the full harvest moon, red as frosted maple leaves through the heated air, slowly rising, lit up the level country softly as by early twilight. Lingeringly, almost reluctantly, Landor got into his saddle. Just to his left, impassive as the night, well to the front of the company as he had been that mortal dragging day, sat Scotchman McPherson. Not once since that early morning scene at Fort Yankton had he spoken a word, not once had he been addressed, had another man shown consciousness of his presence. A pariah, he had so far kept them company; a pariah, he now awaited the end. A moment, fair in his seat, Landor paused; then that which the watchers had expected for hours came to pass. Deliberately he crossed over, drew rein beside the other man.

"McPherson," he said, "this morning I called you coward. That you are not such you have proven, you are proving now. For this reason I ask your pardon. For this reason as well, I give you warning. What we will find-where we are going, I do not doubt, now. I do not believe you doubt. For it I hold you responsible. You had best turn back before belief becomes certainty." Unnaturally precise, cold as November raindrops came the words, the sentences. Deadly in meaning was the pause that followed. "I repeat, you had best turn back."

For a long half minute, face to face there in the moonlight, Landor waited; but no answer came. Just perceptibly he shifted in his place.

"I may forget, give my promise of the morning the lie. Do you understand?"

"Yes, I understand."

Another half minute, ghastly in its significance, passed; then without a word Landor turned. "You have heard, men," he said, "and may God be my judge."

The full moon was well in the sky, showing clear every detail in that scene of desolation, when they arrived. Patter, patter, patter sounded their hoof-beats in the distance. More and more loud they grew, muffled yet penetrating in the silence of night, always augmenting in volume. Out of the shadows figures came dimly into view, taking form against the background of constellations. The straining of leather, the music of steel in bit and buckle, the soft swish of the sun-dried grass proclaimed them very near; then across the trampled corn patch, into the open where had stood the shanty, where now was a thin grey layer of ashes, came the riders, and drew rein; their weary mounts crowding each other in fear at something they saw. Like a storm cloud they came; like the roll of thunder following was the oath which sprang to the lips of every rider save one. Good men they were, God-fearing men; yet they swore like pirates, like humans when ordinary speech is not adequate. In the pause but one man acted, and none intervened to prevent what he did. Out into the open, away from the others, rode Scotchman McPherson; halted, his hand on the holster at his hip. For a second, and a second only, he sat so, the white moonlight drawing clear every line of his grizzled face, his stocky figure. Then deliberately his hand lifted, before him there appeared a sudden blaze of fire, upon the silence there broke a single revolver report, from beneath his lifeless bulk the horse he rode broke free, gave one bound, by instinct halted, trembling in every muscle; then over all, the quick and the dead, returned silence: silence absolute as that of the grave.

How long those twenty men sat there, gazing at that mute, motionless figure on the ground not one could have told. Death was no stranger to them. For years it had lurked behind every chance shrub they passed, in the depths of every ravine, in the darkness of night, from every tangle of rank prairie grass in broad daylight. To it from long familiarity they had become callous; but death such as this, deliberate, cold-blooded, self-inflicted —it awed them while it fascinated, held them silent, passive.

"In God's name!" Again it was Landor who roused them, Landor with his hand on the holster at his hip, Landor who sat staring as one who doubts his own sight. "Am I sane, men? Look, there to your right!"

They looked. They rubbed their eyes and looked again.

"Well, I'll be damned," voiced Crosby; and no man had ever heard him express surprise before. To the north, from the edge of the tall surrounding grass, moving slowly, yet without a trace of hesitation or of fear, coming straight toward them across the trampled earth, were two tiny human figures, hand in hand. No wonder they who saw stared; no wonder they doubted their eyes. One, the figure to the right, was plump and uncertain of step and all in white; white which in the moonlight and against the black earth seemed ghostly. The other was slim and certain of movement and dark-dark as a copper brown Indian boy, naked as when he came on earth. On they came, the brown figure leading, the white following trustfully, until they were quite up to the watchers, halted, still hand in hand.

"How," said a voice, a piping childish voice.

Like rustics at a spectacle the men stared, turned mystified faces each to each, and stared anew. All save one. Off from his horse sprang Landor, caught the bundle of white in his arms.

"Baby Rowland! Baby Bess! And you," —he was staring the other from head to toe, the distance was short, —"who are you?"

"Uncle Billy," interrupting, ignoring, the tiny bit of femininity nestled close, "Uncle Billy, where's papa and mamma! I want them."

Closer and closer the big bachelor arms clasped their burden; unashamed, there with the others watching him, he kissed her.

"Never mind now, Kiddie. Tell me how you came here, and who this is with you."

About the great neck crept two arms, clinging tightly.

"He just came, Uncle Billy. I was calling for papa. Papa put me to sleep and forgot me. The boy heard me and took me out. I was afraid at first, but-but he's a nice boy, only he won't talk and-and —" The narrative halted, the tousled head buried itself joyously. "Oh, I'm so glad you came, Uncle Billy!"

In silence Landor's eyes made the circle of interested watching faces, returned to the winsome brown face so near his own.

"Aren't you hungry, Kid?" he ventured.

On his shoulder the dark poll shook a negative.

"No. We had corn to eat. The boy roasted it. He made a big fire. He's a nice boy, only-only he won't say anything."

Again Landor's eyes made the circle, halted at the intrepid brown waif who, that first word of greeting spoken, had silently stared him back.

"You're sure you don't know anything more, baby? You didn't hear anything until the boy came?"

"No, Uncle Billy. I was asleep. When I woke up it was dark, and I was hungry and-and —" At last it had come: the spattering, turbulent tear storm. Her small body shook, her arms clasped tighter and tighter. "Oh, Uncle Billy, I want my papa and mamma. I tried to find them, and I couldn't. Please find them for me, Uncle Billy, Please! Please!"

It was well past midnight. The big full moon, high now in the sky, cast their shadows almost about their feet when, their labour complete, the party took up the homeward trail. But there were twenty no longer. At their head as before rode Landor, in his arms not a rifle but a blanket; a blanket from which as they journeyed on came now and anon a sound that was alien indeed: the sobs of a baby girl who wept as she slept. Back of him, likewise as when they had come, rode hatchet-faced Crosby; but he, too, was not as before. His saddle had been removed and, in front of him, astride the horse's bare back, warmed by the animal heat, was a brown waif of a boy; not asleep or even drowsy, but wide awake indeed, silently watchful as a prairie owl of every movement about him, every low-spoken word. What whim of satirist chance had put him there, what fate for good or evil, they could only conjecture, could not know, could never know; yet there he was, strangest figure in a land that knew only the bizarre, with whom the unbelievable was the normal. Slowly now, weary to death with the long, long day, depressed with the inevitable reaction from the excitement of the past hours, they moved away, to the south, to the west. In front of them, glittering in the moonlight, seemingly infinite, stretched the waves of the rolling prairie, bare as the sea in a calm. Behind them, growing lesser and lesser minute by minute, merging into the infinite white, were three black dots like tiny boats on the horizon's edge. On they went, a half mile, a mile, looked behind; and, with an awe no familiarity could prevent, faced ahead anew. Back of them now as well as before, uniformly endless, uniformly magnificent, stretched that giant ocean: silent. serene, as mother nature, as nature's master, God himself.

The day of the Indian terror had passed. No longer did the name of Little Crow carry stampede in its wake. The battles of Big Mound, of White Stone Hill, and of the Bad Lands had been fought, had become mere history; dim already to the newcomer as Lexington or Bull Run. Still in the memory, to be sure, was the half-invited massacre of Custer at the Little Big Horn; but the savage genius of Sitting Bull, of Crazy Horse, and of Gall, who had made the last great encounter bloodily unique in the conflict of the red man and the white, was never to be duplicated. Rightly or wrongly deprived of what they had once called their own, driven back, back on the crest of the ever-increasing wave of settlement, facing the alternative of annihilation or of submergence in that flood, the Sioux had halted like a wild thing at bay, with their backs to the last stronghold, the richest plot of earth on the face of the globe, the Black Hills country, and as a cornered animal ever fights, had battled ferociously for a lost supremacy. But, robbers themselves, holding the land on the insecure title of might alone, fighting to the end, they had at last succumbed to the inevitable: the all-conquering invasion of the dominant Anglo-Saxon. Here and there a name stood out: "Scarlet Point," "Strikes-the-Ree," "Little Crow," "Sitting Bull," "Crazy Horse," "Spotted Tail," "Red Cloud," "Gall," "John Grass," names that in multiple impressed but by their fantastic suggestion; but their original pulse-accelerating meaning had long since passed. Now and then a prairie mother, driven to desperation, might incite temporary rectitude in the breast of an incorrigible by a harrowing reference to one or to another; yet to the incoming swarms of land-hungry settlers they were mere supplanted play actors, fit heroes for fiction, for romance perhaps; but like the bison to be kept in small herds safe in the pasture of a reservation, preserved as a relic of a species doomed to extinction.

A thing at which to marvel was the growth of the eastern border of Dakota Territory in this, the time of the great boom. History can scarcely find its parallel. In the space of a decade the census leaped from two-score thousand to nearly a half million. New towns sprang up like fungi in a night. Railroads reached out like the tentacles of an octopus, where a generation before the buffalo had tramped its tortuous trail. Prosperous farms came into being in the meadows where the antelope had pastured. Artesian wells, waterworks, electric lights, street railways, colleges, all the adjuncts of a higher civilisation, blossomed forth under the magic wand of Eastern capital. Doomed to reaction, as an advancing pendulum is doomed to retrace its cycle, was this premature evolution; but temporarily, as a springtime freshet bears onward the driftwood in its path, it carried its predecessor, the unconventional, fighting, wild-loving adventurer, before. On it went, on and on until at last, fairly blocking its path, was the big, muddy, dawdling Missouri. Then for the first time it halted; halted in a pause that was to last for a generation. But it had fulfilled its mission. High and dry on the western side of the barrier, imbued as when they had settled to the east, with the restless spirit of the frontier, unsubdued, unchanged, it cast its burden. There, as they had done before, the newcomers immediately took root, and, after the passage of a year, were all but unconscious of the migration. Over their heads was the same blue prairie sky. Around them, treeless, trackless, was the same rolling, illimitable prairie land. In but one essential were conditions changed; yet that one was epoch-making. Heretofore, surrounded by a common, an alien danger, compelled at a second's warning to band together for life itself, all men were brothers. Now, with the passing of the red peril, with eradication of necessity for any manner of restraint, an abandon of licence, of recklessness, born of the wild life, of overflowing animal vitality i nsufficiently employed, swept the land like a contagion. Unique in the history of man's development was this the era of the cowboy, as fantastic now as the era of the red peril, its predecessor; yet vital, bizarre, throbbing, unconsciously human, as no other period has ever been, as in all probability none will ever be again. Generous, spendthrift, murderous when crossed, chivalrous, fearless, profane, yet fundamentally religious, inebriate, wilful and docile by turns, ceaselessly active, eternally discontented, seeking they knew not what, they were their own evil genius; as certainly as nature surrounded them with Heaven, they supplied their own Hell and, impartial, chose from each to weave the web of their lives.

Of this period, life of this life, was Colonel William Landor; colonel no longer, plain Bill, from the river to the Hills, husband these ten years now, but not father, Cattle King of an uncontested range. Of this life likewise, bred in it, saturated in it, was a dark young woman, his adopted daughter, two years past her majority, Elizabeth Rowland Landor by name. Of it most vitally of all, born of it, rooted in it through unknown centuries of ancestral domicile, was a copper-brown young man, destitute as a boy of twelve of a trace of beard, black as a prairie crow of hair and eyes, deep-lunged like a race-track thoroughbred, wiry as a mustang, garbed as a white man, but bearing the liquid name of a Teton Sioux, "Ma-wa-cha-sa, the lost pappoose," yet known wherever the Santee Massacre and the tale of his appearance was known, as "How" Landor. Of this period, last of all, was the great B.B. —Buffalo Butte-ranch, giant among the giants, whose brand was familiar as his own name to every cowboy west of the Missouri, whose hospitable ranch house, twenty-odd miles from the vest pocket metropolis of Coyote Centre, which in turn, to quote Landor himself, was "a hundred miles from nowhere," was the Mecca of every traveller whom chance drew into this wild, of every curious tenderfoot seeking a glimpse of the reverse side of the coin of life, of every desperate "one lunger," who, with gambler instinct, staked his all on prairie sun and prairie air.

Chapter V
The Land of Licence

For twenty-four hours the two cowmen from the distant Clay Creek ranch had owned Coyote Centre. An hour before sunset on the day previous they had suddenly blown in from the north; a great cloud of yellow dust, lifting lazily on the sultry air, a mighty panting of winded bronchos, a single demoniacal dare-man whoop heralding their coming, a groaning of straining leather, a jingle of great spurs, and an otherwise augmented stillness even in this silent land, marking their arrival. Pete it was, Pete Sweeney, "Long Pete," who first dismounted. Pete likewise it was who first entered the grog shop of Red Jenkins. Pete again it was who, ere ten words had passed, drew cold-blooded, point blank at the only man who saw fit to question the invader's right of absolute ownership. Pete it was once again who, when the smoke had cleared away, assisted in laying out that same misguided citizen, in decent fellowship, beneath the cottonwood bar, and thrust an adequate green roll in the stiffening hand for funeral expenses.

"It's Bill's own fault," he commented lucidly the while. "I don't visit you very often; but when I do I've got the dough to make it square, and this town's my sausage, skin, curl, and all. D'ye understand?" and from Manning, the greybearded storekeeper, to Rank Judge, the one-legged saddler, there was no one to say him nay, none to contest his right of authority.

By no means without an officer of the law was Coyote Centre. Under ordinary conditions its majesty was ably, even aggressively, upheld by its representative, Marshal Jim Burton. Likewise there was no lack of pilgrims, who by devious and circuitous routes sought his residence on this occasion, with tales of distress and petitions for succour; but one and all departed with their mission unfulfilled. The doughty James was not to be found. Urgent business of indefinite duration, at an even more indefinite destination, had called him hence. No one regretted the mischance so much as stalwart Mrs. Burton, who imparted the information, no one deplored the lost opportunity for distinction so much as she; but nevertheless the fact remained. For the time being, Coyote Centre was thrown upon its own resources, was left to work out its own salvation as best it might.

Thus it came about that for a long, long dragging day, and the beginning of a second, the gunpowder had intermittently burned, and that more than intermittently, all but continuously, the red liquor had flowed; to the alternate aggrandisement of Red Jenkins and his straw-haired Norwegian rival across the street-Gus Ericson. Unsophisticated ones there were who fancied that ere this it would all end, that Mr. Sweeney's capacity for absorption had a limit. Four separate gentlemen, with the laudable intention of hastening that much to be desired condition, had sacrificed themselves for the common weal; but to the eternal disgrace of the town, all of them were now down and out, and in various retired spots, where they had been deposited by their sympathising friends, were snoring in peaceful oblivion. Even Len Barker, game disciple of the great master, had reached his limit and, no longer formidable, had, without form of law, been deposited for safekeeping, and with a sigh of relief, in the corporate Bastile; but Mr. Sweeney himself, Mr. Sweeney of the hawk eye and the royal tread, despite a lack of sleep and of solid sustenance, was, to all visible indications, as fresh and aggressive as at the beginning.

Now for the second time night was coming on. Neither up nor down the single business thoroughfare did a street lamp show its face. One and all had succumbed long before to the god of gunpowder. Not a stray dog, and Coyote Centre was plethoric of canines, raised its voice nor showed even a retreating tail near the area of disturbance. Wisdom and a desire for deepest obscurity had come to the many, swift and sudden annihilation to the few. Temporarily, yet effectively as though a cyclone were imminent, business and social life were paralysed. They were a tolerant breed, these citizens of Coyote Centre; repeated similar experience had not been without its effect; moreover, the object lesson of the day before was still vivid in their minds; but at last patience was reaching its limit. In the closed doorway of the town hall a tiny group of men were gathered, a group who spoke scarcely above a whisper, who kept a sharp lookout all surrounding, who stood ready at the twitch of an eyelash to disperse to the four winds. This was revolt incipient. In the single room of Bob Manning's general store was open revolt and plotting. Manning himself, grizzled, grey of hair, shaggy bearded, had the floor.

"You're a bunch of measly cowards," he included indiscriminately. "You come here with your stories and croak and croak, and still not one of you would dare say a word to Pete's face, not one of you but would stand and let him twist your nose if he saw fit." He glowered from one horn of the silent, listening semicircle to the other, with all-including disdain. "If you don't like it, why don't you put a stop to it? If Jim Burton has sneaked, why don't you elect a new marshal? You're damned cowards, I say."

In his place on the cover of a barrel of dried apples, Bud Smith, the weazened little land man, shifted as though the seat hurt him.

"P'raps you're right, dad," he commented imperturbably, "and agin p'raps you're not. It's all well enough to say appoint a new marshal, but as fer's I've been able to discover there's no one hereabouts hankerin' fer the job." He spat at a crack in the cottonwood floor meditatively, struck true, and seemed mildly pleased. "Our buryin' patch is growin' comfortably rapidly as it is, without adding any marshals to the collection. I've known Pete Sweeney fer quite a spell, and my private advice is to let him alone. There ain't coffins enough this side the river to supply the demand, if you was to try to arrest him when he's feelin' as he's feelin' now."

"Who mentioned arresting?" broke in Walt Wagner, the lanky Missourian, who drove the stage. "Pot him, I say. Pot him the first time he isn't looking."

For a long half minute Bud observed the speaker; analytically, meditatively.

"Evidently you ain't been a close observer, my boy," he commented at last, impersonally, "or you wouldn't be talkin' of Pete not lookin'. I ain't no weather prophet, but I'd hint to the feller who tackles that job to say his prayers before he starts. He won't have much time afterwards." With a swifter movement than he had yet made, the speaker slid from his place to the floor, involuntarily cast a glance into the street without. "I ain't perticularly scared, boys," he explained, "and I ain't lookin' fer trouble neither. Between yourselves and myself, it ain't at all healthy to sit here discussin' the matter. Someone's bound to peach on you, and then there's sure to be a call. You better scatter and let it blow over."

"Scatter nothing," exploded Wagner, belligerently. "Slide if you want to, if you've got cold feet. I for one intend staying here as long as I see fit, Sweeney or no Sweeney."

"You do, do you?" It was Manning this time who spoke, Manning with his deep-set eyes flashing over his high cheek bones. "Well, maybe I've got something to say about that." He came out from behind the counter, faced the lanky figure before him, with deliberate contempt. "You're a mighty stiff-backed boy in the daytime, you are, Walt Wagner, but in the dark —" He halted and his mouth curled in bitterest sarcasm. "Why, if you're so anxious for a scrap, don't you run for marshal? Why don't you take the job right now and put Pete out of business?" And his mouth curled again.

Beneath its coat of tan Wagner's face reddened; then went white. Involuntarily his lip curled back like that of a cornered dog, and until it showed the lack of a prominent front tooth.

"Seeing you are so free with your tongue," he retorted, "I might ask you the same question. I ain't no property interest here being destroyed like you have. Why don't you do the trick yourself, dad?"

For a moment there was silence, inaction; then of a sudden the old man stiffened. With an effort almost piteous, he attempted to square his shoulders; but they remained round as before.

"Why don't I?" He held up his right hand-minus the index and middle fingers. He held up his left, stiffened and shrivelled with rheumatism. "Why don't I?" He clumped the length of the tiny storeroom and back again; one crippled leg all but dragging. "Why don't I?" repeated for the third time. "Do you imagine for the fraction of a second, Walt Wagner, that if I was back twenty years and sound like you are, I'd be asking another man why he didn't do the job?" Terrible, almost ghastly, he stood there before them, the picture of bitter rage, of impotent, distorted senility. "Have you got the last spark of manhood left in you, and ask that question of me?"

In the pockets of his trousers Wagner's hands worked nervously. His face went red again, but he gave no answer. Bud Smith it was, Bud Smith, five-feet-two, with a complexion prairie wind had made like a lobster display in a cafe window, who had halted at the door, but who now came back, he it was who spoke.

"And while you're in the talkin' business," he suggested slowly, "you might elab'rate what you meant a bit ago by intimatin' that I had cold feet. We'll listen to that, too, any time you see fit to explain, pardner."

"You want to know, do you?" Wagner's countenance had become normal again, and with an effort at nonchalance he leaned his elbows back against the glass showcase, glancing the while down at the small man, almost patronisingly. "Well, then, for your benefit, I was merely observing that you filled the bill of what dad here said a bit ago we all were." He smiled tantalisingly; again showing the vacancy in his dental arch. "You remember what that was, don't you?"

"P'raps and p'raps not," still deliberately. "I ain't lookin' fer trouble, mind you, but I just like to have things explicit. To be dead sure, I'd like to have you repeat it."

Again there was silence. In it Bob Manning returned to his place behind the counter; his game leg shuffling behind him as he moved. In it likewise there was an interruption from without; the subdued clatter of a horse's feet on the packed earth of the street, the straining of leather, as the man, its rider, alighted, a moment later the click of the door latch as the same man, a stranger if they had noticed, entered and halted abruptly at what he saw. But those within did not notice. Silent as the night without, forgetful for the moment of even Pete Sweeney, they were staring at those two actors there before them.

"I'm listening," repeated Bud Smith gently. "I ain't lookin' fer trouble, you understand; but as fer as I recollect, no feller of my own age ever called me coward. If you think so, I'd like to hear you say it. I'm listenin' fer you to say it now, Walt Wagner."

Again within the room there was silence, and again from without there approached an interruption. From up the street, from out the door of Red Jenkins's joint it came; the patter, patter of many feet, leading it the heavy clump of mighty cowhide boots on the cottonwood sidewalk, the jingle of spurs on those same boots at every step, the deep breathing of a cowman intoxicated at last. Down the walk they came, past the darkened doorways of the deserted shops; wordless, menacing, nearer and nearer. Within the tiny storeroom no one had spoken, no one had noticed. The arms of Walt Wagner were not on the showcase now. In the depths of his pockets they were fumbling again, aimlessly, nervously. His face had gone whiter than before. Once he had opened his lips to speak, revealing the blackness of the vacant tooth; but he had closed them again silently. Now at last he cleared his throat, involuntarily he drew in a long breath. Whether he was about to speak they who watched never knew. What if he had spoken he would have said they likewise never knew; for at that moment, interrupting, compelling, the door to the street swung open with a crash, and fair in the aperture, filling it, blocking it, appeared the mighty, muscular figure of a cowman, while upon their ears, like the menacing bellow of an enraged bull, burst a voice-the challenging, bullying voice of Pete Sweeney, inebriate.

"What the hell be you fellers doin' here?" And when there was no answer repeated, "What the hell be you doin', I say?"

For a space that dragged into a half minute there was inaction while every man within sound of his voice gazed at the speaker; at first almost with fascination, then as the real meaning of the interruption came over them, with sensations as divergent as their various individual minds. There was no need to tell them who looked at that towering, intruding figure that tragedy lurked in the air, that death on the slightest provocation, at the twitch of a trigger finger, dwelt in those big twin Colts lying menacingly across the folded arms. A lunatic escaped was a pleasant companion, a child, to deal with, compared with Pete Sweeney at this time. Malevolent, irresponsible, dare god-bull mastery fairly oozed from his presence. Bad every inch of him, hopelessly, irredeemably bad was this mountain of humanity. Bad from the soles of his misshapen boots to the baggy chaperajos, to the bulging holsters at his hips, to the gleaming cartridge belt around his waist, to the soft green flannel shirt, to the red silk handkerchief about his throat, to the dark unshaven face, to the drink-reddened nose, to the mere slits of eyes, to the upturned sombrero that crowned the shock of wiry hair; bad in detail, in ensemble, was this inebriate cowman, bad.

"Well, why don't you talk?" Himself interrupting the silence he came a step nearer, braced himself with legs far apart. "What've you got to say for yourselves? This ain't no Quaker meeting. Speak up. What're you all doin' here?"

Among the crowd one man alone spoke, and that was lobster-red Bud Smith.

"Tendin' to our own business, I reckon, Pete," he explained evenly.

"You lie!" Narrower and narrower closed the slit-like eyes. "You lie by the clock. You were planning to fix ME, you nest of skunks." From man to man he passed the look, halted at last at the figure of the lanky Missourian. "Some feller here figgered to pot me, and I'm lookin' to see the colour of his hair. Who was it, I'd like to know?"

"Someone's been stuffin' you, Pete." Even, deliberate as before Smith spoke the lie. "We don't give a whoop what you do. You can own the whole county so far as we care. Go back and 'tend to your knittin'. Dad here wants to close up, now."

"He does, does he? Well, he can in just a minute, just as soon as you name the feller I mention." Of a sudden his eyes shifted, dropped like claws on the figure of the little land man. "You know who it is I'm lookin' for. Tell me his name."

"You don't know me very well, Pete."

"I don't, eh? You think I don't know you?" The speaker was inspecting the other as a house cat inspects the mouse within its paws. "In other words, you mean you know, but won't tell me." Lingeringly, baitingly, almost exultingly, he was dragging the *dénouement* on and on. "That's what you mean to imply, is it?"

"You've guessed it, Pete." Not a muscle in the small man's body twitched; there was not the slightest alteration of the even tone. There, facing death as surely as harvest follows seedtime, knowing as he knew that but one man present could interfere to prevent, that that man wouldn't, he spoke those four words: "You've guessed it, Pete." And but minutes before Manning had called this man coward!

For a moment likewise Sweeney did not stir. For a second his slow brain failed to grasp the truth, the deliberate challenge of the refusal; then of a sudden, in a blinding, maddening flood, came comprehension, came action. Swifter than any human being would have thought possible, unbelievably ferocious even in this land of licence, something took place, something which the staring onlookers did not realise until it was done. They only knew that with a mighty backward leap the cowman had reached the single heavy oak door, had sent it shut with a bang. That at the same time there was the vicious spit of a great revolver, that the odour of burnt gunpowder was in their nostrils, that lifting slowly toward the ceiling was a cloud of thin blue smoke; a curtain that once raised made them shudder, made their blood run cold, for it revealed there, stretched on the floor, huddled as it had dropped, lifeless, motionless, the figure of the man who had refused, the weazened face of Land Man Bud Smith! All this they realised in that first second; then something that was almost fascination drew away their eyes to the man who had done this deed, to the man who, his back to the great door, the only means of egress, was covering them, every soul, with the two great revolvers in his hands. For Pete Sweeney was not drunk now. As swiftly as that horrible thing had been done he had gone sober. Yet no man who saw him that instant feared him one whit less. Not a man present, believer or scoffer, but breathed a silent prayer. And there was reason. If Pete Sweeney, Long Pete, had possessed a real friend on earth, he possessed that one no more. Disciples he had, imitators a-plenty; but friends-there had been but one, and now there was none. In an instant of oblivion, of drunken frenzy, he had murdered that friend; murdered him without a chance for self-defence, fair in his tracks. Not another had done this thing but he himself, he, Cowman Pete. Small wonder that they who watched this man prayed, that surreptitious glances sought for an avenue of escape where there was none, that the face of Walt Wagner went whiter and whiter; for as certain as Bud Smith lay dead there upon the floor, there would be a reckoning, —and what that reckoning would be God alone could tell!

And Sweeney himself. After that first, all but involuntary movement, he had not stirred. In his hands the big revolvers did not waver the breadth of a hair. Out of bloodshot, terrible eyes he was looking at that mute figure on the floor; looking at it immovably, indescribably, with an impassivity that was horrible. For the moment he seemed to have forgotten the others' presence, seemed at their mercy; and to the mind of Walt Wagner there came a suggestion. Slowly, surreptitiously one hand came out of his pocket, advanced by the fractions of inches towards his hip; advanced and halted and advanced again, reached almost-almost —.

"That'll do, you!" It was not a voice that spoke, it was a snarl: the snarl of an angry animal. "Put that fist back in your breeches or by God —"

No need to complete that threat. Back went the hand, back as though drawn by a spring, back as though it were a paralysed, useless thing.

"Now line up." At last the move had come, the move they had known was but a question of time. "Toe the crack, every mother's son of you. Step lively."

They obeyed. As Wagner's hand had done, they obeyed. Six men of them there were: surly crippled Manning, with eyes ablaze and jaws set like a trap; lank Wagner with his hands still in his pockets; Rank Judge, stumping on his wooden leg; greasy adipose Buck Walker, who ran the meat market; Slim Simpson, from the eating joint opposite, pale as the tucked-in apron around his waist; last of all the stranger, tall, smooth-shaven, alien in knickerbockers and blouse, his lips compressed, at his throat the arteries pounding visibly through his fair skin. Up they came at the word of command, like children with ill-learned lessons to recite, like sheep with a collie at their heels. Humorous at another time and another place, that compliance would have been; but with that mute, prostrate figure there before them on the floor, with that other menacing, dominating figure facing them, it was far from humorous. It was ghastly in its confession of impotence, in its mute acquiescence to another's will.

The shuffling of feet ceased and silence fell; yet for some reason Pete did not act. Instead he stood waiting; his red-rimmed eyes travelling from man to man, the fissure between them deepening, the heavy lids narrowing, moment by moment. A long half minute he waited, gloating on their misery, prolonging their suspense; then came the interruption. A step sounded on the walk without, a step that was all but noiseless. A hand tried the knob of the door, found it bolted, and tapped gently on the panel.

Not a soul within the room stirred, not even Long Pete; but the narrowing lids closed until they were mere slits, and the unshaven jaws tightened.

Again the knock sounded; louder, more insistent.

This time there was action. One of the revolvers in Pete's hand moved to the end of the line, halted. "Up with your hands," snarled a voice.

Two gnarled, distorted hands, the hands of Bob Manning, lifted in air.

"Up with you," and another pair, and another and another followed, until there were not two but twelve.

"Make a move, damn you," —one of the revolvers had returned to its holster, the free hand was upon the bolt, —"and I'll drop you, every cursed one of you, in your tracks. I'll drop you if I swing the next second." With a jerk, the door opened wide, and like a flash the hand returned to the holster. "Come in, you idiot," he challenged into the darkness without, "come in and take your medicine with the rest."

Within the room the six peered at the blackness of the open doorway, peered and held their breath. For an instant they saw nothing; then of a sudden, fair in the opening, walking easily, noiselessly on moccasined feet, entered a brand new actor, advanced half across the room, while his eyes adjusted themselves to the light, halted curiously. Back of him that instant the door again returned to its case with a crash, the rusty bolt grating in its socket; and above the noise, drowning it, sounded the snarl the others knew so well.

"It's you, is it, redskin? What the hell are you doin' here?"

Deliberately, soundlessly as he had entered, the newcomer turned. From his height of six feet one, an inch below that of Pete himself, he returned the other's look fixedly, without answer. He wore a soft flannel shirt, and a pair of dark brown corduroy trousers, supported by a belt. Unconsciously, as though he were alone, he hitched the corduroys up over his narrow hips, in the motion of one who has been riding. That was all.

Closer and closer came the red lids over Pete's veritable disfigurement. Involuntarily his great nostrils opened.

"Talk up there, Injun," he repeated slowly; and this time his voice was almost gentle. "My name's Sweeney, and I'm speakin' to you. What the devil are you here for?"

No answer, not a sound; not even the twitching of an eyelid or a muscle.

Ten seconds passed, fifteen.

"I'll give you one more chance there, aborigine;" slowly, with an effort, almost gratingly came the words, like the friction of a rusty spring at the striking of a clock; "and I ain't in the habit of doin' that either, pard." He halted and his great chest heaved with the effort of a mighty breath, his whole body leaned a bit forward. "Tell me what you want here, and tell me quick, or by the eternal I'll fill you so full of holes your own mother wouldn't recognise you."

One by one the two repeaters shifted, shifted until they were focussed upon a spot midway between the belt and the rolling collar of the flannel shirt. "I'm listening, How Landor."

At last the moment had come, the climax, the supreme instant in the career of those eight men in that tiny weather-boarded room. No need to tell seven of them at least that it was a moment of life or death. If something, something which seemed inevitable, happened, if one of those curling, itching fingers on the triggers tightened, if but once that took place, their lives were not worth the wording of a curse. If once again that black-visaged, passion-mastered human smelt powder, there would be no end while a target had power to move, while a tiny gleaming cylinder remained in the row within his belt. This they knew; and man by man, as the Creator made them, revealed the knowledge. The jaws of Bob Manning were quiet now, but the old eyes blazed from beneath their sockets like the eyes of a grey timber wolf, the centre of a howling pack. Next to him lank Wagner stood, waiting with closed lips; his lips as grey as those of the dead man on the floor. Rank Judge had not moved, but the harness on his wooden stump creaked softly as his weight shifted from leg to leg. Fat Buck Walker was perspiring almost grotesquely, like an earthenware pitcher. Great drops hung from his chin, from his uptilted nose, and his cotton shirt was dark. Slim Simpson, white before, was like a corpse; only his great boyish eyes stared out, as a somnambulist stares, as one hypnotised. Last of all, at the end of the line was the stranger from the East, representative of another world. Piteous, horrible, the others had been; but he-but for his clothes, his most intimate friend would not have recognised him at that moment. In him, blind, racking terror was personified. To have saved his soul he could not keep still, and his heavy walking shoes grated as they shuffled on the rough floor. He had bitten his lip and the blood stood in his mouth and trickled down, down his clean-shaven face. His eyes, like those of Slim Simpson, were abnormally wide, but shifting constantly in a hopeless search for a place of concealment, of safety. If aught in his life merited retribution, the man paid the price a hundred times over and over that second.

Thus man by man they stood waiting; a background no art could reproduce, no stage manager prodigal of expense. If on earth there ever was a hell, that tiny frontier room with the smoke-blackened ceiling and the single kerosene lamp sputtering on the wall, was the place. Not an imp thereof, but Satan himself, stood in the misshapen boots of Cowman Pete; doubly vicious in the aftermath of a debauch, Pete with the lust of blood in his veins. And against him, scant hope to those who watched, was a man; tall, but not heavy, smooth-cheeked as a boy of fourteen, soft-eyed, soft-handed, without the semblance of a weapon. One branded unmistakably a sleeper, a dreamer, one apparently helpless as a woman. Yet there that night, within the space of minutes, from the time there fell that last speaking silence, with this man the chief actor, there took place something, the report of which spread swifter than wildfire, from the river to the Hills, from the north Bad Lands to the sandy Platte, that will live and be repeated while tales of nerve and of man mastery quicken the pulses of listeners. For after that night Coyote Centre knew Long Pete Sweeney no more; Dakota knew him no more. Not that he was murdered in cold blood as he had murdered others: it was not that. Alone, unmolested, he left, in the starlight of that very night; but he knew, and they who permitted him to go, knew that it had been better —

But we anticipate.

"I'm listening, How Landor," he had said.

But he heard nothing: —yet he saw. He saw a tall, lithe, catlike figure straighten until it seemed fairly to tower. He saw this same figure look at him fully, squarely; as though for the first time really conscious of his presence. He saw two unflinching black eyes, flanked by high cheek bones, out of a copper-brown face meet his own, meet them and hold them; hold them immovably, hold them so he could not look away. He saw the owner of those eyes move-he did not hear, there was no sound, not even a pat from the moccasined feet, he merely saw-and move toward him. He saw that being coming, coming, saw it detour to pass a prostrate body on the floor; always silent, but always coming, always drawing nearer. He saw this thing, he, Pete Sweeney, he, Long Pete, whose name alone was terror. He knew what it meant, he knew what he should do, what he had sworn to do; the muzzles of his two revolvers were already focussed, but he made no move. His fingers lay as before on the triggers. Once in unison they tightened; then loosened again. He did not act, this man. As his maker was his judge, he could not. He was wide awake, preternaturally wide awake; he tried to act, tried to send the message that would make the muscles tense; but he could not. Those two eyes were holding him and he could not. All this he knew; and all the while that other was coming nearer and nearer. He began to have a horror of that coming that he could not halt. The great unshaven jaw of him worked; worked spasmodically, involuntarily. His skin, flaming hot before, of a sudden felt cool. The sweat spurted, stood damp on the hairy hands. Something he had never felt before, something he had observed in others, others like those six in the background, began to grip him; something that whitened his face, that made him feel of a sudden weak-weak as he had never felt before. And still those eyes were upon him, still that dark face came closer and closer. Once more his brain sent the message to kill, once more he battled against the inevitable; and that me ssage was the last. There was no more response than if he were clay, than if his muscles were the muscles of another man. In that instant, without the voicing of a word, the deed was done. That instant came the black chaotic abandon that was terror absolute. In pure physical impotence, his arms dropped dangling at his sides. The other was very near now, so near they could have touched, and the cowman tried to brace himself, tried to prepare for that which he knew was coming, which he read on the page of that other face. But he was too late. Watching, almost doubting their own eyes, the six saw the end. They saw a dark hand of a sudden clench, shoot out like a brown light. They heard an impact, and a second later the thud of a great body as it met the floor. They saw the latter lift, stumble clumsily to its feet, heard a muffled, choking oath. Then for a second time, the last, that clenched fist shot out, struck true. That was all.

For a minute, a long, dragging minute, there was silence, inaction. Then for the first time the victor turned, facing the spectators. Deliberately he turned, slowly, looked at them an instant almost curiously, —but he did not smile. Twelve arms, that had forgotten to lower, were still in the air-but he did not smile. Instead he sought out the stranger in knickerbockers and blouse.

"I came to meet Mr. Craig, Mr. Clayton Craig, and guide him to the B.B. ranch," he explained, "It is Mr. Landor's wish. Is this he?"

Chapter VI
The Red Man and the White

Well out upon the prairie, clear of the limits of the tiny town, two men were headed due west, into the night, apparently into the infinite. There was no moon, but here, with nothing to cast a shadow, it was not dark. The month was late October, and a suggestion of frost was in the air: on the grass blades of the low places, was actually present. As was all but usual at that day, the direction they were going bore no trace of a road; but the man astride the vicious-looking roan cayuse who led the way, the same copper-brown man with the corduroys of Bob Manning's store, showed no hesitation. Like a hound, he seemed to discern landmarks where none were visible to the eye. He rode without saddle or blanket, or spur, or quirt; yet, though he had not spoken a word from the moment they had started, the roan with the tiny ears had not broken its steady, swinging, seemingly interminable lope, had scarcely appeared conscious of his presence. Almost as unit seemed this beast and human. It was as though the man were born in his place, as though, like a sailor on a tiny boat, accustomed through a lifetime to a rolling, uncertain equilibrium, the adjustment thereto had become involuntary as a heart beat, instinctive as breathing. A splendid picture he made there in the starlight and the solitude; but of it the man who followed was oblivious. Of one thing alone he was conscious, and that was that he was very tired; weary from the effect of an unusual exercise, doubly exhausted in the reaction from excitement passed. With an effort he urged his own horse alongside the leader, drew rein meaningly.

"Let's hold up a bit," he protested. "I've come twenty-five miles to-day already, and I'm about beat." He slapped the breast pocket of his coat a bit obviously, and as his companion slowed to a walk, produced a silver-mounted, seal-covered flask and proffered it at arm's length. "The cork unscrews to the left," he explained suggestively.

The dark figure of the guide made no motion of acceptance, did not even glance around.

"Thanks, but I never drink," he declined.

"Not even to be sociable," —the hand was still extended, —"not when I ask you as —a friend?"

"I am a Sioux," simply. "I have found that liquor is not good for an Indian."

For a second the white man hesitated; then with something akin to a flush on his face, he returned the flask to his pocket untasted.

Again, without turning, the other observed the motion.

"Pardon me, but I did not mean to prevent you."

He spoke stiffly, almost diffidently, as on unused to speech with strangers, unused to speech at all; but without a trace of embarrassment or of affectation.

"I do not judge others. I merely know my people-and myself."

Again the stranger hesitated, and again his face betrayed him. He had scratched an aborigine, and to his surprise was finding indications of a man.

"I guess I can get along without it," shortly. "I—" he caught himself just in time from framing a self-extenuation. "I didn't have time-back there," he digressed suddenly, "to thank you for what you did. I wish to do so now." He was looking at the other squarely, as the smart civilian observes the derelict who has saved his life in a runaway. Already, there under the stars, it was difficult to credit to the full that fantastic scene of an hour ago; and unconsciously a trace of the real man, of condescension, crept into the tone. "You helped me out of a nasty mess, and I appreciate it."

No answer. No polite lie, no derogation of self or of what had been done. Just silence, attentive, but yet silence.

For the third time the white man hesitated, and for the third time his face shaded red; consciously and against his will. Even the starlight could not alter the obtrusive fact that he had cut a sorry figure in the late drama, and his pride was sore. Extenuation, dissimulation even, would have been a distinct solace. Looking at the matter now, the excitement past, palliation for what he had done was easy, almost logical. He had not alone conformed. He had but done, without consideration, as the others with him had done. But even if it were not so, back in the land from which he had come, a spade was not always so called. His colour went normal at the recollection. The habitual, the condescending pressed anew to the fore.

He inspected the silent figure at his side ingenuously, almost quizzically; as in his schoolboy days he had inspected his plodding master of physics before propounding a query no mortal could answer.

"I know I waved the white flag back there as hard as any of them," he proffered easily. "I'm not trying to clear myself; but between you and me, don't you think that Pete was merely bluffing, there at the end when you came?" The speaker shifted sideways on the saddle, until his weight rested on one leg, until he faced the other fair. "The fellow was drunk, irresponsibly drunk, at first, when the little chap stirred him up; but afterwards, when he was sober....On the square, what do you think he would have done if-if you hadn't happened in?" For so long that Craig fancied he had not given attention to the question, the guide did not respond, did not stir in his seat; then slowly, deliberately, he turned half about, turned and for the first time in the journey met the other's eyes. Even then he did not speak; but so long as he lived, times uncounted in his after life, Clayton Craig remembered that look; remembered it and was silent, remembered it with a tingling of hot blood and a mental imprecation-for as indelibly as a red-hot iron seals a brand on a maverick, that look left its impress. No voice could have spoken as that simple action spoke, no tongue thrust could have been so pointed. With no intent of discourtesy, no premeditated malice was it given; and therein lay the fine sting, the venom. It was unconscious as a breath, unconscious as nature's joy in springtime; yet in the light of after events, it stood out like a signal fire against the blackness of night, as the beginning of an enmity more deadly than death itself, that lasted into the grave and beyond. For that silent, unwavering look set them each, the red man and the white, in their niche; placed them with an assurance that was final. It was a questioning, analytic look, yet, unconcealed, it bore the tolerance of a strong man for a weak. Had that look been a voice, it would have spoken one word, and that word was "cad."

For a moment the two men sat so, unconscious of time, unconscious of place; then of a sudden, to both alike, the present returned-and again that return was typical. As deliberately as he had moved previously, the Indian faced back. His left arm, free at his side, hung loose as before. His right, that held the reins, lay motionless on the pony's mane. In no detail did he alter, nor in a muscle. By his side, the white man stiffened, jerked without provocation at the cruel curb bit, until his horse halted uncertain; equally without provocation, sent the rowels of his long spurs deep into the sensitive flank, with a curse held the frightened beast down to a walk. That was all, a secondary lapse, a burst of flowing, irresponsible passion like a puff of burning gunpowder, and it was over; yet it was enough. In that second was told the tale of a human life. In that and in the surreptitious sidelong glance following, that searched for an expression in the boyishly soft face of his companion. But the Indian was looking straight before him, looking as one who has seen nothing, heard nothing; and, silent as before the interruption, they journeyed on.

A half hour slipped by, a period wherein the horses walked and galloped, and walked again, ere the white man forgot, ere the instinct of companionship, the necessity of conversation, urban-fostered, gained mastery. Then as before, he looked at the other surreptitiously, through unconsciously narrowed lids.

"I haven't yet asked your name?" he formalised baldly, curtly.

The guide showed no surprise, no consciousness of the long silence preceding.

"The Sioux call me Ma-wa-cha-sa: the ranchers, How Landor."

Craig dropped the reins over his saddle and fumbled in his pockets.

"The Indian word has a meaning, I presume?"

"Translated into English, it would be 'the lost pappoose.'"

The eyebrows of the Easterner lifted; but he made no comment.

"You have been with my uncle, with Mr. Landor, I mean, long?"

"Since I can remember-almost."

The search within the checkered blouse ended. The inquisitor produced a pipe and lit it. It took three matches.

"My uncle never wrote me of that. He told me once of adopting a girl. Bess he called her, was it not?"

"Yes."

Already the pipe had gone dead, and Craig struggled anew in getting it alight, with the awkwardness of one unused to smoking out of doors.

"Do you like this country, this-desert?" he digressed suddenly.

"It is the only one I know."

"You mean know well, doubtless?"

"I have never been outside the State."

Unconsciously the other shrugged, in an action that was habitual.

"You have something to look forward to then. I read somewhere that it were better to hold down six feet of earth in an Eastern cemetery than to own a section of land in the West. I'm beginning to believe it."

No comment.

"I suppose you will leave though, some time," pressed the visitor. "You certainly don't intend to vegetate here always?"

"I never expect to leave. I was born here. I shall die here."

Once more the shoulders of the Easterner lifted in mute thanksgiving of fundamental differ-ence. Of a sudden, for some indefinite reason, he felt more at ease in his companion's presence. For the time being the sense of antagonism became passive. What use, after all, was mere physical courage, if one were to bury it in a houseless, treeless waste such as this? The sense of aloofness, of tranquil superiority, returned. He even felt a certain pleasure in questioning the other; as one is interested in questioning a child. Bob Manning's store and Pete Sweeney were temporarily in abeyance.

"Pardon me, if I seem inquisitive," he prefaced, "but I'll probably be here a month or so, and we'll likely see a good deal of each other. Are you married?"

"No."

"You will be, though." It was the ultimatum of one unaccustomed to contradiction. "No man could live here alone. He'd go insane."

"I eat at the ranch house sometimes, but I live alone."

"You won't do so, though, always." Again it was the voice of finality.

The Indian looked straight ahead into the indefinite distance where the earth and sky met.

"No, I shall not do so always," he corroborated.

"I thought so." It was the tolerant approval of the prophet verified. "I'd be doing the same thing myself if I lived here long. Conformity's in the air. I felt it the moment I left the railroad and struck this-wilderness." Once again the unconscious shoulder shrug. "It's an atavism, this life. I've reverted a generation already. It's only a question of time till one would be back among the cave-dwellers. The thing's in the air, I say."

Again no comment. Again for any indication he gave, the Indian might not have heard.

Craig straightened, as one conscious that he was talking over his companion's head.

"When, if I may ask, is it to be, your marriage, I mean?" he returned. "While I am here?"

For an instant the other's eyes dropped until they were hid beneath the long lashes, then they returned to the distance as before.

"It will be soon. Three weeks from to-day."

"And at the ranch, I presume? My uncle will see to that, of course."

"Yes, it will be at the ranch."

"Good! I was wondering if anything would be doing here while I was here." Craig threw one leg over the pommel of his saddle and adjusted the knickerbockers comfortably. "By the way, how do you-your people-celebrate an event of this kind? I admit I'm a bit ignorant on the point."

"Celebrate? I don't think I understand." The Easterner glanced at his companion suspiciously but the other man was still looking straight ahead into the distance.

"You have a dance, or a barbecue or-or something of that sort, don't you? It's to be an Indian wedding, is it not?"

Pat, pat went the horses' feet on the prairie sod. While one could count ten slowly there was no other sound.

"No, there will be no dance or barbecue or anything out of the ordinary, so far as I know," said a low voice then. "It will not be an Indian wedding."

Craig hesitated. An instinct told him he had gone far enough. Lurking indefinite in the depths of that last low-voiced answer was a warning, a challenge to a trespasser; but something else, a thing which a lifetime of indulgence had made almost an instinct, prevented his heeding. He was not accustomed to being denied, this man; and there was no contesting the obvious fact that now a confidence was being withheld. The latent antagonism aroused with a bound at the thought. Something more than mere curiosity was at stake, something which he magnified until it obscured his horizon, warped hopelessly his vision of right or wrong. He was of the conquering Anglo-Saxon race, and this other who refused him was an Indian. Racial supremacy itself hung in the balance: the old, old issue of the white man and the red. Back into the stirrup went the leg that hung over the saddle. Involuntarily as before he stiffened.

"Why, is it not to be an Indian wedding?" he queried directly. "You seemed a bit ago rather proud of your pedigree." A trace of sarcasm crept into his voice at the thinly veiled allusion. "Have you forsaken entirely the customs of your people?"

Pat, pat again sounded the horses' feet. The high places as well as the low bore their frost blanket now, and the dead turf cracked softly with every step.

"No, I have not forsaken the customs of my people."

"Why then in this instance?" insistently. "At least be consistent, man. Why in this single particular and no other?"

The hand on the neck of the cayuse tightened, tightened until the tiny ears of the wicked little beast went flat to its head; then of a sudden the grip loosened.

"Why? The answer is simple. The lady who is to be my wife is not an Indian."

For an instant Craig was silent, for an instant the full meaning of that confession failed in its appeal; then of a sudden it came over him in a flood of comprehension. Very, very far away now, banished into remotest oblivion, was Pete Sweeney. Into the same grave went any remnants of gratitude to the other man that chanced to remain. Paramount, beckoning him on, one thought, one memory alone possessed his brain: the recollection of that look the other had given him, that look he could never forget nor forgive. "Since you have told me so much," he challenged "you will probably have no objection to telling me the lady's name. Who is it to be?"

Silence fell upon them. Far in the distance, so far that had the white man seen he would have thought it a star, a light had come into being. Many a time before the little roan had made this journey. Many a time he had seen that light emerge from the surface of earth. To him it meant all that was good in life: warmth, food, rest. The tiny head shook impatiently, shifted sideways with an almost human question to his rider at the slowness of the pace, the delay.

"That light you see there straight ahead is in the ranch house," digressed the Indian. "It is four miles away."

Again it was the warning, not a suggestion, but positive this time; and again it passed unheeded.

"You have forgotten to answer my question," recalled Craig.

Swift as thought the Indian shifted in his seat, shifted half about; then as suddenly he remembered.

"No, I have not forgotten," he refuted. "You tell me you have already heard of Bess Landor. It is she I am to marry."

At last he had spoken, had given his confidence to this hostile stranger man; not vauntingly or challengingly, but simply as he had spoken his name. Against his will he had done this thing, despite a reticence no one who did not understand Indian nature could appreciate. Then at least it would not have taken a wise man to hold aloof. Then at least common courtesy would have called a halt. But Clayton Craig was neither wise nor courteous this night. He was a great, weary, passionate child, whose pride had been stung, who but awaited an opportunity to retaliate. And that opportunity had been vouchsafed. Moreover, irony of fate, it came sugar coated. Until this night he had been unconscious as a babe of racial prejudice. Now of a sudden, it seemed a burning issue, and he its chosen champion. His blood tingled at the thought; tingled to the tips of his well-manicured fingers. His clean-shaven chin lifted in air until his lashes all but met.

"Do you mean to tell me," —his voice was a bit higher than normal and unnaturally tense, — "do you mean to tell me that you, an Indian, are to marry a white girl-and she my cousin by adoption? Is this what you mean?"

Seconds passed.

"I have spoken," said a low voice. "I do not care to discuss the matter further."

"But I do care to discuss it," peremptorily. "As one of the family it is my right, and I demand an answer."

Again the tiny roan was shaking an impatient head. It would not be long until they were home now.

"Yes," answered the Indian.

"And that my uncle will permit it, gives his consent?" Again the silence and again the low-voiced "Yes."

Over Craig's face, to his eyebrows and beyond, there swept a red flood, that vanished and left him pale as the starlight about him.

"Well, he may; but by God I won't!" he blazed. "As sure as I live, and if she's as plain as a hag, so long as her skin is white, you'll not marry her. If it's the last act of my life, I'll prevent you!"

The voice of the white man was still, but his heart was not. Beat, beat, beat it went until he could scarcely breathe, until the hot blood fairly roared in his arteries, in his ears. Not until the challenge was spoken did he realise to the full what he had done, that inevitable as time there would be a reckoning. Now in a perfect inundation, the knowledge came over him, and unconsciously he braced himself, awaited the move. Yet for long, eternally long it seemed to him, there was none. The swift reaction of a passionate nature was on, and as in Bob Manning's store, the suspense of those dragging seconds was torture. Adding thereto, recollection of that former scene, temporarily banished, returned now irresistibly, cumulatively. Struggle as he might against the feeling, a terror of this motionless human at his side grew upon him; a blind, unreasoning, primitive terror. But one impulse possessed him: to be away, to escape the outburst he instinctively knew was but delayed. In an abandon he leaned far forward over his saddle, the rowel of his spur dug viciously into his horse's flank. There was a deep-chested groan from the surprised beast, a forward leap-then a sudden jarring halt. As by magic, the reins left his hand, were transferred to another hand.

"Don't," said a voice. "It will not help matters any to do that. It will only make them worse." The two horses, obeying the same hand, stopped there on the prairie. The riders were face to face. "I have tried to prevent this, for the sake of the future, I have tried; but you have made an understanding between us inevitable, and therefore it may as well be now." The voice halted and the speaker looked at his companion fixedly, minutely, almost unbelievingly. "I know I am not as you white men," went on the voice. "I have been raised with you, lived my life so far with you; yet I am different. No Indian would have done as you have done. I cannot understand it. Not three hours ago I saved your life. It was a mere chance, but nevertheless I did it; and yet already you have forgotten, have done-what you have done." So far he had spoken slowly, haltingly; with the effort of one to whom words were difficult. Now the effort passed. "I say I cannot understand it," he repeated swiftly. "Mr. Landor has been very good to me. For his sake I would like to forgive what you have done, what you promise to do. I have tried to forgive it; but I cannot. I am an Indian; but I am also a man. As a race your people have conquered my people, have penned them up in reservations to die; but that is neither your doing nor mine. We are here as man to man. As man to man you have offered me insult-and without reason." For the first time a trace of passion came into the voice, into the soft brown face. "I ask you to take back what you have just said. I do not warn you. If you do so, there is no quarrel between us. I merely ask you to take it back."

He halted expectant; but there was no answer, Craig's lips were twitching uncontrollably, but he did not speak.

Just perceptibly the Indian shifted forward in his seat, just perceptibly the long brown fingers tightened on his pony's mane.

"Will you not take it back?" he asked.

Once more the white man's lip twitched. "No," he said.

"No?"

"No."

That was all-and it was not all. For an instant after the Easterner had spoken the stars looked down on the two men as they were, face to face; then smiling, satiric they gazed down upon a very different scene: one as old and as new as the history of man. Just what happened in that moment that intervened neither the white man nor the red could have told. It was a lapse, an oblivion; a period of primitive physical dominance, of primitive human hate. When they awoke-when the red man awoke-they were flat on earth, the dust of the prairie in their nostrils, the short catch of their breath in each other's ears, out one, the dark-skinned, was above. One, again the dark-skinned, had his fingers locked tight on the other's throat. This they knew when they awoke.

A second thereafter they lay so, flaming eyes staring into their doubles; then suddenly the uppermost man broke free, arose. In his ears was the diminishing patter of their horses' hoofs. They were alone there on the prairie, under the smiling satiric stars. One more moment he stood so; he did not turn; he did not assist the other to rise; then he spoke.

"I do not ask your pardon for this," he said. "You have brought it upon yourself. Neither do I ask a promise. Do as you please. Try what you have suggested if you wish. I am not afraid. Follow me," and, long-strided, impassive as though nothing had happened, he moved ahead into the distance where in the window of the Buffalo Butte ranch house glowed a light.

Chapter VII
A Glimpse of the Unknown

It was very late, so late that the sun entering at the south windows of the room shone glaringly upon the white counterpane of his bed when Craig awoke the next morning. Breakfast had long been over, but throughout the unplastered ranch house the suggestion of coffee and the tang of bacon still lingered. At home those odours would have aroused slight sensations of pleasure in the man, even at this time of day; but now and here they were distinctly welcome, distinctly inviting. With the aid of a tin pail of water and a cracked queensware bowl, he made a hasty toilet, soliloquised an opinion of a dressing-room without a mirror, and descended the creaking stairs to the level below.

The main floor of the ranch house contained but three rooms. Of these, it was the living-room which he entered. No one was about. The pipe which he had smoked with his uncle before retiring the night before remained exactly as he had put it down. His cap and gloves were still beside it. Obviously there was no possibility of breakfast here, and he moved toward the adjoining room. On his way he passed a hook where upon arrival he had hung his riding blouse. Telltale with its litter of dust and grass stems, it hung there now; and unconsciously he scowled at the recollection it suggested.

Opening the door, he was face to face with a little fast-ticking cheaply ornate clock. Its hands indicated eleven, and the man grimaced tolerantly. As in the living-room, no human was present, but here the indications for material sustenance were more hopeful. It was the dining-room, and, although in the main the table had been cleared, at one end a clean plate, flanked by a bone-handled knife and fork and an old-fashioned castor, still remained. Moreover, from the third room, the kitchen, he could now hear sounds of life. The fire in a cook-stove was crackling cheerily. Above it, distinct through the thin partition, came the sound of a girlish voice singing. There was no apparent effort at time or at tune; it was uncultivated as the grass land all about; yet in its freshness and unconsciousness it was withal distinctly pleasing. It was a happy voice, a contented voice. Instinctively it bore a suggestion of home and of quiet and of peace; like a kitten with drowsy eyes purring to itself in the sunshine. A moment the visitor stood silent, listening; then, his heavy shoes clumping on the uncarpeted floor, he moved toward it. Instantly the song ceased, but he kept on, pushed open the door gently, stepped inside.

"Good-morning!" he began, and then halted in an uncertainty he seldom felt among women folk. He had met no one but his uncle the previous night. Inevitably the preceding incident with his guide had produced a mental picture. It was with the expectation of having this conception personified that he had entered, to it he had spoken; then had come the revelation, the halt.

"Good-morning!" answered a voice, one neither abnormally high nor repressedly low, the kind of voice the man seldom heard in the society to which he was accustomed-one natural, un-affected, frankly interested. The owner thereof came forward, held out her hand. Two friendly brown eyes smiled up at him from the level of his shoulder. "I know without your introducing yourself that you're Mr. Craig," she welcomed. "Uncle Landor told me before he left what to expect. He and Aunt Mary had to go to town this morning. Meanwhile I'm the cook, and at your service," and she smiled again.

For far longer than civility actually required, to the extreme limit of courtesy and a shade beyond, in, fact, until it unmistakably sought to be free, Clayton Craig retained that proffered hand. Against all the canons of good breeding he stared. Answering, a trace of colour, appearing at the brown throat, mounted higher and higher, reached the soft oval cheeks, journeyed on.

"I beg your pardon," apologised the man. He met the accusing eyes fairly, with a return of his old confidence. "You had the advantage of me, you know. I was not forewarned what to expect."

It was the breaking of the ice, and they laughed together. The girl had been working with arms bare to the elbow, and as now of a sudden she rolled the sleeves down Craig laughed again; and in unconscious echo a second later she joined. Almost before they knew it, there alone in the little whitewashed kitchen with the crackling cook-stove and the sunshine streaming in through the tiny-paned windows, they were friends. All the while the girl went about the task of preparing a belated breakfast they laughed and chatted-and drew nearer and nearer. Again while Craig ate and at his command the girl sat opposite to entertain him, they laughed and chatted. Still later, the slowly eaten meal finished, while Elizabeth Landor washed the dishes and put everything tidy and Craig from his seat on the bottom of an inverted basket reversed the position of entertainer, they laughed and chatted. And through it all, openly when possible, surreptitiously when it were wise, the man gave his companion inspection. And therein he at first but followed an instinct. Very, very human was Clayton Craig of Boston, Suffolk County, Massachusetts, and very, very good to look upon was brown-eyed, brown-skinned, brown-haired Elizabeth Landor. Neither had thought of evil, had other thought than the innocent pleasure of the moment that first morning while the tiny clock on the wall measured off the swift-moving minutes. Good it is to be alive in sun-blessed South Dakota on a frosty warm October day, doubly good when one is young; and these two, the man and the girl, were both young. Months it takes, years sometimes, in civilisation, with barriers of out on the prairie, alone, with the pulse of nature throbbing, throbbing, insistently all about, the process is very swift, so swift that an hour can suffice. No, not that first hour wherein unconsciously they became friends, did the angel with the big book record evil opposite the name of Clayton Craig; not until later, not until he had had time to think, not until —.

But again we anticipate.

"I'm so glad you've come," the girl had ejaculated, "now when you have." At last the work was over, and in unconscious comradery they sat side by side on the broad south doorstep; the sun shining down full upon their uncovered heads-smiling an unconscious blessing more potent than formula of clergy. She was looking out as she spoke, out over the level earth dazzling with its dancing heat waves, mysterious in its suggestion of unfathomable silence, of limitless distance. "It's such a little time now before I am going away, and Uncle Landor has talked of you so much, particularly of late." A pause, a hesitating pause. "I suppose you'll laugh at me, but I hope you'll stay here, for a time, anyway, after I'm gone."

Clayton Craig, the listener, was not gazing out over the prairie. The object at which he was looking was very near; so near that he had leaned a trifle back the better to see, to watch. He shifted now until his weight rested on his elbow, his face on his hand.

"You are going away, you say?" he echoed.

"Yes. I supposed you knew-that Uncle had told you." Despite an effort, the tiny ears were reddening. She was very human also, was Elizabeth Landor. "I am to be married soon."

"Married?" A long pause. "And to whom, please?" The voice was very low.

Redder than before burned the tiny ears. No more than she could keep from breathing could she prevent telling her secret, her happiness, this prairie girl; no more than she could prevent that accompanying telltale scarlet flood.

"You didn't know it, but you've met him already," she confided. "You met him last night." To her at this time there was no need of antecedent. There was but one to whom the pronoun might refer. "It was he who showed you here-How Landor."

For a long time-for he was thinking now, was Clayton Craig, and did not answer-there was silence. Likewise the girl, her confession voiced, said no more; but her colour came and went expectantly, tantalisingly, and the eyes that still looked into the distance were unconscious of what they saw. From his place the man watched the transparent pantomime, read its meaning, stored the picture in his memory; but he did not speak. A minute had already passed; but still he did not speak. He was thinking of the night before, was the man, of that first look he had received-and of what had followed. His eyes were upon the girl, but it was of this he was thinking. Another minute passed. A big shaggy-haired collie, guardian of the dooryard, paused in his aimless wandering about the place to thrust a friendly muzzle into the stranger's hand; but even then he did not respond. For almost the first time in his irresolute life a definite purpose was taking form in the mind of Clayton Craig, and little things passed him by. A third minute passed. The colour had ceased playing on the face he watched now. The silence had performed its mission. It was the moment for which he was waiting, and he was prepared. Then it was the angel of the great book opened the volume and made an entry; for then it was the watcher spoke.

"I met him last, night, you say?" It was the hesitating voice of one whose memory is treacherous, "I have been trying to recall-Certainly you must be mistaken. I saw no one last night except Uncle Landor and an Indian cow-puncher with a comic opera name." He met the brown eyes that were of a sudden turned upon him, frankly, innocently. "You must be mistaken," he repeated.

Searchingly, at first suspiciously, then hesitatingly, with a return of the colour that came as easily as a prairie wind stirs the down of a milk-weed plant, Elizabeth Landor returned his look. It was an instinct that at last caused her eyes to drop.

"No, I was not mistaken," she voiced. "How Landor is an Indian. It is he I meant."

For a carefully timed pause, the space in which one recovers from hearing the unbelievable, Craig was silent; then swiftly, contritely he

roused. "I beg a thousand pardons," he apologised. "I meant no disrespect. I never dreamed-Forgive me." He had drawn very near. "I wouldn't hurt you for the world. I —Please forgive me." He was silent.

"There's nothing to forgive." The girl's colour was normal again and she met his eyes frankly, gravely.

"But there is," protested the man humbly. "Because he happened to be minus a collar and had a red skin —I was an ass; an egregious, blundering ass."

"Don't talk that way," hurriedly. "You merely did not know him, was all. If you had been acquainted all your life as I have —" Against her will she was lapsing into a defence, and she halted abruptly. "You were not at fault."

Again for a carefully timed pause the man was silent. Then abruptly, obviously, he changed the subject.

"You said you were going away," he recalled. "Is it to be a wedding journey?"

"Yes," tensely.

"Tell me of it, please; I wish to hear."

"You would not be interested."

"Elizabeth —" syllabalised, reproachfully. "Am I not your cousin?"

No answer.

"Haven't you forgiven me yet?" The voice was very low. Its owner was again very near.

"You'd laugh at me if I told you," repressedly. "You wouldn't understand."

Slowly, meaningly, Clayton Craig drew away-resumed the former position; the place from which, unobserved, he could himself watch.

"We're going away out there," complied the girl suddenly, reluctantly. Her hand indicated the trackless waste to the right. "Just the two of us are going: How and I. We'll take a pack horse and a tent and How's camp kit and stay out there alone until winter comes." Against her will she was warming to the subject, was unconsciously painting a picture to please the solitary listener. "We'll have our ponies and ammunition and plenty to read. The cowboys laugh at How because ordinarily he never carries a gun; but he's a wonderful shot. We'll have game whenever we want it. We'll camp when we please and move on when we please." Again unconsciously she glanced at the listener to see the effect of her art. "We'll be together, How and I, and free-free as sunshine. There'll be nothing but winter, and that's a long way off, to bring us back. It's what I've always wanted to do, from the time I can remember. How goes away every year, and he's promised this once to take me along." Suddenly, almost challengingly, she turned, facing the man her companion. "Won't it be fine?" she queried abruptly.

"Yes," answered a voice politely, a voice with a shade of listlessness in its depths, "fine indeed. And if you want anything at any time you can go to the nearest ranch house. One always does forget something you know."

"That's just what we can't do," refuted the girl swiftly. "That's the best of it all. The Buffalo Butte is the last ranch that way, to the west, until you get to the Hills. We probably won't see another human being while we're gone. We'll be as much alone as though we were the only two people in the world."

Craig hesitated; then he shrugged self-tolerantly.

"I'm hopelessly civilised myself," he commented smilingly. "I was thinking that some morning I might want toast and eggs for breakfast. And my clean laundry might not be delivered promptly if I were changing my residence so frequently." He lifted from his elbow. "Pardon me again, though," he added contritely. "I always do see the prosaic side of things." The smile vanished, and for the first time he looked away, absently, dreamily. As he looked his face altered, softened almost unbelievably. "It would be wonderful," he voiced slowly, tensely, "to be alone, absolutely alone, out there with the single person one cared for most, the single person who always had the same likes and dislikes, the same hopes and ambitions. I had never thought of such a thing before; it would be wonderful, wonderful!"

No answer; but the warm colour had returned to the girl's face and her eyes were bright.

"I think I envy you a little, your happiness," said Craig. Warmer and warmer tinged the brown cheeks, but still the girl was silent.

"Yes, I'm sure I envy you," reiterated the man. "We always envy other people the things we haven't ourselves; and I —" He checked himself abruptly.

"Don't talk so," pleaded the girl. "It hurts me."

"But it's true."

Just a child of nature was Elizabeth Landor; passionate, sympathetic, unsophisticated product of this sun-kissed land. Just this she was; and another, this man with her, her cousin by courtesy, was sad. Inevitably she responded, as a flower responds to the light, as a parent bird responds to the call of a fledgling in distress.

"Maybe it's true now-you think it is," she halted; "but there'll be a time —"

"No, I think not. I'm as the Lord made me." Craig laughed shortly, unmusically. "It's merely my lot."

The girl hesitated, uncertain, at a loss for words. Distinctly for her as though the brightness of the day had faded under a real shadow, it altered now under the cloud of another's unhappiness. But one suggestion presented itself; and innocently, Instinctively as a mother comforts her child, she drew nearer to the other in mute human sympathy.

The man did not move. Apparently he had not noticed.

"The time was," he went on monotonously, "when I thought differently,

when I fancied that some time, somewhere, I would meet a girl I understood, who could understand me. But I never do. No matter how well I become acquainted with women, we never vitally touch, never become necessary to each other. It seems somehow that I'm the only one of my kind, that I must go through life so-alone."

Nearer and nearer crept the girl; not as maid to man, but as one child presses closer to another in the darkness. One of her companion's hands lay listless on his knee, and instinctively, compellingly, she placed her own upon it, pressed it softly.

"I am so selfish," she voiced contritely, "to tell you of my own love, my own happiness. I didn't mean to hurt you. I simply couldn't help it, it's such a big thing in my own life. I'm so sorry."

Just perceptibly Craig stirred; but still he did not look at her. When he spoke again there was the throb of repression in his voice; but that was all.

"I'm lonely at times," he went on dully, evasively, "you don't know how lonely. Now and then someone, as you unconsciously did a bit ago, shows me the other side of life, the happy side; and I wish I were dead." A mist came into his eyes, a real mist. "The future looks so blank, so hopeless that it becomes a nightmare to me. Anything else would be preferable, anything. It's so to-day, now." He halted and of a sudden turned away so that his face was concealed. "God forgive me, but I wish it were over with, that I were dead!"

"No, no! You mustn't say that! You mustn't!" Forgetful entirely, the girl arose, stood facing him. Tears that she could not prevent were in the brown eyes and her lip twitched. "It's so good to be alive. You can't mean it. You can't."

"But I do. It's true." Craig did not stir, did not glance up. "What's the use of living, of doing anything, when no one else cares, ever will care. What's the use —"

"But somebody does care," interrupted the girl swiftly, "all of us here care. Don't say that again, please don't. I can't bear to hear you." She halted, swallowed hard at a lump which rose hinderingly in her throat. "I feel somehow as though I was to blame, as though if you should mean what you said, should-should —" Again she halted; the soft brown eyes glistening, the dainty oval chin trembling uncontrollably, her fingers locked tight. A moment she stood so, uncertain, helpless; then of a sudden the full horror of the possibility the other had suggested came over her, swept away the last barrier of reserve. Not the faintest suspicion of the man's sincerity, of his honesty, occurred to her, not the remotest doubt. In all her life no one had ever lied to her; she had never consciously lied to another. The world of subterfuge was an unread book. This man had intimated he would do this terrible thing. He meant it. He would do it, unless-unless —

"Don't," she pleaded in abandon. "Don't!" The hand was still lying idle on the man's knee, and reaching down she lifted it, held it prisoner between her own. It was not a suggestion she was combating now. It was a certainty. "Promise me you won't do this thing." She shook the hand insistently; at first gently, then, as there was no response, almost roughly. "Tell me you won't do it. Promise me; please, please!"

"But I can't promise," said the man dully. "I'm useless absolutely; I never realised before how useless. You didn't intend to do it, but you've made me see it all to-day. I don't blame you, but I can't promise. I can't."

Silence fell upon them; silence complete as upon the top of a mountain, as in the depths of a mine, the absolute silence of the prairie. For seconds it remained with them, for long-drawn-out, distorted seconds; then, interrupting, something happened. There was not a cloud in the sky, nor the vestige of a cloud. The sun still shone bright as before; yet distinctly, undeniably, the man felt a great wet spattering drop fall from above upon his hand-and a moment later another. He glanced up, hesitated; sprang to his feet, his big body towering above that of the little woman already standing.

"Elizabeth!" he said tensely. "Cousin Bess! I can't believe it." He took her by the shoulders compellingly, held her at arm's length; and the angel who watched halted with pen in air, indecisive. "We've known each other such a ludicrously short time-but a few hours. Can it be possible that you really meant that, that at least to someone it does really matter?" It was his turn to question, to wait breathlessly when no answer came. "Would you really care, you, if I were dead? Tell me, Bess, tell me, as though you were saying a prayer." One hand still retained its grip on her shoulder, but its mate loosened, instinctively sought that averted, trembling chin, as hundreds of men, his ancestors, had done to similar chins in their day, lifted it until their eyes met. Had he been facing his Maker that moment and the confession his last, Clayton Craig could not have told whether it were passion or art, that action. "Tell me, Bess girl, is it mere pity, or do you really care?"

Face to face they stood there, eye to eye as two strangers, meeting by chance in darkness and storm, read each the other's mind in the glitter of a lightning flash. It was all so swift, so fantastic, so unexpected that for a moment the girl did not realise, did not understand. For an instant she stood so, perfectly still, her great eyes opening wider and wider, opening wonderingly, dazedly, as though the other had done what she feared-and of a sudden returned again to life; then in mocking, ironic reaction came tardy comprehension, and with the strength of a captured wild thing she drew back, broke free. A second longer she stood there, not her chin alone, but her whole body trembling; then without a word she turned, mounted the single step, fumbled at the knob of the door. "Bess," said the man softly, 'Cousin Bess!" But she did not glance back nor speak, and, listening, his ear to the panel, Craig heard her slowly climb the creaking stairs to her own room and the door close behind her.

Chapter VIII
The Skeleton Within the Closet

Comparatively few men of cheerful outlook and social inclination attain the age of five and fifty without contracting superfluous avoirdupois and distinctive mannerism. That Colonel William Landor was no exception to the first rule was proven by the wheezing effort with which he made his descent from the two-seated canvas-covered surrey in front of Bob Manning's store, and, with a deftness born of experience, converted the free ends of the lines into hitch straps. That the second premise held true was demonstrated ten seconds later in the unconscious grunt of soliloquy with which he greeted the sight of a wisp of black rag tacked above the knob of the door before him.

"Mourning, eh," he commented to his listening ego. "Looks like a strip of old Bob's prayer-meeting trousers." He tried the entrance, found it locked, and in lieu of entering tested the badge of sorrow between thumb and finger. "Pant stuff, sure enough," he corroborated. "It can't be Bob himself, or they'd have needed these garments to lay him out in. Now what in thunder, I wonder —"

He glanced across the street at Slim Simpson's eating house. Like the general store, the door was closed, and just above the catch, flapping languidly in a rising prairie breeze, was the mate to the black rag dangling at his back. The spectator's shaggy eyebrows tightened in genuine surprise, and with near-sighted effort he inspected the fronts of the short row of other buildings along the street.

"Civilisation's struck Coyote Centre good and proper, at last, evidently," he commented. "They'll be having a bevel plate hearse with carved wood tassels and a coon driver next!" He halted, indecisive, and for the first time became conscious that not a human being was in sight. In the street before him a pair of half-grown cockerels with ludicrously long legs and abbreviated tails were scratching a precarious living from amid the litter. On the sunny expanse of sidewalk before Buck Walker's meat market a long-eared mongrel lay stretched out luxuriously in the physical contentment of the subservient unmolested; but from one end of the single street to the other not a human being was in sight; save the present spectator, not a single disturber of the all-pervading quiet. Landor had seen the spot where the town now stood when it was virgin prairie, had watched every building it boasted rise from the earth, had hitherto observed it through the gamut of its every mood from nocturnal recklessness to profoundest daybreak remorse; but as it was now with the sun nearing the meridian, deserted, dead —.

"Well, I'm beat!" he exploded as emphatically as though another were listening. "There must have been a general cleanup this time. I fear that the report of my respected nephew —" He checked himself suddenly, a bit guiltily. Even though no one was listening, he was loath to voice an inevitable conclusion. Decision, however, had triumphed over surprise at last, and, leaving the main street, he headed toward what the proud citizens denominated the residence quarter — a handful of unpainted weather-stained one-story boxes, destitute of tree or of shrub surrounding as factory tenements. The sun was positively hot now, and as he went he unbuttoned his vest and sighed in unconscious satisfaction at the relief. At the second domicile, a residence as nearly like the first as a duplicate pea from the same pod, he turned in at the lane leading to the house unhesitatingly, and without form of knocking opened the door and stepped inside.

The room he entered was bare, depressingly so; bare as to its uncarpeted cottonwood floor, bare in its hard-finished, smoke-tinted walls. In it, to the casual observer, there were visible but four objects: an old-fashioned walnut desk that had once borne a top, but which did so no longer; two cane-bottomed chairs with rickety arms; and, seated in one thereof, a man. The latter looked up as the visitor entered, revealing an unshaven chin and a pair of restless black eyes over the left of which the lid drooped appreciably. He was smoking a long black stogie, and scattered upon his vest and in a semicircle surrounding his chair was a sprinkling of white ash from vanished predecessors. Though he looked up when the other entered, and Landor returned the scrutiny, there was no salutation, not even when, without form of invitation, the rancher dropped into the vacant seat opposite and tossed his broad felt hat familiarly amid the litter of the desk. A moment they sat so, while with an effort the newcomer recovered his breath.

"I thought I'd find you here, Chantry," he initiated eventually. "I've noticed that the last place to look for a doctor is in the proximity of a funeral." He fumbled in his pocket and produced a stogie, mate to that in the other's mouth. "This particular ceremony, by the way, I gather from the appearance of the metropolis, must have been of more than ordinary interest." And lighting a match he puffed until his face was concealed.

"Rather," laconically.

"Never mind the details," Landor prevented hurriedly. The haze had cleared somewhat, and he observed his taciturn companion appreciatively. "I left Mary up with Jim Burton's wife, and I think she can be trusted to attend to such little matters."

Chantry smoked on without comment, but his restless black eyes were observing the other shrewdly. Not without result had the two men known each other these five years.

"It's a great convenience, this having women in the family," commented Landor impersonally. "It's better than a daily paper, any time." Again the deliberate, appreciate look. "You haven't decided yet to prove the fact for yourself, have you?"

Still Chantry smoked in silence, waiting. The confidence that had brought the other to him was very near now, almost apparent. Only too well he knew the signs-the good-natured satire that ill concealed a tolerance broad as the earth, the flow of trivialities that cleared the way later of non-essentials. In silence he waited; and, as he had known the moment that big figure appeared in the doorway, it came.

Deliberately Landor removed the stogie from his lips, as deliberately flicked off the loose ash onto the floor at his side, inspected the burning tuck critically.

"Supposing," he introduced baldly, "a fellow-an old fellow like myself," he corrected precisely, "was to be going about his business as an old fellow should, in a two-seated surrey with canvas curtains such as you've seen me drive sometimes." The speaker paused a second to clear his throat. "Supposing this old fellow was just riding through the country easy, taking his time and with nothing particular on his mind, and all of a sudden he should feel as though someone had sneaked up and stuck him from behind with a long, sharp knife. Supposing this should happen, and, although it was the middle of the day, everything should go black as night and he should wake up, he couldn't tell how much later, and find himself all heaped up in the bottom of the rig and the team stock still out in the middle of the prairie." Deliberately as it had left, the cigar returned to the speaker's lips, was puffed hard until it glowed furiously; and was again critically examined. "Supposing such a fat old fellow as myself should tell you this. As a doc and a specialist, would you think there was something worth while the matter with him?"

Still Chantry did not speak, but the burned-out stump in his fingers sought a remote corner of the room, consorted with a goodly collection of its mates, and the drooping eyelid tightened.

"Supposing," continued Landor, "the thing should happen the second time, and the old fellow, who wasn't good at walking, should be spilled out and have to foot it home three miles. What would you think then?"

One of Chantry's hands, itself not over clean, dusted the ash off his vest absently.

"When was it, this last time?" he questioned.

"Yesterday," impassively. "I'd started for here to meet my nephew when the thing struck me; and when I managed to get home I sent How over instead." He halted reminiscently. "I wrote the boy to come a couple of weeks ago-that's when it caught me first."

"Your nephew, Craig, knows about it, does he?"

Landor puffed anew with a shade of embarrassment.

"No. I thought there was no call to tell the folks at the ranch. Mary'd have a cat-fit if she knew. I told them I got out to shoot at a coyote, and the bronchos ran away." He glanced at the other explanatorily, deprecatingly. "Clayton is my sister's son and the only real relative I have, you know. I just asked him to come on general principles."

Chantry made no comment. Opening a drawer of the desk, he fumbled amid a litter of articles useful and useless, and, extracting a battered stethoscope, shifted his chair forward until it was close to the other and stuck the tiny tubes to his ears. Still without comment he opened the rancher's shirt, applied the instrument, listened, shifted it, listened, shifted and listened the third time-slid his chair back to the former position.

"What else do you know?" he asked.

Landor buttoned up the gap in his shirt methodically.

"Nothing, except that the thing is in the family. My father went that way when he was younger than I am, and his father the same." The stogie had gone dead in his fingers, and he lit a fresh one steadily. "I've been expecting it to catch up with me for years."

"Your father died of it, you say?"

"Yes; on Thanksgiving Day." The big rancher shifted position, and in sympathy the rickety chair groaned dismally. "Dinner was waiting, I remember, a regular old-fashioned New England dinner with a stuffed sucking pig and a big turkey with his drumsticks in the air. Mother and Frances-that's my sister-were waiting, and they sent me running to call father. He was a lawyer, and a great hand to shut himself up and work. I was starved hungry, and I remember I hot-footed it proper upstairs to his den and threw open the door." Puff! puff! went the big stogie. "An Irish plasterer with seven kids ate that turkey, I recollect," he completed, "and I've never kept Thanksgiving from that day to this."

"And your grandfather?" unemotionally.

"Just the same. He was a preacher, and the choir was singing the opening anthem at the time."

The doctor threw one thin leg over the other and stared impassively out the single window. It faced the main street of the town.

"The doings are over for this time, I fancy," he digressed evenly. "I see a row of bronchos tied down in front of Red's place."

Landor did not look around.

"Mary and Mrs. Burton will count them, never fear," he recalled in mock sarcasm. "What I want to know is your opinion."

"In my opinion there's nothing to be done," said Chantry.

Landor shifted again, and again the chair groaned in mortal agony.

"I know that. What I mean is how long is it liable to be before —" he halted and jerked his thumb over his shoulder —"before Bob and the rest will be doing that to me?"

Chantry's gaze left the window, met the shrewd grey eyes beneath the other's drooping lids.

"It may be a day and it may be ten years," he said.

Unconsciously Landor settled deeper into his seat. His jaws closed tight on the stump of the stogie. Unwaveringly he returned the other's gaze.

"You have a more definite idea than that, though," he pressed. "Tell me, and let's have it over with."

For five seconds Chantry did not speak; but the restless black eyes bored the other through and through, at first impersonally, as, scalpel in hand, he would have studied a patient before the first incision in a major operation; then, as against the other's will, a great drop of sweat gathered on the broad forehead, personally, intimately.

"Yes, my opinion is more definite than that," he corroborated evenly. He did not suggest that he was sorry to say what he was about to say, did not qualify in advance by intimating that his prognosis might be wrong. "I think the next attack will be the last. Moreover, I believe it will come soon, very soon." Impassively as he had spoken, he produced a book of rice paper from his pocket and a rubber pouch of tobacco. The long fingers were skilful, and a cigarette came into being as under a machine. Without another word he lit a match and waited until the flame was well up on the wood. Of a sudden a great cloud of kindly smoke separated him from the other.

With an effort the big rancher lifted in his seat, passed his sleeve across his forehead clumsily.

"Thank you, Chantry." He cleared his throat raspingly. "As I said, I expected this; that's why I came to see you to-day." For the second time his cigar was dead, but he did not light it again. There was no need of subterfuge now. "I want you to do me a favour." He looked at the other steadily through the diminishing haze. "Will you promise me?"

"No," said Chantry.

Landor stared as one who could not believe his ears.

"No!" he interrogated.

"I said so."

A trace of colour appeared in the rancher's mottled cheeks as, with an effort, he got to his feet.

"I beg your pardon then for disturbing you," he said coldly. "I was labouring under the delusion that you were a friend."

The brief career of the cigarette was ended. Chantry's long fingers had locked over his knee. He did not move.

"Sit down, please," he said. "It is precisely because I am your friend that I will not promise."

Landor halted, a question in every line of his face.

"I think I fail to understand," he groped. "I suppose I'm dense."

"No, you're merely transparent. You were going to ask the one thing I can't promise you."

Landor stared, in mystified uncertainty.

"Please sit down. You were going to ask me to take charge of your affairs if anything was to happen. Is it not so?"

"Yes. But how in the world —" "Don't ask it then, please," swiftly. He ignored the other's suggestion. "Get someone else, someone you've known for a long time."

"I've known you for a long time-five years."

"Or leave everything in your wife's hands." Again Chantry scouted the obvious. "If there should be need she could get a lawyer from the city —"

"Lawyer nothing!" refuted Landor. "That's just what I wish to avoid. Mary or the girl, either one, have about as much idea of taking care of themselves as they have of speaking Chinese. They'd be on the county inside a year, with no one interested to look out for them."

"But How —"

"He's as bad. He can ride a broncho, or stalk a sandhill crane where there isn't cover to hide your hat, or manage cattle, or stretch out in the sun and: dream; but business-He wouldn't know a bank cheque if he saw one; and, what's worse, he doesn't want to know."

"Craig, then, your nephew —" It was not natural for Chantry to be perfunctory, and he halted.

For a moment the big rancher was silent. In his lap his fingers met unconsciously, tip to tip, in the instinctive habit of age.

"I anticipated that," he said wearily. "I realise it's the obvious thing to do. I never adopted How as I did the girl —I was willing to, but he didn't see the use-and so Craig's the only man kin I have." The life and magnetism, usually so noticeable in Landor's great figure, had vanished. It was merely an old man facing the end who settled listlessly into his seat. "I had big hopes of the boy. I hadn't seen him since he was a youngster, and Frances, while she lived, was always bragging about his doings. That's why I sent for him." Pat, pat went the big fingers in his lap against each other. "I've always felt that if worst came to worst the women folks would have someone practical to rely on; but somehow, when I saw him last night, from what he said and what he didn't say, from the way he acted and the way he explained-what happened here last evening —" The speaker caught himself. A trace of the old shrewdness crept into the grey eyes as he inspected his companion steadily. "I know How pretty well, and when someone intimates to me that he is a grand-stand player, or goes out of his way to pick a quarrel, or meddles with someone else's affairs —" Again the big man caught himself. The scrutiny became almost a petition. "I cut you off short about what went on here yesterday," he digressed. "I didn't want to hear. I guess I was afraid to hear. It's been foolish, I know, but I've depended a good deal upon the boy, and I'm afraid he's going to be a —disappointment."

With the old machine-like precision Chantry rolled another cigarette, lit it, sent a great cloud of smoke tumbling up toward the ceiling. That was all.

"You see for yourself how it is," said the rancher. "I wouldn't ask you again if there was anyone else I could go to; but there isn't. Maybe I'm only borrowing trouble, maybe there won't be anything for you or anyone to do; but it would be a big load off my mind to know that if anything should happen. —" He halted abruptly. It was not easy for this man to discuss his trouble, even to a friend. "It isn't such a big thing I'm asking," he hurried. "I'm sure if positions were reversed and you were to request me —"

"I know you would. I realise I seem ungrateful. I —" Of a sudden, interrupting, Chantry arose precipitately: a thin, ungainly figure in shiny, thread-bare broadcloth, exotic to the point of caricature. Unconsciously he started pacing back and forth across the room, restlessly, almost fiercely. Never in the years he had previously known the man had Landor seen him so, seen him other than the impassive, almost forbidding practitioner of a minute ago. For the time being his own trouble was forgotten in surprise, and he stared at the transformation almost unbelievingly. Back and forth, back and forth went the thin, ungainly shape, the ill-laid floor creaking as he moved, paused at last before the single dust-stained window, stood like a silhouette looking out over the desolate town. Watching, Landor shifted uncomfortably in his seat. Once he cleared his throat as if to speak. An instinct told him he should say something; but he was in the dark absolutely, and words would not come. Reaching over to the desk he took up his broad felt hat and sat twirling it in his fingers, waiting.

As suddenly as he had arisen Chantry returned, resumed his seat. His face had grown no-ticeably pale, and his left eyelid drooped even more than normally.

"I feel I owe you an apology," he said swiftly. "In a way we've been friends, and as you say, it's not a big thing you ask of me; but nevertheless I can't grant it. Please don't ask me."

The hat in Landor's hands became still, significantly still.

"I admit I don't understand," he accepted, "but of course if you feel that way, I shall not ask you again." Unconsciously a trace of the former stiffness returned to his manner as he arose heavily. "I think I'd better be going." His mouth twitched in an effort at pleasantry. "Mary'll be dying to give me the details."

Chantry did not smile, did not again ask the other to resume his seat. Instead, he himself arose, stood facing his guest squarely.

"I feel that I owe you an explanation as well," he said repressedly. "Would you like to hear?"

"Yes-if you don't mind. If you'd prefer not to, however —"

"No, I'd rather you-understood than to go that way." The doctor cleared his throat in the manner of one who smokes overmuch. "We all have our skeleton hid away somewhere, I suppose. At least I have mine, and it keeps bobbing out at times like this when I most wish —" He caught himself, met his companion's questioning look fairly. "Haven't you wondered why I ever came here; why, having come, I remain?" he queried suddenly. "You know that I barely make enough to live, that sometimes I don't have a case a week. Did it never occur to you that there was something peculiar about it all?"

"Peculiar?" The hat in the rancher's hand started revolving again. He had, indeed, thought of it before, thought of it tolerantly, with a vague sense of commiseration-an attitude very similar to that with which the uninitiated observe a player at golf; but that there might be another, a sinister meaning —.

"If it hasn't occurred to you before, doesn't it seem peculiar, now that you consider it?" The question came swiftly, tensely, with a significance there was no misunderstanding. "Tell me, please."

"Yes, perhaps; but —"

"But you do see, though," relentlessly. "You can't help but see." The speaker started anew the restless, aimless pace. "The country is full of us; all new countries are." He was still speaking hurriedly, tensely, as we tell of a murder or a ghastly tragedy; something which in duty we must confide, but which we hasten to have over. "It's easier to get here than to Mexico or to Canada, and until the country is settled, until people begin to suspect —" He halted suddenly opposite the other, his face deathly pale, deathly tortured. "In God's name, don't you understand now?" he questioned passionately. "Must I tell you in so many words why I refused, why I don't dare do anything else but refuse?"

"No, you don't need to tell me." Absently, unconsciously, the rancher produced a red bandana handkerchief and wiped his face; then thrust it back into his pocket. "I think I understand at last." His eyes had dropped and he did not raise them again to his companion. "I'm sorry, very sorry, that I asked you; sorry most of all that —" He halted diffidently, his great hands hanging loose at his side, his broad shoulders drooping wearily. He was not glib of speech, at best, and this second blow was hard to bear. A full half minute he stood so, hesitant, searching for words; then heavily, clumsily, he turned, started for the door. "I really must be going," he concluded.

Chantry did not ask him to stay, made no motion to prevent his going. Tense, motionless, he stood where he had last paused, waited in silence until the visitor's hand was upon the knob.

"Good-bye Landor," he said then simply.

Not the words themselves, but something in the tone caused the rancher to halt, to look back.

"Good-day, you mean, rather," he corrected.

"No, good-bye. You will not see me again."

"You don't mean —"

"No. I'm too much of a coward for that, or I should have done so long ago. I merely mean I'll move on to-morrow."

Face to face the two men stood staring at each other. Seconds drifted by. It was the doctor who spoke at last.

"God knows that if I could, I'd change with you even now, Landor," he said repressedly. "I'd change with you gladly." A moment he stood so, tense as a wire drawn to the point of breaking, ghastly tense; then of a sudden he went lax. Instinctively his fingers sought his pockets, and there where he stood he started swiftly to roll a cigarette.

"Go, please," he requested. "Good-bye."

Chapter IX
The Voice of the Wild

Eight miles out on the prairie, out of sight of the Buffalo Butte ranch house-save for a scattering herd of grazing cattle in the distance, and a hobbled mouse-coloured broncho feeding near at hand, out of sight of every living thing—a man lay stretched full length upon the ground. It was the time of day that Landor had tried the door of Bob Manning's store, and the broad brim of the man's hat was pulled far forward to keep the glitter from his eyes. Under his head was a rolled-up blanket; an Indian blanket that even so showed against the brown earth in a blot of glaring colour. His hands were deep in his pockets; his moccasined feet were crossed. At first sight, an observer would have thought him asleep; but he was not asleep. The black eyes that looked forth motionless from beneath the hat brim, that apparently never for an instant left that scattering blot where, distorted, fantastic from distance and through the curling heat waves the herd grazed, were very wide awake indeed. They were not even drowsy or off guard. They were merely passive, absolutely passive. The whole body was passive, motionless, relaxed in every muscle and every nerve; and therein lay the marvel-to all save the thousandth human in this restless age, the impossibility. To be awake and still motionless, to do absolutely nothing, not even sleep-seemingly the simplest feat in life, it is one of the most difficult. A wild thing can do it, all wild things when need is sufficient; but man, modern man-Here and there one retains the faculty, as here and there one worships another God than wealth; but here and there only. Yet it was such an one that lay alone out there on the Dakota prairie that October day; one who, as Craig had said, hinted unfortunately of comic opera, but who never, even in remotest conception, fancied that comic opera existed, a dreamer and yet, notwithstanding, a doer, an Indian, and still not an Indian; Ma-wa-cha-sa by name.

With the approach of midday a light wind had arisen, and now, wandering northward, it tugged at the pony's long, shaggy mane and tail, set each individual hair of the little beast vibrating in unjustified ferocity; and, drifting aimlessly on, stirred the brittle grass stalks at the man's feet with the muffled crackling of a far-distant prairie fire. The herd, a great machine cutting clean every foot of the sun-cured grass in its path, moved on and on, reached a low spot in the gently rolling country, and passed slowly from view; then, still moving forward, took shape on the summit of the next rise, more distinct than before.

Time passed as the man lay there, time that to another would have been interminable, that to him was apparently unnoted. Gradually, as the full heat of the day approached, the breeze became stronger, set the heat waves dancing to swifter measure, sang audibly in the listener's ears its siren song of prairie and of peace. The broncho, its appetite temporarily satisfied, lay down fair in its tracks, groaned lazily in the action, and shut its eyes. It was the rest time of the wild, and the same instinct appealed to the leader of the distant herd. Down it went where it stood as the pony had done, disappeared absolutely from view. A moment later another followed, and another, and another. It was almost uncanny, there in the fantastic glimmer, that disappearance. In the space of minutes, look where one would, the horizon was blank. Where the herd had been there was nothing, not even a blot. It was as the desert, and the vanished herd a mirage. It was like the far northland tight in the grip of winter, like the ocean at night. It was the Dakota frontier at midday.

Again time passed and, motionless as at first, wide eyed, the man lay looking out. The pony was sound asleep now. Its nostrils widened and narrowed rhythmically and it snored at intervals. Save for this and the soft crackle of the grass and the aeolian song of the wind the earth was still; still as death; so still that, indescribably soft as it was immeasurably distant, the man detected of a sudden against it a new sound. But he did not stir. The black eyes looked out motionless as at first. He merely waited a minute, two-and it came again: a bit louder this time, more distinct, unmistakable.

This time the listener moved. Deftly, swiftly, he unrolled the gaudy blanket, spread it thin upon the ground, covered it completely with his body. In lieu of a pillow his arms crossed under his head, and, leaning back, the hat brim still shading his eyes, he lay gazing up into the sky, motionless as a prairie boulder.

Again the sound was repeated; not a single note, but a medley, a chorus. It was still faint, still immeasurable as to distance; but nearer than before and approaching closer second by second. Not from the earth did it come, but from the air. Not by any stretch of the imagination was it an earthly sound, but aërial. It was an alien note and still it was not alien. There upon the silent earth with its sunshine and its illimitable distances, it seemed very much a part of the whole. Its keynote was the keynote of the time and place, its message was their message, the thrill it bore to the listener the thrill of the whole. It was not a musical call, that steadily approaching sound. No human being has ever been able to locate it in pitch or metre; yet to such as the listening man upon the ground, to those who have heard it year by year, it is nevertheless the sweetest, most insistent of music. Beside it there is no other note which will compare, none other which even approaches its appeal. It is the spirit of the wild, of magnificent distances, of freedom impersonate. It is to-day, it was then; for the sound that the man heard drawing nearer and nearer that October afternoon was the swelling, diminishing note of the migrant on its way south, of the grey Canada honker en route from the Arctic circle to the Gulf of Mexico.

"Honk! honk!" Sonorous, elusive, came the sound. It was within a half mile now, and there was no mistaking the destination, the intent of its makers. "Honk! honk! honk! honk!" from many throats, in many keys, louder and louder, confused as children's voices at play; then in turn diminishing, retreating. Very mystifying to one who did not understand would have been that augmenting, lessening sound; but to that waiting human boulder it was no mystery. As plainly as though he could see, he knew every movement of that approaching triangle. As certainly as the broncho near by and the herd in the distance had responded to the sunshine and the time of day, he knew they were responding. To all wild things it was the rest hour, and to those a half mile high in the air as inevitably as to the beast on earth instinct had said "halt." They were still going southward, still drawing nearer and nearer; but it would not be for long. Already they were circling, descending, searching here and there for a place to alight, to rest. Suspicious even here, they were taking their time; but distinct now amid the confusion was the sound of their great wings against the denser air, and the "Honk! honk! honk!" was a continuous chatter.

Circle after circle made the flock. Once their noise all but ceased, and the listener fancied for an instant they were down, but in a moment it was resumed louder than before, and he knew they were still a-wing. "Honk! honk! honk! honk! honk! honk!" They were very near indeed, so near that the sleeping pony was aroused at the clamour and, lifting its head, looked about curiously.

"Honk! honk! honk! Flap! flap! Swish!" Between the sun and the watcher there fell a moving shadow and another-then a multitude. The clamour was all-surrounding, the flap of great wings a continuous beating, the whistle of air like that in a room with a myriad buzzing electric fans. Temporarily the prairie breeze was lost; swallowed up in the greater movement. Surprised, for the moment frightened, the broncho sprang to his feet-paused irresolute. For an instant the sky was hid. Overhead, to right, to left, all-obscuring, was nothing but a blot of great grey bodies, of wide wings lighter on the under surface, of long, curious necks, of dangling feet; then, swiftly as it had come it passed; the sun shone anew; the cloud and the shadow thereof, going straight in the face of the wind, wandered on. "Honk! honk! honk! honk! honk! honk!" they repeated; but it was the voice of departure. The thing was done. There on the level earth, fair in view, they had passed overhead within twenty feet of their arch-enemy, man; and had not known. Now less than a quarter of a mile away they were circling for the last time. One big gander was already down and stretching his long neck from side to side. Another, with a great flapping of wings, was beside him; and another, and another. The prairie wind carried along the sound of their chatter; but it was subdued now, entirely different from the clamour of a bit ago. Against the blue of the sky where they had been a blot only, the curling, dancing heat waves arose. One and all had answered the siesta call.

Up to this time the man who watched had not stirred. As they had gone over, the wide-open eyes had stared up at them; but not in the twitching of a muscle had the long body betrayed him. Not even now that it was over did he move. Instead, low at first, then louder, a whistle sounded. The pony, wide awake now, was grazing contentedly; but he paused. The whistle sounded for the third time, and reluctantly he drew near, halted obediently. Then at last there was action. With one motion the Indian was on his feet. Swiftly as it was spread the blanket was rolled and replaced in the waterproof pouch with the remnants of the lunch and a book of odds and ends which he carried always with him. The whole was strapped to the pony's bare back. As swiftly the hobble was removed and, not a minute from the time the last bird was down, the man and the beast, the latter only visible from the direction in which they were going, were moving on a zigzag, circuitous trail toward the resting yet ever-watchful flock before them.

On they went, the pony first, the crouching man beside, his body even with the pony's front legs, his eyes peering through the wind-tossed mane. First to the right, then to the left they tacked, halting at intervals, as a pony wandering aimlessly will halt now and then to feed; but never losing the general direction, always bit by bit drawing nearer and nearer. A half hour passed by and in it they covered forty rods-half the distance. Thirty minutes more elapsed and they had crossed an equal portion of the remaining space. Then it was they halted and a peculiar thing happened.

The wind had gradually risen during the day, and now, the middle of the afternoon, was blowing steadily. Light objects unattached move easily across the level prairie at this time of year, and here and there under its touch one after another of a particular kind were already in motion. Fluffy, unsubstantial objects they were, as large as a bushel measure and rudely circular. Looking out over the level earth often a half dozen at a time were visible, rolling and halting and rolling again on an endless journey from nowhere to nowhere. They were the well-named tumble weeds of the prairie; as distinctive as the resting flock of late autumn, of approaching winter. One of these it was now that came tumbling in lazily from the south and, barely missing the indifferent birds themselves, dawdled languidly on toward the pony beyond. On it came, would have passed to the right; but, under an impulse he in no way understood, the broncho moved to intercept it. Fair in its path, the little beast would still have shifted to give it right of way, for the weed is very prickly; but again the authority he did not question held him in his place, and the three, the man, the horse, and the plant, came together. Then it was the *finale* began, the real test, the matching of human cunning and animal watchfulness.

Left alone there upon the prairie, the indifferent broncho resumed its feeding. Away from it, foot by foot, so slowly that a careful observer could barely have seen it stir, moved the great weed. No animal on the face of earth save man himself would have been suspicious of that natural blind; even he would have overlooked it had he not by chance noted that while every other of its kind was moving with the wind, it slowly but surely was advancing against it. The scene where the drama was taking place was level as a floor, the grazed grass that covered it scarcely higher than a man's hand; yet from in front not an inch of the Indian's long body was visible, not a sound marked its advance. In comparison with its movement time passed swiftly; a third half hour while it was advancing ten rods. Already the short autumn afternoon was drawing to a close. The sun was no longer uncomfortably hot. The heat waves had ceased dancing. In sympathy the prairie breeze, torn of the sun, was becoming appreciably milder. As certainly as it had come, the brief rest period was drawing to a close.

But the long figure that gave the blind motion showed no haste. Inch by inch it advanced, never still, yet never hurrying. The great unsuspicious birds were very near now, so near that a white hunter would have lost his equanimity in anticipation. Through the meshwork of the blind the stalker counted them. Twenty-seven there were together, and near to him another, a sentinel. He was within half the distance of a city block of the latter, so close that he could see the beady, watchful eyes, the pencillings of the plumage, the billowing of feathers as the long neck shifted from side to side. Verily it was a moment to make a sportsman's blood leap-to make him forget; but not even then did the Indian show a sign of excitement, not for a minute did the lithe body cease in its soundless serpentine motion. It was splendid, that patient, stealthy approach, splendid in its mastery of the still hunt; but beyond this it was more, it was fearful. Had an observer been where no observer was, it would inevitably have carried with it another suggestion-the possibilities of such a man were a real object, one vital to his life, and not a mere pastime, at stake. What would this patient, tireless, splendid animal do then? What if another man, his enemy, were the object, the quarry?

The rest time at last was over. Insidiously into the air had crept a suggestion of coolness, of approaching night. In the background the pony ceased feeding, stood patiently awaiting the return of its rider. Far in the distance, the herd, a darker blot against the brown earth, were once more upon their feet. The flock, that heretofore like a group of barnyard fowls in the dust and the sun had remained indolently resting and preening their plumage, grew alert. One after the other they began wandering here and there aimlessly, restlessly. The subdued chatter became positive. Two great ganders meeting face to face hissed a challenge. Here and these a big bird spread its great wings tentatively, and folded them again with distinct reluctance. The cycle was all but complete. The instinct that in the beginning had bid them south, that had for this brief time sent them to earth, was calling again. In sympathy the restless head of the sentinel went still. Another minute, another second even, perhaps, and they would be gone. Through the filmy screen the stalker saw it all, read the meaning. He had ere this drawn unbelievably near. Barely the width of a narrow street separated him from the main flock-less than the breadth of a goodly sized room the motionless sentinel. It was the moment for action.

And action followed. Like a mighty spring the slim muscular body contracted in its length. Toes and fingers dug into the earth like a sprinter awaiting the starting pistol. He drew a long breath. Then of a sudden, straight over the now useless blind, unexpected, startling as a thunderclap out of a cloudless sky, directly toward the nearest bird bounded a tall brown figure, silent as a phantom. For a second the entire flock stared in dumb paralytic surprise; then following there came a note of terror from eight and twenty throats that rose as one voice, that over the now silent prairie could have been heard for miles. It was the signal for action, for escape, and, terror-mad, they broke into motion. But a flock of great Canada geese cannot, like quail, spring directly a-wing. They must first gather momentum. This they attempted to gain-in its accomplishment all but one succeeded. That one, the leader, the sentinel, was too near. Almost before that first note of terror had left his throat the man was upon him. Ere he could rise two relentless hands had fastened upon his beating wings and held him prisoner. Hissing, struggling, he put up the best fight he could; but it was useless. "Honk! honk! honk! honk! honk! honk!" shrilled the flock now safe in the air. "Honk! honk! honk!" as with wings and feet they climbed into the sky. "Honk! honk! honk!" softer and softer. "Honk! honk! honk!" for the last time, faint as an echo; and they were gone. Behind them the human and the wild thing his prisoner stood staring at each other alone.

For a long, long time neither moved. Its first desperate effort to escape past, the bird ceased to struggle, stood passive in its place; passive as the man himself had remained there on the ground a few hours before. Its long neck swayed here and there continuously, restlessly, and its throat was a-throb; but no muscle of the body stirred. It had made its fight-and lost. For the time being resistance was fatuous, and it accepted the inevitable. Silent as its captor, it awaited the move of the conqueror. It would resist again when the move came, resist to the last ounce of its strength; but until then in instinctive wisdom it would husband its energy.

Yet that move was very slow in coming. It was the time of day when ordinarily the herder collected his drove and returned toward the home corral; still he showed no intention of haste. The broncho was shaking his head at intervals restlessly; too well trained to leave, yet impatient as a hungry child for the return-and was ignored. For the time being the man seemed to have forgotten all external considerations. Not savagely nor cruelly, but with a sort of fascination he stood gazing at this wild thing in his power. For a long, long time he did nothing more, merely looked at it; looked admiringly, intimately. No trace of blood hunger was in his face, no lust to kill; but pure appreciation-and something more; something that made the two almost kin. And they were much alike; almost startlingly alike. Each was graceful in every movement, in every line. Each was of its kind physical perfection. Each unmistakably bore a message of the wild; of solitude, of magnificent distances. Each was a part of its setting; as much so as the all-surrounding silence. Last of all, each stood for one quality dominant, one desire overtowering all others; and that was freedom, unqualified, absolute.

Long as it was they stood there so, the bird was true to its instinct of passive inaction. It was the human that made the first move. Gently, slowly, one hand freed itself, stroked the silky soft plumage; stroked it intimately, almost lovingly-as an animal mother caresses its young. The man did not speak, made no sound, merely repeated the motion again and again. Under the touch the restless head became still, the watchful black eyes more watchful. That was all. Slowly as it had moved before, the man's hand shifted anew, passed down, down, the glossy throat to the breast-paused over the heart of the wild thing. There it remained, and for the first time a definite expression came into the mask-like face; a look of pity, of genuine contrition. A moment the hand lay there; then, childish as it may seem, absurd, if you please, the man spoke aloud.

"You're afraid of me, deathly afraid, aren't you, birdie?" he queried softly. "You think because I'm bigger than you and a cannibal, I'm going to kill you." Kneeling, he looked fair into the black eyes-deep, mysterious as the wild itself. "You think this, and still you don't grovel, don't make a sound. You're brave, birdie, braver than most men." He paused, and one by one his hands loosened their grip. "I'm proud of you; so proud that I'm going to say good-bye." He straightened to his full height. Unconsciously his arms folded across his chest. "Go, birdie; you're free."

A moment longer there was inaction. Unbelieving, still a captive, the great bird stood there motionless as before; then of a sudden it understood; it was free. By some chance, some Providence, this great animal, its captor, had lost the mastery, and it was free. Simultaneously with the knowledge the pent-up energy of the last minutes went active, fairly explosive. With a mighty rush it was away; feet and wings beating the earth, the air. Swifter and swifter it went, gaining momentum with each second. It barely touched the frost-brown prairie; it cleared it entirely, it rose, rose, with mighty sweeps of mighty wings. Oh, it was free! free! free! "Honk! honk!" Free! free! "Honk! honk! honk!"

Like a statue, silent again as death, the man watched as the dark spot on the horizon grew dimmer and dimmer until it faded at last into the all-surrounding brown.

Chapter X
The Curse of the Conquered

It was late, very late on the prairie, when How Landor returned that evening. The herd safely corralled for the night, he rode slowly toward the ranch house, and, without leaving the pony's back, opened and closed the gate of the barb wire fence surrounding the yard and approached the house. There was a bright light in the living-room, and, still without dismounting, he paused before the uncurtained window and looked in. Mrs. Landor, looking even more faded and helpless than usual, sat holding her hands at one side of the sheet-iron heater, and opposite her, his feet on the top rim of the stove, sat Craig. The man was smoking a cigarette, and even through the tiny-paned glass the air of the room looked blue. Obviously the visitor and his aunt were not finding conversation easy, and the former appeared distinctly bored. Neither Landor himself nor the girl was anywhere visible, and, after a moment, the spectator moved on around the corner. The dining-room as he passed was dark, likewise the kitchen, and the rider made the complete circuit of the house, pausing at last under a certain window on the second floor facing the south. It was the girl's room, and, although the shade was drawn, a dim light was burning behind. For perhaps a minute the man on the barebacked broncho hesitated, looking up; then rolling his wide-brimmed hat into a cylinder he moved very close to the weather-boarded wall. The building was low, and, by stretching a bit, the tip of the roll in his hand reached the second story. He tapped twice on the bottom of the pane.

No answer, but of a sudden the room went dark.

Tap! tap! repeated the hat brim gently.

Still no answer.

Again the man hesitated, and, the night air being a bit frosty, the pony stamped impatiently.

"Bess," said a low voice, "it is I, How. Won't you tell me good-night?"

This time there was response. The curtain lifted and the sash was opened; a face appeared, very white against the black background.

"Good-night, How," said a voice obediently.

The man settled back in his seat and the sombrero was unrolled.

"Nothing wrong, is there, Bess?" he hesitated. "You're not sick?"

"No, there's nothing wrong," monotonously. "I'm a bit tired, is all."

For a long minute the man said nothing, merely sat there, his black head bare in the starlight, looking up at her. Repressed human that he was, there seemed to him nothing now to say, nothing adequate. Meanwhile the pony was growing more and more impatient. A tiny hoof beat at the

half-frozen ground rhythmically.

"All right, then, Bess," he said at last. "You mustn't sit there in the window. It's getting chilly. Good-night."

The girl drew back until her face was in shadow.

"Good-night," she echoed for the second time, and the shade closed as before.

For five minutes longer the Indian sat as he was, bare of head, motionless; but the light did not return, nor did he hear a sound, and at last he rode slowly out the gate and toward his own quarters.

The place where he lived was exactly a half mile from the Buffalo Butte ranch house, and due north. Originally a one-room shack, grudgingly built according to government requirements to prove up on a homestead, it had recently been enlarged by the addition of a second larger room, and as a whole the place further improved by the building of a sod and weather-board barn. The reason for this was obvious, to one acquainted with the tenant's habits particularly so. Just how long the Indian had remained separate, just why he had first made the change, Landor himself could hardly have told. Suffice it to say it had been for years, and in all that time, even in the coldest weather, the voluntary exile had never lived under a roof. Primitive or evolved as it might be, as youth and as man, the Indian was a tent-dweller. Just now the little house was being fitted up for occupancy, How himself doing it at odd moments of the day and at evenings; but as yet he still lived, as always, under eight by ten feet of canvas near at hand.

A lighted tent stands out very distinctly by contrast against a dark horizon, and almost before he had left the ranch house yard the man on the impatient, mouse-coloured broncho knew that he had company; yet, characteristic in his every action, he did not hurry. Methodically he put up the pony in the new barn, fed and bedded him for the night. From the adjoining stall, out of the darkness, there came a nasal puppyish whine and the protest of a straining chain. Had it been daylight, an observer would have seen a woolly grey ball with a pointed nose and a pair of sharp eyes tugging at the end of that tether; but as it was, two gleaming eyes, very close together, were all that were visible. It was to the owner of these eyes that the man gave the scraps from his lunch remaining in the saddlebag. For it, as for the pony, he made a bed; then-though the little beast was only a grey prairie wolf, it was a baby and lonely-he knelt down and for a moment laid his own face against the other's softly shaggy face.

When, a bit later, he arose and went toward the light there was a moist spot on his cheek where a rough little tongue had inscribed its affection.

On the tent wall was a shadow such as that made by a big man with his back to the light, and as the newcomer opened the flap and stepped inside the maker of the shadow roused himself in the manner of one whose thoughts had been far away.

"You're late to-night," he commented.

"Yes."

Characteristic of the two men, no explanation was offered or expected, and the subject dropped.

There was a small soft-coal stove in one corner, and in silence the Indian threw in fresh fuel. The lantern hanging opposite was burning low, and, turning it higher, he shifted the tin reflector so that the light would play on the scene of operations. Leaving the tent for a moment, he returned with a young grouse, and, dressing it skilfully, put it in a skillet to fry. From the chest where he had been sitting he produced a couple of cold boiled potatoes and sliced them into the opposite side of the same pan. He did not hurry, he rather seemed to be dawdling; yet almost before the observer awoke to the fact that supper was under preparation a tiny folding table with a turkey red cloth was set, the odour of coffee-cheap coffee, yet surprisingly fragrant-was in the air, and the bird and potatoes were temptingly brown. It was almost uncanny the way this man accomplished things. Landor himself never ceased to marvel. How always seemed unconscious of what he was doing, seemed always thinking of something else; yet he never wasted a motion, and when the necessity arose the thing required was done. It was so in small things. It was identical in large.

Up to this time, since that first perfunctory greeting not a word had been spoken. Now, the meal complete, its maker halted hospitably.

"Better join me," he invited simply. "You must have had an early supper. I noticed the kitchen was dark at the house."

"Yes. I'm not hungry, though." The big man sank lower into his seat wearily. "I'm not feeling very well to-night."

In silence the younger man sat down to eat alone. He did not press his invitation, he did not express sympathy at the other's admission. Either would have been superfluous. Instead he ate with the hearty appetite of a healthy human, and thereafter, swiftly and methodically as he had prepared the meal, cleared the table and put all in order. Then at last, the fire replenished and a couple of long-haired buffalo robes thrown within the radius of its heat, he stretched full length thereon in the perfect contentment of one whose labor for the day is done, and awaited the something he knew had brought the other to him at this unusual hour. "There's a pipe and tobacco in the drawer of the little table at your right," he assisted.

Landor roused with a trace of surprise.

"I didn't know you ever smoked," he commented.

"I don't," simply. Again there was no suggestion of the superfluous, the obvious explanation.

Nervously, almost jerkily, Landor filled the brier bowl and pressed the brown flakes tight with his little finger. The match he lit crackled explosively, and he started at the unexpected sound as one whose nerves were on edge. The pipe aglow, he still sat for a moment puffing hard.

"How," he initiated then abruptly, "I wish you would do me a favour. Will you promise me?"

The younger man did not hesitate, did not question. "If in my power, yes, sir," he said.

That was all, yet better than a complete chapter it told the relation of the two men; the unquestioning confidence of the younger, the trace of almost patriarchal respect that never left his manner when, addressing the elder. "If in my power, yes, sir."

"It isn't much I'm going to ask," continued Landor hurriedly. "It's simply that you and Bess be married at once instead of waiting until the day set." Puff, puff went the pipe as though the speaker were uncertain whether or no to say more. "I have a particular reason for wishing it," he completed inadequately.

For a moment the Indian hesitated; but even then no question was voiced; there was no probing of the confidence the other preferred not to give.

"I will speak to Bess to-morrow if you wish," he said.

Landor lit another match absently and held it to the already glowing bowl; then threw it away, unconscious of what he had done.

"Another thing," he introduced hurriedly. "I'm pretty strong now, but nevertheless I'm getting to be an old man, and so to-day while I was in

town I had Bob Manning witness my will. I know it's all form, but I feel better to have things settled." With forced matter of factness he knocked the burned contents of the pipe into the grate and filled the bowl afresh. "Mary isn't used to having any responsibility, so I left practically everything to Bess. I know that if anything should happen to me you'd take care of her mother."

No answer, though Landor waited expectantly.

"I don't need to ask your promise to be good to Bess." Very different from his usual peremptory self was the big rancher to-night, very obvious, pathetically so, his effort to appear natural. "I know you'll make her happy, my boy."

Even yet there was no response, and the visitor shifted uncomfortably. As well as he knew his own name he knew that his secret was secret no longer. Yet with the instinct of the wild thing that hides itself to die alone he avoided direct mention of the fact, direct wording of the inevitable. But something in the attitude of the motionless figure before him prevented further dissimulation. Some influence urged him to hasten the *dénouement* which he knew was but postponed. With an effort he straightened in his seat and for the first time met the other's black eyes steadily.

"I did right, don't you think, How?" he questioned directly.

"Right, perhaps; I don't know." A pause. "What I do know is that I'm sorry you did as you did."

"Sorry, How?"

"Yes, sir. Very sorry."

"And why?"

No answer.

The light from the tin reflector had been playing full upon the Indian's face, and now, rising, he shifted it until the corner by the stove was in shadow. "I will tell you why." He returned to his place and stretched himself as before, his hands locked beneath his head. "You are a rich man, Mr. Landor, and Bess is human. She doesn't know what money is yet, but you will compel her to learn. From what I have read and the little I have seen, I think she would be happier if she never knew."

For the third time Landor filled the pipe bowl and lit it with a fragment of coal from the grate.

"I don't see why, How," he refuted.

"You do, though, sir."

"No. Tell me."

There was a long pause, so long that Landor fancied the other would not answer; then of a sudden he found the intense black eyes fixed upon him unshiftingly.

"The reason is because not only Bess but others are human. As we are now I can make her happy, very happy. I know it because —I love her." He paused, and into the tent there came the long-drawn-out wail of the baby prisoner. Silence returned. "As surely as that little wolf is lonely, Bess will know the trouble money brings if you do as you intend. Not myself, but other men will teach her."

Landor was not smoking now. The pipe had gone dead in his fingers.

"Once more I ask why, How?"

The other's eyes did not shift, nor a muscle of his body.

"Because she is white and they are white, and I —am an Indian."

At last it had come: the thing Landor had tried to avoid, had hitherto succeeded in avoiding. Yet face to face the big man could ignore it no longer. It was true, as true as human nature; and he knew it was true. Other men, brothers of his own race, would do this thing-as they would do anything for money; and he, Landor, he who had raised her from a child, who had adopted her as his own daughter, he it was who would make it possible!

Involuntarily the big man got to his feet. He did not attempt to move about, he did not speak. There, standing, he fought himself inch by inch; battled against the knowledge of the inevitable that had been dogging him day by day, hour by hour. A long time he stood so, his great hands locked, his face toward the blank tent wall opposite; then at last he turned.

"I realise what you mean, How," he said swiftly, "and understand the way you feel. God knows I wish it were different, wish I did not believe what you say true; but things are as the are. What we have to do now is the best thing possible under the circumstances." He sat down in the chair again heavily, his hands still locked in his lap. "If wrong has been done I am to blame, I myself, in raising you and Bess together. I might have known that it was inevitable, you two here alone to care for each other; but I was poor then, and I never thought that Bess —"

"Mr. Landor —"

The big man halted. For the first time he realised the admission of what he had been saying, the inevitable implication-and he was silent. For seconds likewise the Indian was still; but in them he was looking at the other steadily, in a way he had never looked at him before, with an intensity that was haunting.

"So you, too, feel that way," he said at last slowly. There was no anger in the voice, nor menace; merely wonder, and, yes, pathos-terrible, gripping pathos. "I knew that everyone else felt so-everyone except Bess herself; but you-you —I did not know that before, Mr. Landor."

Mute as before the big man sat motionless, listening. From the bottom of his soul he wished to say something in refutation, in self-defence; but he could not. There was nothing to say.

"No, I never even dreamed of such a thing," went on the repressed voice, "not even when at first you were slow to give your consent to our marriage. I fancied it was merely because you thought me impractical, because I cared nothing for a life that was different, was not my own. Nor again, even a bit ago when you asked me to promise-what I did promise —I did not suspicion such a thing. I thought it a compliment, the sincerest compliment I had ever received in my life: the fact that you should trust me so, with all that was dear to you in the world." Just perceptibly he halted, but his eyes did not leave the white man's face. "But I see it all now. I was blind before, but I see at last. You are like the rest, like everyone with a white skin. The fact that we've lived together for half a generation makes no difference. You're square, square to the end. You even like me in a way. You've given your word and won't go back on it; but nevertheless you're sorry. Even while you urge us to marry, to have the thing over, to have a responsibility off your mind, you feel you are sacrificing Bess to an inferior." He halted for a second, and even at this time Landor was conscious that it was infinitely the longest speech he had ever heard the man make. "I don't blame you, Mr. Landor; you can't help it; it's the instinct of your race; but nevertheless, nevertheless —"

The voice halted abruptly, repressedly. The intense black eyes were of a sudden looking directly past the other, straight up at the roof of the tent. No power on earth could have made him complete that sentence, made him admit the deadly hurt it suggested. From the unusual confidence of a bit ago he merely lapsed into the normal, his own repressed, impassive self. Yet as plainly as though he had spoken Landor recognised the difference, realised as well that while outwardly there would be no change, from this moment on so long as they both lived the confidence of the Indian would be as dead to him as though he had ceased to exist. He had seen it happen before. He knew the signs. With the knowledge for the first time in the years they two had lived together he realised how much after all he had grown to depend upon this laconic human, how much he had lost. It was the last drop in his cup of bitterness, the crushing straw. His great ungainly body dropped forward until his face was hid in his hands. On the walls of the tent a distorted, exaggerated shadow marked the movement of his shoulders as they rose and fell with his deep, irregular breathing. Again silence fell upon them, silence that by word of mouth was to remain unbroken. In it from the stable there sounded again the wail of the lonely baby, and a moment later, muffled, echo-like from the distance, the answering call of one of its own kind free upon the infinite prairie; but apparently neither man noticed, neither man cared-and the silence returned. Long minutes passed. The fire in the stove burned lower and lower. Into the tent crept a suggestion of the coolness without. Then at last Landor roused. Without a word he put on his hat and buttoned his coat. His fingers were unnaturally clumsy and he found the task difficult. Just for a moment he had a wild idea of asking the other's forgiveness, of attempting an explanation where none was possible; but he realised it would but make matters worse, and desisted. The Indian, too, had arisen, and repressedly co urteous, stood ready to open the flap of the tent for the other to pass. For a moment, the last moment they were ever to see each other alive, they stood so, each waiting for the other to speak, each knowing that the other would not speak; then heavily, shufflingly, Landor took a step forward.

The tent curtain opened before him, was held back while he passed; then closed again, shutting him out.

For five long dragging minutes after he was gone the other man remained as he stood, motionless as a bronze statue, as an inanimate thing. The kerosene lamp was burning low now and sputtered dismally; but he did not notice, did not hear. For the third time, tremulous against the background of night and of silence, came the wail of the lonely little captive. It was a kindred sound, an appealing sound, and at last the figure responded. Hatless as he was he left the tent, returned a minute later with something tagging at his heels: a woolly, grey, bright-eyed something, happy as a puppy at release and companionship. Methodically the man banked the coal fire and put out the lantern. He did not make a bed, did not undress. Instead, weary as Landor himself, he dropped amid the buffalo robes, lay still. "Sniff, sniff," sounded a pointed, inquiring nose in the darkness, "sniff, sniff, sniff." There was no response, and becoming bolder, its owner crept close to the face of the silent being on the ground, squirmed a moment contentedly-and likewise became still.

Chapter XI
The Tree of Knowledge

The darkness that precedes morning had the prairie country in its grip when Howard, the gaunt foreman of the B.B. ranch, drew rein before the silent tent, and with the butt end of his quirt tapped on the heavy canvas.

"Wake up," he called laconically. "You're wanted at the ranch house."

Echo-like, startling in its suddenness, an inverted V opened in the white wall and in it, fully dressed, vigilant, appeared the figure of its owner.

"What is it?" asked a voice insistently.

The Texan stared in unconcealed surprise.

"In Heaven's name, man, don't you ever sleep?" he drawled. "The boss is dead," he added baldly at second thought.

The black V closed again, and distinct in outline against the white background appeared the silhouette of the listener. His arms were folded across his chest in a way that was characteristic, and his moccasined feet were set close together. He spoke no word of surprise, asked no question; merely stood there in the silence and the semi-darkness waiting.

The foreman was by no means a responsive soul, yet, watching, there instinctively crept over him a feeling akin to awe of this other silent human. There was the mystery of death itself in that motionless, listening shadow.

"It was just before I came over to tell you that Mrs. Landor raised the house," he explained. "She woke up in the night and found the boss so-and cold already." Unconsciously his voice had lowered. "She screamed like a mad woman, and ran down-stairs in her nightdress, chattering so we could hardly understand her." He slapped at his baggy chaperajos with his quirt absently. "That's all I know, except there's no particular use to hurry. It's all over now, and he never knew what took him."

Silently as before the aperture in the tent opened and closed and the listener disappeared; to reappear a moment later with a curled-up woolly bundle in his arms. Without a word of explanation he strode toward the barn, leaving Howard staring after him uncertainly. Listening, the latter heard a suppressed little puppyish protest, as though its maker were very sleepy, a moment later the soft, recognising whinny of a broncho, and then, startlingly sudden as the figure had first emerged from the tent, it appeared again, mounted, by his side.

For half the distance to the ranch house not a word was said; then of a sudden Howard drew his horse to a walk meaningly.

"I suppose it's none of my business," he commented without preface, "but unless I'm badly mistaken there'll be hell to pay around the Buffalo Butte now."

Again, as at the tent door, his companion made no answer; merely waited for the something he knew was on the other's mind. The east was beginning to lighten now, and against the reddening sky his dark face appeared almost pale.

Howard shifted in his saddle seat and inspected the ground at his right as intently as though there might be jewels scattered about.

"The boss's relative-Craig," he added, "has taken possession there as completely as if he'd owned the place a lifetime instead of been a visitor two days." The long moustaches that gave the man's face an unmeritedly ferocious expression lifted characteristically. "I like you, How, or I wouldn't stick my bill into your affairs. That boy is going to make you trouble, take my word for it."

Even then there was no response; but the overseer did not seem surprised or offended. Instead, the load he had to impart off his mind, his manner indicated distinct relief. But one thing more was necessary to his material comfort-and that solace was at hand. Taking a great bite of plug tobacco, a chew that swelled one of his thin cheeks like a wen, he lapsed into his normal attitude of disinterested reverie.

The ranch house was lighted from top to bottom, abnormally brilliant, and as the Indian entered the odour of kerosene was strong in his nostrils. In the kitchen as he passed through were the other two herders. They sat side by side in uncomfortable inaction, their big sombreros in their hands; and with the suppression of those unused to death nodded him silent recognition. The dining-room was empty, likewise the living-room; but as he mounted the stairs, he could hear the muffled catch of a woman's sobs, and above them, intermittent, authoritative, the voice of a man speaking. His moccasined feet gave no warning, and even after he had entered the room where the dead man lay none of the three who were already present knew that he was there.

Just within the doorway he paused and looked about him. In one corner of the room, well away from the bed, sat Mary Landor. She did not look up as he entered, apparently did not see him, did not see anything. The first wild passion of grief past, she had lapsed into a sort of passive lethargy. Her fingers kept picking at the edge of the loose dressing sack she had put on, and now and then her thin lips trembled; but that was all.

Only a glance the newcomer gave her, then his eyes shifted to the bed; shifted and halted and, unconsciously as he had done when Howard first broke the news, his feet came close together and his arms folded across his chest in characteristic, all-observing attention. Not a muscle moved, he scarcely seemed to breathe. He merely watched.

And this was what he saw: The shape of a dead man lying as at first beneath the covers; only now the sheet had been raised until the face was hid. Beside it, stretched out in abandon as she had thrown herself down, her head all but buried from view, was the girl Bess. She was sobbing as though her heart would break: sobbing as though unconscious of another human being in the world. Above her, leaning over her, was the form of a man: Craig. His uncle had brought his belongings from the tiny town the day before, and even at this time his linen and cravat were immaculate. He was looking down at the little woman before him, looking and hesitating as one choosing between good and evil.

"Bess," he was saying, "you must not. You'll make yourself sick. Besides, it's nearly morning and people will be coming. Don't do so; please!"

No answer, no indication that he had been heard; only the muffled, racking, piteous sobs.

"Bess," insistently, "Bess! Listen to me. I can't have you do so. Uncle Landor wouldn't like it, I know he wouldn't. He'd be sorry if he knew. Be brave, girlie. You're not alone yet."

Still no response of word or of action. Still the dainty, curved shoulders trembled and were quiet and trembled again.

The man's hand dropped to the coverlet beside him. His face went very close.

"Cousin Bess," he repeated for the last time tensely, "I can't let you cry so. I won't. I care for you too much, little girl; infinitely too much. It hurts me to have you feel so terribly, hurts me more than I can tell." Just for a moment he hesitated, and like an inexperienced gambler his face went tense and white. "You must listen to me, Elizabeth, Uncle has gone, but there are others who will take care of you. I myself will take care of you, girlie. Listen, Bess, for there's something I must tell you, something you make me tell you now." Swiftly, unhesitatingly, he leaned still nearer; with one motion his arm passed about her and he clasped her close, so close she could not struggle, could not prevent. "I love you, little girl. Though I've only known you two days, I love you. That is what you compel me to tell you. This is why it hurts me to have you cry so. I love you, Bess; I love you!"

This is what, there in that tiny unplastered bed-room next the roof, came to pass that October morning. Just so the four living actors remained for a second while the first light of day sifted in through the tiny-paned windows; the elderly woman unconscious of the drama enacting before her eyes, unconscious of anything, her thin fingers still picking at the edge of her sack; the motionless watcher rigid as a casting in bronze: the passionate gambling stranger man holding the girl to him tightly, so tightly she could not but remain so, passive; then came the climax. Of a sudden the image that had been lifeless resolved itself into a man. Muscles played here and there visibly beneath the close-fitting flannel shirt he wore. Swiftly, yet still without a sound, one moccasined foot moved forward, and its mate-and again the first. Unexpected as death itself would have been at that instant, Craig felt two mighty irresistible hands close on his shoulders; close with a grip that all but paralysed. Irresistibly again he felt himself turned about, put upon his feet; realised of a sudden, too suddenly and unexpectedly even to admit of a cry, that the girl was free, that, not a foot distant, he was staring into the face of the one being on earth from whom he had most to fear. All this in seconds; then, mercifully intervening, a Providence itself, the tense wet face of the girl came between. The first sound that had been spoken came to his ears.

"How! In God's name don't! He didn't mean any harm; I know he didn't. Forgive him, How; please, please," and repeated: "Forgive him-for my sake."

The lamps had long been out, but the odour of low-test kerosene still hung about the closed living-room where the same four people sat in council. No effort had as yet been made to put the place to rights, and in consequence it was stuffy and disordered and proportionately depressing. The mound of cigarette stumps which Craig had builded the night before lay unsightly and evil of odour on the table. The faded rag carpet was littered with the tobacco he had scattered. His gaudy riding blouse and cap reposed on a lounge in one corner. His ulster and hat, which he had unpacked the last thing before retiring, lay across a chair. Look where one might about the place, there were evidences of his presence, of his dominant inhabitance. Already after two days' residence, as Howard had said, he had taken complete possession. Whosoever may have possessed the voice of authority in the past, concerning the future there was to be no doubt. That voice was speaking now.

"To be sure I shall take him East," it said. "His father is buried in Boston, and his grandfather, and his grandfather's father." The voice halted, lowered. "Besides, my mother and his other sister, who died years and years ago, are both there." Obviously, too obviously, he turned away until his face was hid. Into the voice there crept a throb that was almost convincing. "They'd all want him with them, I'm sure, even though he wouldn't have cared; and I think he would. He mentioned it the first night I came, but of course I didn't realise-then —" The voice was silent.

As hours before in the room above, Mary Landor showed no emotion, did not speak. Not even yet had her sorrow-numbed brain awakened, had she grasped the full meaning of the thing which had happened to her. Later, indefinitely later, the knowledge would come, and with it the hour of reckoning; but for the present she was a mere puppet in the play. Craig, the dominant, had told her to dress, and she had dressed. He had summoned her to the council, and she had obeyed. But it was not to her now that he had spoken, nor to the other man who, silent as he had entered, stood erect, his arms folded, listening. To yet another he had spoken. She it was, Elizabeth, who answered.

"But to take him clear back there, away from everyone who cares for him or ever has cared for him." The soft lower lip was becoming unmanageable and the girl halted, winking hard. "It seems cruel."

"Not if he would have wished it, Bess."

"But if he hadn't wished it —"

"I repeat I think he would." Craig shifted until his back was toward the other man. "I think that his mentioning the possibility at all, the first night I came, proves that he wished it."

"Perhaps....I don't know." ...A long pause; then of a sudden the girl arose and walked to the window. But subterfuge was from her a thing apart, and she merely leaned her face against the casement. "I can't bear to think of it," she trembled.

Craig moved half way toward her; then remembered, and halted.

"Yes, let's decide, and not talk about it," he returned swiftly. "You agree with me after all, don't you, Bess?"

The girl did not look up.

"Don't ask me. You and How and Aunt Mary decide." With an effort she resumed her former place; but even yet she did not glance at him. "Wherever you take him I shall go along, is all."

Swiftly, exuberantly swiftly, Craig took her up.

"Yes, I think he would have liked that. I ... You agree with me too, don't you, Aunt Mary?"

The older woman started at sound of her name, looked up vacantly. "What?" she queried absently.

Craig repeated the question perfunctorily.

"Yes, he was always good to me, very good to me," she returned monotonously.

In sympathy, the girl's brown eyes moistened anew; but Craig turned away almost impatiently. "Let's consider it settled then," he said.

For the first time the girl glanced up; but it was not at Craig that she looked. It was at that other figure in the background, the figure that not once through it all had stirred or made a sound. "What shall we do, How? what ought we to do?" she asked.

For ten seconds there was silence; but not even then did Craig recognise the other's presence by so much as a glance. Only the look of exultation left his face, and over his blue eyes the lids tightened perceptibly.

"Don't consider what I think, Bess," said a low voice at last. "Do what you feel is right."

It was the white man who had decided, but it was another who brought the decision to pass. How Landor, the Indian, it was who, alone in the dreary chamber beneath the roof, laid the dead man out decently, and for five dragging minutes thereafter, before the others had come, stood like a statue gazing down at the kindly, heavy face, with a look on his own

that no living human had ever seen or would ever see. How Landor, the Indian, it was who, again alone in the surrey, with the closely drawn canvas curtains, drove all that day and half the night to the nearest undertaker at the railroad terminus beyond the river, seventy-five miles away. How Landor, the Indian, again it was who, with a change of horses, but barely a pause to eat, started straight back on the return trail, and ere it was again light was within the limits of Coyote Centre, knocking at the door of Mattie Burton, the one woman friend of Mary Landor he knew. How Landor it was once more who, before twenty-four hours from the time he had left, had passed, with the unwilling visitor by his side, re-entered the Buffalo Butte ranch yard. Last of all, How Landor, the Indian, it was who faced the old surrey once more to the east, and with still another team before him and a cold lunch in his pocket, sat waiting within the hour to take the departing ones away.

Through it all he scarcely spoke a word, not one that was superfluous. What he was thinking of no one but he himself knew. That he had expected what had taken place in his absence, his bringing Mrs. Burton proved. At last realisation had come, and Mary Landor was paying the price of the brief lethargic respite; paying it with usury, paying it with the helpless abandon of the dependent. The dreary weather-coloured ranch house was not a pleasant place to be in that day. Craig left it thankfully, with a shrug of the shoulders beneath the box-fitting topcoat, as the door closed behind him. The other passenger, the one who should have left also and did not, the girl Elizabeth —.

How Landor it was again who, when minutes of waiting had passed, minutes wherein Craig consumed cigarettes successively, tied the team and disappeared within doors. What he said none save the girl herself knew; but when he returned he was not alone, and though the eyes of his companion were red, there was in her manner no longer a trace of hesitation.

The two passengers comfortably muffled in the robes of the rear seat, the driver buttoned the curtains tight about them methodically. The day was very still, not a sound came to them from over the prairie, and of a sudden, startlingly clear, from the house itself there came an interruption: the piteous, hopeless wail of a woman in a paroxysm of grief, and a moment later the voice of another woman in unemotional, comforting monotone.

"How," said a choking, answering voice, "I can't go after all, I can't!"

Within the carriage, safe from observation, her companion took her hand authoritatively, pressed it within his own.

"Yes, you can, Bess," he said low. "Aunt Mary will have to fight it out for herself. You couldn't help her any by staying."

But already the Indian was gone. Within the house as before, even keen-eared Mattie Burton failed to catch what he said. Had she done so, she would have been no wiser, for apparently that moment a miracle took place. Of a sudden, the hysterical voice was silent. The man spoke again and-the watcher stared in pure unbelief-her own hand in her companion's hand, Mary Landor followed him obediently out to the surrey.

"We haven't any time to lose," he said evenly, as he drew back the flap of the curtain. "You'd better say good-bye now."

"Mother!"

"Bessie, girl. Bessie!"

Again within the ranch house, Mary Landor sank into a seat with the utter weariness of a somnambulist awakened. Fully a half minute the Indian stood looking down at her. For one of the few times in his life his manner indicated indecision. His long arms hung loose from his shoulders. His wide-brimmed hat hid his eyes. The watcher thought he looked very, very weary. Then of a sudden he roused. Bending over-did he foresee what was to come, that moment? —he did something he had never done before.

"Good-bye, mother," he said, and kissed her on the lips.

The door closed behind him noiselessly, and a half minute later the loose-wheeled old surrey went rumbling past the door. Mrs. Burton was feminine and curious, and she went to the window to watch it from sight. The Indian, alone on the front seat, sat looking straight ahead. The bronchos, fresh from the stall, and but a few weeks before wild on the prairie, tugged at the bit wickedly, tried to bolt; but the driver did not stir in his place. The left hand, that held the reins, rose and fell with their motion, as an angler takes up slack in his line; that was all. The woman had lived long on the frontier. She was appreciative and pressed her face against the pane the better to see. They were through the gate now, well out on the prairie. The clatter of the waggon had ceased, the figure of the driver was concealed by the curtains; but the bronchos were still tugging at the bit, still —.

"Mary! In heaven's name!" The sound of a falling body had caught her ear and she had turned. "Mary Landor!" The dishes in the cupboard against the wall shook as something heavy met the floor. "Mary!" A pause and a tongue-tied examination. "My God! The woman is dead!"

It was ten minutes before starting time. The old-fashioned engine, contemptuously relegated to the frontier before going to the junk heap, was puffing at the side of the low sanded station platform. The rough cottonwood box was already in the baggage car. How himself had assisted in putting it there, had previously settled for its transportation. Likewise he had bought the girl's ticket, and checked her scanty baggage. The usual crowd of loafers was about the place, and his every action was observed with the deepest interest. Wherever he moved the spectators followed. Urchins near at hand fought horrible mimic duels for his benefit; duels which invariably ended in the scalping of the vanquished-and with expressions of demoniacal exultation playing upon the face of the conqueror. From far in the rear a war whoop sounded; and when the effort was to all evidence ignored, was repeated intrepidly near at hand. They put themselves elaborately in his way, to move at his approach with grunts of guttural protestation. Already, even here on the frontier, the Sioux and his kind were becoming a novelty. Verily they were rare sportsmen, those mimicking loafers; and for Indians it was ever the open season. All about sounded the popping of their artillery; to be, when exhausted, as often reloaded and fired again.

But through it all, apparently unseeing, unconscious, the man had gone about his business. Now as he left the ticket window and approached the single coach, it was nearly starting time. The girl had already entered and sat motionless in her seat watching him through the dusty window glass. Craig, his feet wide apart, stood on the platform smoking a last cigarette. He shrugged in silence as the other passed him and mounted the steps.

Save for the girl, the coach was empty; but, destitute of courtesy, the spectators without stared with redoubled interest. Without a word the man handed over the ticket and checks. Still in silence he slipped a roll of bills into her passive hand. Until that moment the girl had not thought of money; but even now as she accepted it, there never occurred the wonder from whence it had come. Had she known how those few dollars had been stored up, bit by bit, month by month-But she did not know. Unbelievably unsophisticated, unbelievably innocent and helpless, was Elizabeth Landor at this time. Sitting there that morning on the threshold, she had no more comprehension of the world she was entering, she had entered, than of eternity itself. She was merely passive, trusting, waiting to be led. Like a bit of down from the prairie milkweed plant, she was to be the sport of every breath of wind that blew. And already that wind was blowing. She had watched the scene on the platform, had understood the intent of the mimicry, had seen the winks and nudges, had heard the mocking war whoop. All this she had seen, all this had been stored away in her consciousness to recur again and again in the future. Even now her cheeks had burned at the knowledge, and at last she had watched the man's coming with a feeling of repression she had never known before, whose significance she did not try to analyse, did not in the least understand. She did not thank him for the money. To do so never occurred to her. It was the moment for parting, but she did not throw her arms about his neck in abandon, as she would have done a week before. Something, she knew not what, prevented. She merely sat there, repressed, passive, waiting. A moment, by her side, the Indian paused. He did not speak, he did not move. He merely looked at her; and in his dark eyes there was mirrored a reflection of the look there had been in the eyes of the wild thing he had stalked and captured that day alone on the prairie. But the girl was not looking at him, did not se e. A moment he stood so, unconsciously as so many, many times before, in pose; then deliberately, gently, ignoring the row of curious observant eyes, he took her hand and raised it to his lips.

"Good-bye, Bess," he said low. "Come back as soon as you can; and don't worry. Everything will come right." Gently as he had lifted the hand, he released it. A smile-who but he could have smiled at that moment? —played for an instant over his face. Then, almost before the girl realised the fact, before the repressive something that held her in its grip gave release, he was gone. As he left the coach, Craig, who was waiting, started without a word or a hint of recognition to enter. His foot was already on the step, when he felt a hand upon his arm; a hand with a grip whose meaning there was no misinterpreting. Against his will he drew back. Against his will he met the other, face to face, eye to eye. For what seemed to him minutes, but which in reality was only a second, they stood so. Not a word was spoken, of warning or of commonplace. There was no polite farce for the benefit of the spectators. The Indian merely looked at him; but as once before, alone under the stars, that look was to remain burned on the white man's memory until he went to his grave.

"A'board," bawled the conductor, and as though worked by the same wire, the engineer's waiting head disappeared within the cab window.

Side by side, Clayton Craig and Elizabeth Landor sat watching the weather-stained station and the curious assembled group, as apparently they slowly receded. The last thing they saw was the alien figure of an Indian in rancher's garb, gazing motionless after them; and by his side, in baiting pantomime, one gawky urchin engaged in the labour of scalping a mate. The last sound that reached their ears was the ironic note of a war whoop repeated again and again.

Chapter XII
Within the Conqueror's Own Country

It was the day set for the wedding, the eighteenth since the girl had left, the sixteenth since a new mound had arisen on the bare lot adjoining that beneath which rested Landman Bud Smith, the twelfth since How Landor had arrived to haunt the tiny railway terminus. The one train from the East was due at 8:10 of the morning. It was now eight o'clock. Within the shambling, ill-kept hotel, with its weather-stained exterior and its wind-twisted sign, the best room, paid for in advance and freshly dusted for the occasion, awaited an occupant. In a stall of the single livery, a pair of half-wild bronchos, fed and harnessed according to directions, were passively waiting. An old surrey, recently oiled and tightened in all its senile joints, was drawn up conveniently to the door. In a tiny room, designated the study, of the Methodist parsonage, on the straggling outskirts of the town, the only minister the settlement boasted sat staring at the unpapered wall opposite. He was a mild-featured young man of the name of Mitchell, recently graduated from a school of theology, and for that reason selected as a sacrifice to the frontier. In front of him on the desk lay a duly prepared marriage licence, and upon it a bright gold half eagle. From time to time he glanced thereat peculiarly, and in sympathy from it to the tiny fast-ticking clock at its side. He did so now, and frowned unconsciously.

At the station the crowd of loafers that always preceded the arrival or departure of a train were congregated. In some way suggestions of the unusual had passed about, and this day their number was greatly augmented. Just what they anticipated they did not know; they did not care. Restless, athirst for excitement, they had dumbly responded to the influence in the air and come. In the foreground, where a solitary Indian stood motionless, waiting, there was being repeated the same puerile pantomime and horse-play of a former occasion. At intervals, from the rear, sounded the war whoop travesty. It was all the same as that afternoon eighteen days before, when the girl had left, similar even to the cloud of black smoke in the distance lifting lazily into the sky; only now the trail, instead of growing thinner and lighter, became denser and blacker minute by minute. In sympathy, the humorists on the platform redoubled their efforts. The instinct of anticipation, of Anglo-Saxon love of excitement that had brought them there, urged them on. Not one throat but many underwent simultaneous pantomimic bisection. A half dozen voices caught up the war whoop, passed it on from throat to throat. Almost before they realised what they were doing, the thing became a contagion, an orgy. Many who had not taken part before, who had come from mere curiosity, took part now. The crowd pressed closer and closer about the alien, the centre of attraction. When he moved farther along the platform to avoid them, they followed. Heretofore passive, the innate racial hostility became active. One youth with a dare-devil air jostled him-and disappeared precipitately. There was no response, no retaliation, and another followed his example. The confusion redoubled, drowned the roar of the approaching train. Spectators in the rear began mounting trucks and empty barrels the better to see. Within the station itself the shirt-sleeved agent surreptitiously locked the door to the ticket-room and sprung the combination of the safe. Beginning harmless ly, the incident was taking on a sinister aspect, and he had lived too long in this semi-lawless land to take any chances. Re-turning to his place of observation at the window, he was just in time to see a decayed turnip come hurtling over the heads of the crowd and, with enviable accuracy, catch the Indian behind the ear. Simultaneously, with a roar and a puff of displaced air, the light train drew into the station, on time.

Through it all the Indian had not spoken a word. Save to move twice farther away along the platform, he had not stirred. Unbelievable as it may seem, even when the missile had struck him, though it had left a great red welt, he gave no sign of feeling. For a space following the arrival of the train there was a lull, and in it, as though nothing had happened, he approached the single coach and stood waiting.

It was the last of the week and travel was very light.

A dapper commercial salesman with an imitation alligator grip descended first, looked about him apprehensively, and disappeared with speed. A big rancher with great curling moustaches and a vest open save at the bottom button followed. He likewise took stock of the surroundings, and discreetly withdrew. Following him there was a pause; then of a sudden onto the platform, fair into view of the crowd, appeared one for whom apparently they had been looking, one who on the instant caused the confusion, temporarily stilled, to break forth anew: the figure of a dainty brown girl with sensitive eyes and a soft oval chin, of Elizabeth Landor returned alone!

"Ah, there she is," shouted a voice, an united voice, the refound voice of the expectant crowd.

"Yes, there she is," repeated the intrepid youth who had introduced the jostle. "Go to, redskin. Kiss her again. Kiss her; we don't mind."

A great shout followed this sally, a shout that was heard far up the single street, and that brought curious faces to a half score of doors.

"No, we don't mind, redskin," they guffawed. "Go to! Go to!" Hesitant, hopelessly confused, the girl halted as she had appeared. Her great eyes opened wider than before, her face shaded paler momentarily, the soft oval chin trembled. Another minute, another second even.

"Come Bess," said a low voice. "Come on; don't mind them. I'll take care of you."

It was the first speech the man had made, and from pure curiosity the crowd went silent, listening-silent until he was silent; then with the lack of originality ever manifest in a mob, they caught up his words themselves.

"Yes, Bess," they baited, "he'll take care of you. Come, don't keep him waiting."

But the girl did not stir. Had empires depended upon it that moment, she could not have complied. Could she have cried, as the chin had at first presaged, she might perhaps have done so; but she was beyond the reach of tears now. The complete meaning of the scene had come to her at last, the realisation of personal menace; and a fear such as she had never before known, gripped her relentlessly. She could hear, hear every word; but her muscles refused to act. She merely stood there, the old telescope satchel she carried gripped tight in her hand, her great eyes, wide and soft as those of a wild thing, staring out into the now rapidly accumulating rabble; merely stared and waited.

"Bess," repeated the persuading voice, "come, please. Don't stand there, come."

At last the girl seemed to hear, to understand. Hesitatingly, with trembling steps, she came a pace forward, and another; then of a sudden she gave a little cry and her free hand lifted defensively. But she was not quick enough, had seen too late; and that instant came the *dénouement*. A second turnip, decayed like its predecessor, aimed likewise unerringly, caught her fair in the mouth, spattered, and broke into fragments that fell to the car steps. Following, swift as rain after a thunderclap, a spurt of blood came to her lips and trickled down her face.

Simultaneously the crowd went silent; silent as the still prairie about them, awed irresistibly by the thing they had themselves wittingly or unwittingly done. Save one, not a human being stirred. That one, no need to tell whom, transformed visibly; transformed as they had never seen a human being alter before. With not a step, but a bound, he was himself on the platform of the coach; the girl, protected behind him, hid from sight. She was sobbing now; sobbing tumultuously, hysterically. In the stillness every listening ear on the platform could hear distinctly. For an instant after he had reached her the Indian stood so, his left arm about her, his back toward them. He did not say a word, he did not move. For the first time in his life he dared not. He did not see red that moment, this man; he saw black-black as prairie loam. Every savage instinct in his brain was clamouring for freedom, clamouring until his free hand was clenched tight to keep it from the bulging holster behind his right hip. Before this instant, when they were baiting him alone, it was nothing, he could forgive; but now-now-He stared away from them, stared up into the smiling, sarcastic prairie sky; but, listening, they, who almost with fascination watched, could hear beneath the catch of the girl's sobs the sound of his breathing.

Ever at climaxes time seems suspended. Whether it was a second or a minute he stood there so, they who watched could never tell. What they did know was that at last he turned, stood facing them. All their lives they had seen passion, seen it in every phase, seen it until it was commonplace. It was in the very air of the frontier, to be expected, life of the life; but as this man shifted they saw a kind of which they had never dreamed. For How Landor was master of himself again, master, as well-they knew it, every man and youth who saw, —of them. For another indefinitely long deathly silent space he merely looked at them; looked eye to eye, individual by individual, into every face within the surrounding semi-circle. Once before another man, a drunken cowman, had seen that identical look. Now not one but a score saw it, felt a terrible ice-cold menace creep from his brain into their brains. Even yet he did not speak, did not make a sound; nor did they. Explain it as you will, he did this thing. Another thing he did as well; and that was the end. Slowly, deliberately, he stepped to the platform and held out his hand. Obediently the girl followed. She was not crying now. Her eyes were red and a drop of blood came now and then to her lips; but she had grown wonderfully quiet all at once, wonderfully calm-almost as much so as the man. Deliberately as he had stepped down into the spectators' midst, the Indian took the old telescope from the girl's hand and, she following by his side, moved a step forward. He did not touch her again nor did she him. They merely moved ahead toward the sidewalk that led up the single street; moved deliberately, leisurely, as though they were alone. Not around the crowd, but straight through it they passed; through a lane that opened as by magic as they went, and as by magic closed behind them, until they were within a solid human square. But of all the assembled spectators that day, an aggregation irresponsible, unchivalrous as no other rabble on earth—a mob of the frontier,—not on e spoke to challenge their action, not one attempted to bar their way. The complete length of the platform they went so, turned the corner by the station-and, simultaneously, the crowd disappeared from view, hid by the building itself. Then in sudden reaction, the girl weakened. Irresistibly she caught at the man's arm, held it fast.

"Oh, How! How!" she trembled, "is it to be always like this with you and me? Is it to be always, everywhere, so?"

But the man said never a word.

Two hours had passed. The girl had breakfasted. A wood fire crackled cheerfully in the sheet iron heater of the tiny room where the same two people sat alone. Already the world had taken on a different aspect. Not that Elizabeth Landor had forgotten that recent incident at the depot. She would never forget it. It had merely passed into temporary abeyance, taken its proper place in the eternal scheme of things. Another consideration, paramount, all-compelling, had inevitably crowded it from the stage. It was this consideration that had held her silent far longer than was normal. It was its overshadowing influence that at last prompted speech.

"How did you know I was coming to-day?" she queried suddenly.

"How did *you* know I would be at the train to meet you?" echoed a voice.

The girl did not answer, did not pursue the subject.

"Tell me of Aunt Mary, please," she digressed. "I felt somehow when you wrote as if I —I —" A swiftly gathered shower called a halt. Tear drops, ever so near, stood in her eyes. "Please tell me," she completed.

The man told her. It did not take long. As of her prosaic life, so there was little to record of the death of Mary Landor. "It was best that you were away," he ended. "It was best for her that she went when she did."

"You think so, How, honestly?" No affectation in that anxious query. "You think I didn't do wrong in leaving as I did?"

"No, you did no wrong, Bess." A pause. "You could not."

A moment the girl sat looking at him; in wonder and something more.

"I believe you knew all the time Aunt Mary would-go while I was away," she said suddenly, tensely. "I believe you helped me away on purpose."

No answer.

"Tell me, How. I want to know."

"I thought so, Bess," simply.

For a long time the girl sat so; silent, marvelling. A new understanding of this solitary human stole over her, an appreciation that drowned the sadness of a moment ago. "How you must care for me," she voiced almost unconsciously. "How you must care for me!"

She did not expect an answer. She was not disappointed. Again a silence fell; a silence of which she was unconscious, for she was thinking. Minutes passed. In the barn the bronchos were passively waiting. At the parsonage the young minister still sat scowling in his study. No time had been set for the visit he expected. There was no apparent reason why he should not have gone about his work; but for some reason he could not. Angry with himself, he thrust the new half eagle into his pocket and, placing the offending licence beneath a pile of papers, he walked over to the window and stood staring out into the sunshine.

Within the tiny room at the hotel the gaze of the girl shifted, dropped to her feet. Despite an effort her face tinged slowly red.

"Did you think," she queried abruptly, "when you expected me to-day that I would come alone?"

The Indian showed no surprise.

"Yes, Bess," he answered. "I knew you would be alone."

"Why, How?" The question was just audible.

"Because I trusted you, Bess."

Silence again. Surreptitiously, swiftly, the girl's brown eyes glanced up; but he was not looking at her, and again her glance fell. A longer pause followed, a pause wherein the girl could not have spoken if she would. A great preventing lump was in her throat, an obstacle that precluded speech. Many things had happened in the short time since she had last been with this man, some things of which she was not proud; and beside such a trust as this Bess Landor was speechless. Without volition upon her part, the cup of life had been placed to her lips and, likewise without knowledge of what it contained, she had tasted. The memory of that draught was with her now. Under its influence she spoke.

"You are better than I am, How," she said.

If the man understood he gave no evidence of the knowledge. He did not even look at her. Time was passing, time which should have found them upon their way, but he showed no impatience. It was his day, his moment, his by right; but no one looking at him would have doubted that he himself would never first suggest the fact. Conditions had changed very rapidly in the recent past, altered until, from his view-point, it was impossible for him to make the move toward the old relation, to even intimate its desirability. With the patience of his race he waited. In the fulness of time he was rewarded.

"How," of a sudden initiated a voice, withal an embarrassed voice, "will you do me a favour?"

"What is it, Bess?"

The girl coloured. Instinctively the man knew that at last the recall had come, and for the first time he was looking at her steadily.

"Promise me, please," temporised the girl.

"I promise."

Even yet Elizabeth Landor found it difficult to say what she wished to say.

"You won't be-offended or angry, How?"

"No, Bess. You could hurt me, but you couldn't make me angry."

"Thank you, How. It's a little thing, but I'd like to have you humour me." She met his look directly. "It's when we are married to-day you'll be dressed-well, not the way you usually dress." Her colour came and went, her throat was a-throb. "Dressed like-You understand, How."

Of a sudden the Indian was upon his feet; then as suddenly he checked himself. Characteristically, he now ignored the immaterial, went, as ever, straight to fundamentals without preface or delay. Scarce one human in a generation would have held aloof at that moment. It was his, his by every right; but even yet he would not take it, not until —.

"Bess," he said slowly. "I want to ask you a question and I want you to answer me—as you would answer your mother were she alive." Once again, unconsciously, he fell into pose, his arms across his breast, his great shoulders squared. "I have seen Mr. Landor's will. He has left you nearly everything. You are rich, Bess; I won't tell you how rich because you wouldn't understand. You are young and can live any life you wish. You know what marrying me means. I am as I am and cannot change. You know what others, people of your own race, think when you are with me. They have shown you to-day. Answer me, Bess, have you thought of all this? Was it duty that brought you back, or did you really wish to come? Don't take me into consideration at all when you answer. Don't do it, or we shall both live to regret. Tell me, Bess, as you know I love you, whether you have thought of all this and still wish to marry me. Tell me." He was silent. Once again it was a climax, and once again came oblivion of passing time. For minutes passed, minutes wherein, with wide open eyes, the girl made her choice. Not in hot blood was the decision made, not as before in ignorance of what that decision meant. Deliberately, with the puerile confidence we humans feel in our insight of future, she chose; as she believed, honestly.

"Yes, How," she said slowly. "I have thought of it all and I wish to marry you. I've no place else in the world to go. There's no one in the world that I trust as I trust you. I wish to marry you to-day, How."

Then, indeed, it was the man's moment. Then, and not until then, he accepted his reward. "Bess!" She was in his arms. "Bess!" He tasted Paradise. "Bess!" That was all.

For the second time that day the air of the tiny town tingled with portent of the unusual. For the second time a crowd was gathered; only now it was not at the station, but at a place of far more sinister import, within and in front of the "Lost Hope" saloon. Again in personnel it was different, notably different from that of the first occasion. The same irresponsibles were there, as ever they are present at times of storm; but added to the aggregation now, outnumbering them, were others ordinarily responsible, men typical in every way of the time and place. A second difference of even greater portent was the motif of gathering. For it was not a mere rumour, an idle curiosity, that had brought them together now. On the contrary they had at last, these dominant Anglo-Saxons, begun to take themselves seriously. Rumour, inevitable in a place where days were as much alike as the one-story buildings on the main street, had begun when How Landor had commenced to haunt the station at the time of the incoming train. The incident of the morning had familiarised the rumour into gossip. Hard upon this had followed a report from the hotel landlord, and gossip had become certainty. Then it was that horse-play had ceased, and, save at the point of congregation, a silence, unwonted and sinister, had taken its place. So marked was the change that when at last the Indian and the girl left the hotel together on their way to the parsonage the street through which they passed was as still as though it were the street of a prairie dog town. So quiet it was that the girl was deceived; but the ears of the Indian were keener, and faint as an echo beneath it, as yet well in the distance, he detected the warning of an alien note. Not as on that other day out on the prairie when he caught the first trumpet call of the Canada goose, did he recognise the sound from previous familiarity. Never in his life had he heard its like; yet now an instinct told him its meaning, told him as well its menace. Not once did he look back, not one word of prophecy did he speak to the girl at his side; yet as surely as a grey timber wolf realises what is to come when he catches the first faint bay of the hounds on his trail, How Landor realised that at last for him the hour of destiny had struck, that as surely as the wild thing must battle for life he must do likewise—and that soon, very, very soon.

Up the street they went: a small dark girl garbed as no woman was ever garbed in a fashion-plate, a tall copper-brown man all but humorously grotesque in a ready-made suit of clothes that were far from a fit and the first starched shirt and collar he had ever worn. Laughable unqualifiedly, this red man tricked out in the individuality-destroying dress of the white brother would have been to an observer who had not the key to the situation; but to one who knew the motive of the alteration it was far as the ends of the earth from humorous. On they went, silent now, each in widely separated anticipation; and after them, at first silent likewise, then as it advanced growing noisier and noisier, followed the crowd which had congregated at the Lost Hope saloon. As on the day of the little landman's funeral when Captain William Landor had passed up the street of Cayote Centre, ahead where the Indian and the girl advanced not the figure of a human being was in sight, unless one were suspicious and looked closely, not a face; but to the Indian eyes were everywhere. Every house they passed-for they were in the residence section now-had its pair or multiple pairs peering out through the slats of a blind, or, as in a theatre preceding a performance, at the side of a drawn curtain. Like wildfire the news had spread; like turtles timid women folk had drawn close within their shells; yet everywhere curiosity they could not repress prompted them to take a last look before the storm. Once, and once only, the pedestrians were interrupted. Then a house dog came bounding across the lawn to pause at a safe distance and growl a menace; and again the all-noting Indian had observed the cause of the unwonted bravery, had heard the low voice from the kitchen that had urged the beast on.

Thus nearer and nearer that sunny fall morning the storm approached. Long before this, unobservant though she was, had the girl not been living in the future instead of the present, she would have recognised its coming. For the pursuers were gaining rapidly now. They had crossed onto the same street, the principal residence thoroughfare, and were coming as a crowd ever moves: swiftly, those in the rear exerting themselves to get to the fore, and so again. Far from silent by this time, the man ahead, the man who never deigned a backward glance, could hear their voices in a perpetual rumble; could distinguish at intervals, interrupting it, above it, a voice commanding, inflaming. Without seeing, he knew that at last his persecutors had found a commander, a directing spirit-and as well as he knew his own name he knew who that leader was. Unsophisticated absolutely in the ways of the world was this man; but in the reading of his fellows he was a master.

Apparently oblivious when a part of this same crowd had congregated at the train, he had nevertheless observed them individual by individual; and in his own consciousness had known that the moment, his moment, had not come: for a leader, the leader, was not there. Again when the train had pulled in he had watched-and still the leader did not appear. But he was not deceived. As he had trusted in the girl's coming he had trusted in another's following surreptitiously; and as now he heard that one voice sounding above the other voices he knew he had been right. For the man at the head of that pursuing mob which gained on them so rapidly block by block, the man whose influence in those brief hours the Indian and the girl had been alone in the tiny room at the hotel had vitalised the lukewarm racial hostility into a thing of menace, was the same man whose life he had once saved, the same man about whose throat ere the identical night had passed his fingers had closed: Clayton Craig by name, one time of Boston, Mass., but now, by his uncle's will, master of the Buffalo Butte ranch house!

Meanwhile in the study of the parsonage Clifford Mitchell was again looking out the single window. Time and time again he had tried to work-and as often failed. At last he had conformed to the inevitable and was merely waiting. The house was on the outskirts of the town and the window faced the open prairie; bare and rolling as far as the eye could reach. He was city bred, this mild-faced servant of God, and as yet the prairie country was a thing at which to marvel. He was looking out upon it now, absently, thoughtfully, wondering at its immensity and its silence-when of a sudden he became conscious that it was no longer silent. Instead to his ears, growing louder moment by moment, penetrating the illy constructed walls, came an indistinct roar; rising, lowering, yet ever constant: a sound unlike any other on earth, distinctive as the silence preceding had been typical-the clamour of angry, menacing human voices *en masse*. Once, not long before, in a city street the listener had heard that identical sound; and recognition was instantaneous. Swift as memory he recalled the strike that had been its cause, the horde of sympathisers who had of a sudden appeared as from the very earth, the white face and desperate figure of the solitary "scab" fighting a moment, and a moment only, for life, in their midst. Swift as memory came that picture; and swift upon its heels, blotting it out, the present returned. Clifford Mitchell had not been among this people long; yet already he had caught the spirit of the place, and as he listened he knew full well what a similar gathering among them would mean. He was not a brave man, this blue-eyed pastor; not a drop of fighting blood was in his veins; and as moment after moment passed and the sound grew nearer and nearer, the first real terror of his life came creeping over him. Not in his mind was there a doubt as to the destination of that oncoming multitude. Premonition had been too electric in the air that day for him to question its meaning. They were coming to him, to him, Clifford Mitchell, these irresponsible menacing humans. It might be another for whom they had gathered; but he as well would share in their displeasure, in their punishment: for he was a party to the thing of which they disapproved. All the day, from the time the Indian had called and almost simultaneously, vague rumours of trouble had come floating in the visitor's wake; he had been in anticipation; and now the thing anticipated had become a certainty. Answering he felt the cold perspiration come pouring out on his forehead; and absently, he wiped it away with the palm of his hand. Following came a purely physical weakness; and stumbling across the room he took the seat beside the desk. Unconsciously nervous, restless, his fingers fumbled with the pile of papers before him until they came to a certain one he had buried. Almost as though impelled against his will to do so he spread this one flat before him and sat staring at it, dumbly waiting.

Nearer and nearer came the roar as he sat there, irresistible, cumulatively menacing as a force of nature; and instinctively, by it alone, the listener marked the approach of its makers. He could hear them down the street at the other end of the block before the residence of Banker Briggs. He knew this to a certainty because part of those who came were on the sidewalk, and that was the only piece of cement in town. Again, by the same token, he knew when they passed the only other house in the block besides his own. There was a gap in the boardwalk there, and when the leaders reached it the patter of their footsteps went suddenly muffled on the bare earth. It was his turn next, his in a moment; yes, the feet were already on the confines of his own yard, the roar of their owners' voices was all about. He could even distinguish what they were saying now, could catch names, his own name.

Of a sudden, expected and yet unexpected, a dark shadow passed before his window, and another; then a swarm. Simultaneously faces, not a few but as many as could crowd into the space, appeared outside the panes, staring curiously in. Involuntarily he arose to draw the shade; and at that moment, interrupting, startlingly loud, there came a knock at his front door.

Clifford Mitchell paused on his way to the window, stood irresolute; and, seemingly impossible as it was, the number of curious faces multiplied.

The knock was repeated; not fearfully or frantically, but deliberately and with an insistence there was no misunderstanding.

This time the minister responded. He did not pause to blot out the faces of the curious. The licence he had been absently holding was still in his hand; but he did not delay to put it down. There was something compelling in that knock; something that demanded instant obedience, and he obeyed. The living-room through which he passed on his way had two windows and, identical with that of his study, each was black with humanity; but he did not even glance at them. His legs trembled involuntarily and his throat was dry as though he had been speaking for hours; yet, nevertheless, he obeyed. With a hand that shook perceptibly he turned the button of the spring lock, and, opening the door onto the street, looked out.

While Clifford Mitchell lived, while lived every man of the uncounted throng gathered there beneath the noon-time sun that October day, they remembered that moment, the moments that followed. As real life is ever stranger than fiction, so off the stage occur incidents more stirring than at the play. Standing there in the narrow doorway, white-faced, hesitant, awaiting a command, the minister himself exemplified the fact beyond question; yet of his own grotesque part he was oblivious. He had thought for but one thing that moment, had room in his consciousness for but one impression; and that was for the drama ready there before him. And small wonder, for, looking out, this was what he saw:

An uneven straggling village street, mottled with patches of dead grass and weeds. Along it, here and there, like kernels of seed scattered on fallow ground, a sprinkling of one-story houses. This the background. In the midst of it all, covering his lawn, overflowing into the yards of his neighbours, dense, crowding the better to see, all-surrounding, was a solid zone of motley humanity. Old men with weather-beaten faces and untrimmed beards were there, young men with the marks that dissipation and passion indelibly stamp, awkward, gawky youths unconsciously aping their elders, smooth-faced youngsters in outgrown garments; all ages and conditions of the human frontier male were there-but in that zone not a single woman. Ranchers there were in corduroys and denims, cowboys in buckskin and flannel, gamblers in the glaring colours distinctive of their kind, business men with closely cropped moustaches, idlers in anything and everything; but amid them all not a friendly face. This the surrounding zone, the mongrel pack that had brought the quarry to bay.

In the centre of the half circle they formed, within a couple of paces of the now open doorway, were three people. Two of them, a rather small brown girl and a tall wiry Indian in a new suit of ready-made clothes and a derby hat of the model of the year before, were nearest; so near that the door, which swung outward, all but touched them. The other, a well-built, smooth-faced Easterner with a white skin and delicate hands, was opposite. His dress was the dress of a man of fashion, his cravat and patent leather buttoned shoes were of the latest style; but his linen was soiled now, and a two-days' growth of beard covered his chin. Moreover, his eyes were bloodshot and, despite an effort to prevent, as he stood there now he wavered a bit to right and left. One look told his story. He had been drinking, drinking for days; and, worst of all, he had been drinking this day, drinking in anticipation of this very moment, swallowing courage against the necessity of the now. All this the stage and its setting, upon which the white-faced minister raised the curtain. Simultaneously, as ever an audience grows silent when the real play begins, it grew silent now. The hinges of the little-used front door were rusty and had squeaked startlingly. Otherwise not a sound marked the opening of the drama.

A moment following the silence was intense, a thing one could feel; then of a sudden it was broken-not by words, but by action. One step the white-skinned man took forward; a step toward the girl. A second step he advanced, and halted; for, preventing, the hand of the other man was upon his own.

"Stand back, please," said an even voice. "It's not time for congratulations yet. Stand back, please."

Answering there was a sound; but not articulate. It was a curse, a challenge, a menace all in one; and with a hysterical terrified little cry the girl shrank back into the doorway itself. But none other, not even the minister, stirred.

"Mr. Craig," the words were low, almost intimately low, but in the stillness they seemed fairly loud. "I ask you once more to stand back. I don't warn you, I merely request-but I shall not ask it again." Of a sudden the speaker's hand left the other's arm, dropped by his own side. "Stand back, please."

Face to face the two men stood there; the one face working, passionate, menacing; the other emotionless as the blue sky overhead. A moment they remained so while the breathless onlookers expected anything, while from the doorstep the minister's white lips moved in a voiceless prayer; then slowly, lingeringly, the man who had advanced drew back. A step he took silently, another, and his breathing became audible, still another, and was himself amid the spectators. Then for the first time he found voice.

"You spoke your own sentence then, redskin," he blazed. "We'd have let you go if you'd given up the girl; but now-now-May God have mercy on your soul now, How Landor!"

Again there was silence; silence absolute. As at that first meeting on the car platform, the girl had turned facing them. It was the crisis, and as before an instinct which she did not understand, which she merely obeyed, brought her to the Indian's side; held her there motionless, passive, mysteriously unafraid. Her usually brown face was very pale and her eyes were unnaturally bright; but withal she was unbelievably calm-calm as a child with its hand in its father's hand. Not even that solid zone of menacing, staring eyes had terror for her now. Whether or no she loved him, as she believed in God she trusted in that motionless, dominant human by her side.

A moment they stood so in a silence wherein they could hear each other breathe, wherein the prayer that had never left the minister's lips became audible; then came the end. Incredible after it was over was that *dénouement*, inexplicable to a legion of old men, then among the boys, who witnessed it, to this day. Yet as the incredible continues to take place in this world it took place then. As one man can ever dominate other men it was done that silent noon hour. For that moment the first challenge that had ever passed the lips of How Landor was spoken. The only challenge that he ever made to man or woman in his life found voice; and was not accepted. One step he took toward that listening, expectant throng and halted. With the old, old motion his arms folded across his chest.

"Men," he said, "I don't want trouble here to-day. I've done my best to avoid it; but the end has come. I've stood everything at your hands, every insult which you could conceive, things which no white man would have permitted for a second; and so far without resentment. But I shall stand it no more. I'm one to a hundred; but that makes no difference. Bess Landor and I are to be married now and here; here before you all. I shall not talk to you again. I shall not ask you to leave us in peace; but as surely as one of you speaks another word of insult to her or to me, as surely as one of you attempts to interfere or prevent, I shall kill that man. No matter which of you it is, I shall do this thing." A moment longer he stood so, observing them steadily, with folded arms; then, still facing, he moved back a step. "Mr. Mitchell," he said, "we are ready."

And there that October noonday, fair in the open with two hundred curious eyes watching, in a silence unbroken as that of prairie night itself, Bess Landor and Ma-wa-cha-sa the Sioux were married. The minister stumbled in the ritual, and though he held the book close before his face, it was memory alone that prompted the form; for the pages shook until the letters were blurred. Yet it was done, and, save one alone, every spectator who had come with a far different intent stayed and listened to the end. That one, a tall, modish alien with a red, flushed face covered with a two-days' growth of bread, was likewise watching when it began. But when it was over he was not there; and not one of those who had followed his lead had noticed his going.

Chapter XIII
The Mystery of Solitude

Westward across the unbroken prairie country, into the smiling, sun-kissed silence and emptiness, two people were driving: a white girl of two-and-twenty summers and an Indian man a few years older. Back of them, in the direction from which they had come, was the outline of a straggling, desolate village. Ahead, to either side, was the rolling brown earth; and at the end of it, abrupt apparently as a material wall, the blue of a cloudless October sky. The team they were driving, a mouse-coloured broncho and a mate a shade darker, were restless after three days of enforced inactivity and tugged at the bit mightily. Though the day was perfectly still, the canvas curtains of the old surrey flapped lazily in a breeze born of the pace alone. The harness on the ponies shuffled and creaked with every move. Though the bolts of the ancient vehicle had been carefully tightened, it nevertheless groaned at intervals with the motion; mysteriously, like the unconscious sigh of the aged, apparently without reason. Beneath the wheels the frost-dried grass rattled continuously, monotonously; but save this last there was no other sound. Since the two humans had left the limits of the tiny town there had been no other sound. Now and then the girl had glanced behind, instinctively, almost fearfully; but not once had the man followed her example, had he stirred in his place. Swiftly, silently, he was leaving civilisation behind him; by the scarce visible landmarks he alone distinguished was returning to his own, to the wild that lay in the distance beyond.

Thus westward, direct as a tight cord, on and on they went; and back of them gradually, all but unconsciously, the low-built terminus grew dimmer and dimmer, vanished detail by detail as completely as though it had never been. Last of all to disappear, already a mere black dot against the blue, was the water tank beside the station. For three miles, four, it held its place; then, as, with the old unconscious motion the girl turned to look back, she searched for it in vain. Behind them as before, unbroken, limiting, only the brown plain and the blue surrounding wall met her gaze. At last, there in the solitude, there with no observer save nature and nature's God, she and the other were alone.

As the first man and the first woman were alone they were alone. From horizon to horizon was not a sign of human handiwork, not a suggestion of human presence. They might live or die, or laugh or weep, or love or hate-and none of their kind would be the wiser. All her life that she could remember the girl had lived so, all her life she had but to lift her eyes above her feet to gaze into the infinite; yet in the irony of fate never until this moment, the moment when of all she should have been the happiest, did the immensity of this solitude appeal to her so, did appreciation of the terrible, haunting loneliness it concealed touch her with its grip. Care free, thoughtless, never until the whirl of the last fortnight had the future, her future, appealed to her as something which she herself must shape or alter. Heretofore it had been a thing taken for granted, preordained as the alternate coming of light and of darkness. But in that intervening time, short as it was, she had awakened. Rude as had been the circumstances that had aroused her, they had nevertheless been effective. Without volition upon her part the panorama of another life had been unrolled before her eyes. Sensations, thoughts, impulses of which she had never previously dreamed had been hers. Passions unconceived had stalked before her gaze. More a nightmare on the whole than an awakening it had all been; yet nevertheless the experience had been hers. Much of its meaning had passed her by. Events had crowded too thickly for her to grasp the whole; but *en masse* the effect had been definite-startlingly definite. Unbelievable as it may seem, for the first time in her existence she had aroused to the consciousness of being an individual entity. The inevitable metamorphosis of age, the thing which differentiates a child from an adult, belated long in her passive life, had at last taken place. Bewilderingly sudden, so sudden that as yet she had not adjusted herself to the change, had barely become conscious thereof, yet certain as existence it self, the transformation had come to pass. Looking back there that afternoon, looking where the town had been and now was not, mingling with the impressions of a day full to overflowing, there came to the girl for the first time a definite appreciation of this thing that she had done. And that moment from the scene, never to appear again, passed Bess Landor the child; and invisibly into her place, taking up the play where the other had left, came Elizabeth Landor the woman.

Very, very long the girl sat there so; unconsciously long. With the swift reaction of youth, the scene of the excitement vanished, the personal menace gone, the impression it had made passed promptly into abeyance. As when she and the man had sat alone in the tiny room of the hotel, another consideration was too insistent, too vital, to prevent dominating the moment. Any other diversion, save absolute physical pain itself, would have been inadequate, was inadequate. Gradually, minute by minute, as the outline of the town itself had vanished, the depressing impression of that jeering frontier mob faded; and in its stead, looming bigger and bigger, advancing, enfolding like a storm cloud until it blotted out every other thought, came realisation of the thing she had done: came appreciation of its finality, its immensity. Then it was that the infinite bigness of this uninhabited wild, the sense of its infinite loneliness, pressed her close. Despite herself, against all reason, as a child is afraid of the dark there grew upon her a terror of this intangible thing called solitude that stretched out into the future endlessly. Smiling as it was this day, unchangeably smiling, she fancied a time when it would not smile, when its passive eventless monotony would be maddening. Swiftly, cumulatively as with every intense nature impressions reproduce, this one augmented. Again into the consideration intruded the absolute finality, the irrevocability of her choice. More distinctly than when she had listened to the original, memory recalled the vow of the marriage ceremony she had taken: "For better or for worse, in sickness or in health, until death do us part." No, there was no escape, no possible avenue that remained unguarded. The knowledge overwhelmed her, suffocated her. Vague possibilities, recently born, became realities. Closer and closer gripped the solitude. For the first time in her existence the dead surrounding silence became unbearable. Almost desperately she shifted back in her seat. Instinctively she sought the hand of her companion, pressed it tight. A mist came into her eyes, until the very team itself was blotted out.

"Oh, How," she confessed tensely, "I'm afraid!"

The man roused, as one recalled from reverie, as one awakened but not yet completely returned.

"Afraid, Bess? Afraid of what?"

"Of the silence, of the future; of you, a bit."

"Afraid of me, Bess?" Perplexed, wondering, the man held the team to a walk and simultaneously the side curtains ceased flapping, hung close. "I don't think I understand. Tell me why, Bess."

"I can't. A child doesn't know why it's afraid of the dark. The dark has never hurt it. It merely is."

At her side the man sat looking at her. He did not touch her, he did not move. In the time since they had come into his own a wonderful change had come into the face of this Indian man; and never was it so wonderful as at this moment. He still wore the grotesque ready-made clothes. The high collar, galling to him as a bridle to an unbroken cayuse, had made a red circle about his throat; yet of it and of them he was oblivious. Very, very young he looked at this time; fairly boyish. There was a colour in his beardless cheeks higher than the bronze of his race. The black eyes were soft as a child's, trusting as a child's. In the career of every human being there comes a time supreme, a climax, a period of exaltation to which memory will ever after recur, which serves as a standard of happiness absolute; and in the career of How Landor the hour had struck. This he knew; and yet, knowing, he could scarcely credit the truth. His cup of happiness was full, full to overflowing; yet he was almost afraid to put it to his lips for fear it would vanish, lest it should prove a myth.

Thus he sat there, this Indian man with whom fate was jesting, worshipping with a faith and love more intense than a Christian for his God; yet, with instinctive reticence, worshipping with closed lips. Thus the minutes passed; minutes of silence wherein he should have been eloquent, minutes that held an opportunity that would never be his again. Smiling, ironic, fate the satirist looked on at her handiwork, watched to the end; and then, observing that *finale*, laughed-and with the voice of Elizabeth Landor.

"Don't work at it any more, How," derided destiny. "You don't understand, and I can't tell you."

She straightened in her seat and shrugged her shoulders with a gesture she had never used before, that had come very lately: come concomitantly with the arrival of the woman Elizabeth. "Anyway, I think it will be all right. I at least am not afraid of your eloping with someone else." She laughed again at the thought and folded her hands carefully in her lap. "It's quite impossible to think of you interfering with the property of someone else; even though that property were a girl."

Mechanically the Indian chirruped to the team and shook the reins. On his face the look of perplexity deepened. Instinctively he realised that something was wrong; but how to set it right he did not know, and, true to his instincts, waited. "You wouldn't be afraid in the least to do so," wandered on the girl, "even though the woman were another man's wife. You aren't afraid of anything. You'd take her from before his very eyes if you'd decided to do so, if you saw fit. It's not that. It merely would never occur to you; not even as possibility."

Still groping, the man looked at her, looked at her full; but no light came.

"Yes, you're right, Bess," he corroborated haltingly. "It would never occur to me to do so."

More ironically than before laughed fate; and again with the voice of Elizabeth Landor.

"You're humorous, How, deliciously humorous; and still you haven't the vestige of a sense of humour." She laughed again involuntarily. "I hadn't myself a few weeks ago. I think I was even more deficient than you; but now-now—" Once again the tense-strung laugh, while in her lap the crossed hands locked and grew white from mutual pressure. "Now of a sudden I seem to see humour in everything!"

More than perplexed, concerned, distressed from his very inability to fathom the new mood, the man again brought the team to a walk, fumbled with the reins impotently.

"Something's wrong, Bess," he hesitated. "Something's worrying you. Tell me what it is, won't you?"

"Wrong?" The girl returned the look fair, almost defiantly. "Wrong?" Still again the laugh; unmusical, hysterical. "Certainly nothing is wrong. What could be wrong when two people who have so much in common as you and I, who touch at so many places, are just married and alone? Wrong: the preposterous idea!"

She was silent, and of a sudden the all-surrounding stillness seemed to be intensified. For at last, at last the man understood and was looking at her; looking at her wordlessly, with an expression that was terrible in its haunting suggestion of unutterable sadness, of infinite pain. He did not say a word; he merely looked at her; but shade by shade as the seconds passed there vanished from his face to the last bit every trace of the glory that had been its predecessor. Not until it was gone did the girl realise to the full what she had done, realise the mortal stab she had inflicted; then of a sudden came realisation in a gust and contrition unspeakable. Swiftly as rain follows a thunderclap her mood changed, her own face, hysterically tense, relaxed in a flood of tears. In an abandon of remorse her arms were about him, her face was pressed close to his face.

"Forgive me, How," she pleaded. "I didn't mean to hurt you. I'm nervous and irresponsible, that's all. Please forgive me; please!"

At a dawdling little prairie stream, superciliously ignored by the map-maker, yet then and now travelling its aimless journey from nowhere to nowhere under the name of Mink Creek, they halted for the night.

Though they had been driving steadily all the afternoon, save once when, far to the south, they had detected the blot of a grazing herd, they had seen no sign of human presence. They saw no indication now. The short fall day was drawing to a close. The sun, red as maple leaf in autumn, was level with the earth when How Landor pulled up beside the low sloping bank, and, the girl watching from her observation seat in the old surrey, unharnessed and watered the team and hobbled them amid the tall frost-cured grass to feed.

"Now for the tent," he said on returning. "Will your highness have it face north, south, east, or west?"

"East, please, How. I want to see the sun when it first comes up in the morning."

With the methodical swiftness of one accustomed to his work the man set about his task. The tent, his own, was in the rear of the waggon box. The furnishings, likewise his own, were close packed beside. More quickly than the watcher fancied it possible the whole began to take shape. Long before the glory had left the western sky the tent itself was in place. Before the chill, which followed so inevitably and swiftly, was in the air the diminutive soft coal heater was installed and in service. Following, produced from the same receptacle as by legerdemain, vanishing mysteriously within the mushroom house, followed the blanket bed, the buffalo robes, the folding chairs and table, the frontier "grub" chest. Last of all, signal to the world that the task was complete, the battered lantern with the tin reflector was trimmed and lit and, adding the final touch of comfort and of intimacy that light alone can give, was hung from its old hook on the ridge pole. Then at last, the first shadows of night stealing over the soundless earth, the man approached the lone spectator and held out his arms for her to descend.

"Come, Bess," he said. He smiled up at her as only such a man at such a time can smile. "This is my night. I'm going to do everything; cook supper and all. Come, girlie."

The meal was over, and again, as on that other occasion when Colonel William Landor had called, the two people within the tent occupied the same positions. In the folding rocking chair sat the girl, the light from the single lantern playing upon her brown head and soft oval face. In the partial darkness of the corner, stretched among the buffalo robes, lay the man. His arms were locked behind his head. His face was toward her. His eyes-eyes unbelievably soft and innocent for a mature man-were upon her. As he had said, this was his night, and he was living in it to the full. Ever taciturn with her as with others, he was at this time even more silent than usual, silent in a happiness which made words seem sacrilege. He merely looked at her, wonderingly, worshipfully, with the mute devotion of a dog for its master, as a devout Catholic gazes upon the image of the Virgin Mother. Since they had entered the tent he had scarcely spoken more than a single sentence at a time. Only once had he given a glimpse of himself. Then he had apologised for the meagreness of the meal. "To-morrow," he had said, "we will have game, the country is full of it; but to-day —" he had looked down as he had spoken —"to-day I felt somehow as though I could not kill anything. Life is too good to destroy, to-day."

Thus he lay there now, motionless, wordless, oblivious of passing time; and now and then in her place the girl's eyes lifted, found him gazing at her-and each time looked away. For some reason she could not return that look. For some reason as each time she caught it, read its meaning, her brown face grew darker. As truly as out there on the prairie she was afraid of the infinite solitude, she was afraid now of the worship that gaze implied. She had awakened, had Elizabeth Landor; and in the depths of her own soul she knew she was not worthy of such love, such confidence absolute. She expected it, she wanted it-and still she did not want it. She longed for oblivion such as his, oblivion of all save the passing minute; and it was not hers. Prescience, without a reason therefor which she would admit, prevented forgetfulness. She tried to shake the impression off; but it clung tenaciously. Instinctively, almost under compulsion, she even went ahead to meet it, to prepare the way.

"You mustn't look at me that way, How," she laughed at last forcedly. "It makes me afraid of myself-afraid of dropping. Supposing I should fall, from up in the sky where you fancy I am! No one, not even you, could ever put the pieces together."

"Fall," smiled the man, "you fall? You wouldn't; but if you did, I'd be there to catch you."

"Then you, too, would be in fragments. I'm very, very far above earth, you know."

"I'd want to be so, if you fell," said the man. "You're all there is in the world, all there is in life, for me. I'd want to be annihilated, too, then."

The girl's hands folded in her lap; as they had done that afternoon, very carefully.

"You don't know me even yet, How," she guided on. "You think I'm perfect, but I'm not. I know I'm very, very human, very-bad at times."

The other smiled; that was all.

"I'm liable to do anything, be anything. I'm liable to even fancy I don't like you and run away."

"If you did you'd return very soon."

"Return?" She looked at him fully. "You think so?"

"I know so."

"Why, How?"

"Because you care for me."

"But it would be because I didn't care for you that I'd go, you know."

"You'd find your mistake and come back."

The clasped hand locked, as once before they had done.

"And when I did-come back-you'd forgive me, How?"

"There'd be nothing to forgive."

"It wouldn't be wrong-to leave you that way?"

"To me you could do no wrong, Bess."

"Not if I did anything, if I —ran away with another man?"

The listener smiled, until the beardless face was very, very boyish.

"I can't imagine the impossible, Bess."

"But just supposing I should?" insistently. "You'd take me back, no matter what I'd done, and forgive me?"

For a half minute wherein the smile slowly vanished from his face the man did not answer, merely looked at her; then for the first time since they had been speaking his eyes dropped.

"I could forgive you anything, Bess; but to take you back, to have everything go on as before —I am human. I could not."

A moment longer the two remained so, each staring at their feet; then of a sudden, interrupting, the girl laughed, unmusically, hysterically.

"I'm glad you said that, How," she exulted; "glad I compelled you to say it. As you confess, it makes you seem more human. A god shouldn't marry a mortal, you know."

The man looked up gravely, but he said nothing.

"I'm going to make you answer me just one more thing," rushed on the girl, "and then I'm satisfied. You'd forgive me, you say, forgive me anything; but how about the other man, the one who had induced me to run away? Would you forgive him, too?"

Silence, dead silence; but this time the Indian's eyes did not drop.

"You may as well tell me, How. I'm irresponsible to-night and I won't give you any peace until you do. Would you forgive the other man, too?"

Once more for seconds there was a lapse; then slowly the Indian lifted in his place, lifted until he was sitting, lifted until his face stood out clear in the light like the carving of a master.

"Forgive *him*, Bess?" A pause. "Do you think I am a god?"

That was all, neither an avowal nor a denial; yet no human being looking at the speaker that moment would have pressed the query farther, no human being could have misread the answer. With the same little hysterical, unnatural laugh the girl sank back in her seat. The tense hands went lax.

"I'll be good now, How," she said dully. "One isn't married every day, you know, and it's got on my nerves. I'm finding out a lot of things lately, and that's one of them: that I have nerves. I never supposed before that I possessed them."

Deliberately, without a shade of hesitation or of uncertainty, the man arose. As deliberately he walked over and very, very gently lifted the girl to her feet.

"Bess," he said low, "there's something that's troubling you, something you'd feel better to tell me. Don't you trust me enough to tell me now, girlie?"

Very long they stood so, face to face. For a time the girl did not look up, merely stood there, her fingers locked behind her back, her long lashes all but meeting; then of a sudden, swiftly as the passing shadow of an April cloud, the mood changed, she glanced up.

"I thought I could scare you, How," she joyed softly, "and I have." She smiled straight into his eyes. "I wanted to see how much you cared for me, was all. I've found out. There's absolutely nothing to tell, How, man; absolutely nothing."

For another half minute the man looked at her deeply, silently; but, still smiling, she answered him back, and with a last lingering grip that was a caress his hands dropped.

"I trust you, Bess, completely," he said. "It makes me unhappy to feel that you are unhappy, is all."

"I know, How." Tears were on the long lashes now, tears that came so easily. "I'll try not to be bad again." She touched his sleeve. "I'm very tired now and sleepy. You'll forgive me this once again, won't you?"

"Forgive you! —Bess!" She was in his arms, pressed close to his breast, the presence of her, intense, feminine, intoxicating him, bearing him as the fruit of the poppy to oblivion. "God, girl, if you could only realise how I love you. I can't tell you; I can't say things; but if you could only realise!"

Passionate, throbbing, the girl's face lifted. Her great brown eyes, sparkling wet, glorious, looked into his eyes. Her lips parted.

"Say that again, How," she whispered, "only say that again. Tell me that you love me. Tell me! tell me!"

Chapter XIV
Fate, the Satirist

Four months drifted by. The will of Colonel William Landor had been read and executed. According to its provisions the home ranch with one-tenth of the herd, divided impartially as they filed past the executor, were left to Mary Landor; in event of her death to descend to "an only nephew, Clayton Craig by name." A second fraction of the great herd, a tenth of the remainder, selected in the same manner, reverted at once "unqualifiedly and with full title to hold or to sell to the aforementioned sole blood relative, Clayton Craig." All of the estate not previously mentioned, the second ranch whereon How Landor had builded, various chattels enumerated, a small sum of money in a city bank, and the balance of the herd, whose number the testator himself could not give with certainty, were willed likewise unqualifiedly to "my adopted daughter, Elizabeth Landor." That was all. A single sheet of greasy note paper, a collection of pedantic antiquated phrases, penned laboriously with the scrawling hand of one unused to writing; but incontrovertible in its laconic directness. Save these three no other names were mentioned. So far as the Indian Ma-wa-cha-sa, commonly called How Landor, was concerned he might never have existed. In a hundred words the labour was complete; and at its end, before the single sheet was covered, sprawling, characteristic, was the last signature of him who at the time was the biggest cattleman west of the river: William Landor of the Buffalo Butte.

Craig himself did not appear, either at the reading or the execution. Instead a dapper city attorney with a sarcastic tongue and an isolated manner was present to conserve his interests; and, satisfied on that score, and ere the supply of Havanas in a beautifully embossed leather case was exhausted, in fact, to quote his own words, "as quickly as a kind Providence would permit," he vanished into the unknown from whence he came. Following, on the next train, came a big-voiced, red-bearded Irishman who proclaimed himself the new foreman and immediately took possession. Simultaneously there disappeared from the scene the Buffalo Butte ranch and the brand by which it had been known; and in its place upon the flank of every live thing controlled, stared forth a C locked to a C (C-C): the heraldry of the new master, Clayton Craig.

Likewise the long-planned wedding journey had taken place and become a memory. Into the silent places they went, this new-made man and wife-and no one was present at the departure to bid them adieu. Back from the land of nothingness they came-and again no one was at hand to welcome their return. In but one respect did the accomplishment of that plan alter from the prearranged; and that one item was the consideration of time. They did not stay away until winter, as the girl had announced. Starting in November, they did not complete the month. Nor did they stay for more than a day in any one spot. Like the curse of the Wandering Jew, a newborn restlessness in the girl kept calling "On, on." Battle against it as she might, she was powerless under its dominance. She knew not from whence had come the change, nor why; but that in the last weeks she had altered fundamentally, unbelievably, she could not question. The very first night out, ere they had slept, she had begun to talk of change on the morrow. The next day it was the same-and the next. When they were moving the morbid restlessness gradually wore away; for the time being she became her old careless-happy self; and in sympathy her companion opened as a flower to the sun. Then would come a pause; and the morbid, dogging spirit of unrest would close upon her anew. Thus day by day passed until a week had gone by. Then one morning when camp was struck, instead of advancing farther, the man had faced back the way they had come. He made no comment, nor did she. Neither then nor in days that followed did he once allude to the reason that had caused the change of plan. When the girl was gay, he was gay likewise. When she lapsed listlessly into the slough of silence and despond, he went on precisely as though unconscious of a change. His acting, for acting it was, even the girl could not but realise at that time, was masterly. What he was thinking no human being ever knew, no human being could ever know; for he never gave the semblance of a hint. Probably not sinc e man and woman began under the sanction of law and of clergy to mate, had there been such a honeymoon. Probably never will there be such another.

That the whole expedition was a piteous, dreary failure neither could have doubted ere the first week dragged by. That the marriage journey which it ushered in was to be a failure likewise, neither could have questioned, ere the second week, which brought them home, had passed. The Garden of Eden was there, there as certainly in its frost-brown sun-blessed perfection as though spread luxuriously within the tropics. Adam was there, Adam prepared to accept it as normally content as the first man; but Eve was not satisfied. Within the garden the serpent had shown his face and tempted her. For very, very long she would not admit the fact even to herself, deluded herself by the belief that this newborn discontent was but temporary; yet bald, unaltering as the prairie itself, the truth stood forth. Thus they went, and thus they returned. Thus again thereafter the days went monotonously by.

One bright spot, and one alone, appeared on their firmament; and that was the opening of the new house. This was to be a surprise, a climax boyishly reserved by its builder for their return. The man had intentionally so arranged that the start should be from the old ranch, and in consequence the girl had never seen either the new or its furnishings, until the November day when the overloaded surrey drew up in the dooryard, and the journey was complete. Pathetic, indescribable, in the light of the past, in the memory of the solitary hours that frontier nest represented, the moment must have been to the man when he led the way to the entrance and turned the key. Yet he smiled as he threw open the door; and, standing there, ere she entered, he kissed her.

"It isn't much, but it was mine, Bess, and now it's yours," he said, and, her hand in his, he crossed the threshold.

A moment the girl stood staring around her. Crude as everything was, and cheap in aggregate, it spoke a testimony that was overwhelming. Never before, not even that first night they had been alone, had the girl realised as at this moment what she meant to this solitary, impassive human. Never before until these mute things he had fashioned with his own hands stood before her eyes did she realise fully his love. With the knowledge now came a flood of repentance and of appreciation. Her arms flew about his neck. Her wet face was hid.

"How you love me, man," she voiced. "How you love me!"

"Yes, Bess," said the other simply; and that was all.

For that day, and the next, and the next, the mood lasted, an awakening the girl began to fancy permanent; then inevitably came the reaction. The man took up his duties where he had laid them down: the supervision of a herd scattered of necessity to the winds, the personal inspection of a range that stretched away for miles. Soon after daylight, his lunch for the day packed in the pouch he slung over his shoulder, he left astride the mouse-coloured, saddleless broncho; not to return until dark or later, tired and hungry, but ever smiling at the home-coming, ever considerate. Thus the third night he returned to find the house dark and the fire in the soft coal stove dead; to find this and the girl stretched listless on the bed against the wall, staring wide-eyed into the darkness.

"I was tired and resting, How," she had explained penitently, and gone about the task of preparing supper; but the man was not deceived, and that moment, if not before, he recognised the inevitable.

Yet even then he made no comment, nor altered in the minutest detail his manner. If ever a human being played the game, it was How Landor. With a blindness that was masterly, that was all but fatuous, he ignored the obvious. His equanimity and patience were invulnerable. Silent by nature, he grew fairly loquacious in an effort to be companionable. Probably no white man alive would have done as he did, would have borne what he did; perhaps it would have been better had he done differently; but he was as he was. Day after day he endured the galling starched linen and unaccustomed clothing, making long journeys to the distant town to keep his wardrobe clean and replenished. Day after day he polished his boots and struggled with his cravat. Puerile unqualifiedly an observer would have characterised this repeated farce; but to one who knew the tale in its entirety, it would have seemed very far from humorous. All but sacrilege, it is to tell of this starved human's doing at this time. The sublime and the ridiculous ever elbow so closely in this life and jostled so continuously in those stormy hours of How Landor's chastening. Suffice it to repeat that every second through it all he played the game; played it with a smiling face, and the ghost of a jest ever trembling on his lips. Played it from the moment he entered his house until the moment he daily disappeared, astride the vixenish undersized cayuse. Then when he was alone, when there were no human eyes to observe, to pity perchance, then-But let it pass what he did then. It is another tale and extraneous.

Thus drifted by the late fall and early winter. Bit by bit the days grew shorter; and then as a pendulum vibrates, lengthened shade by shade. No human being came their way, nor wild thing, save roving murderers on pillage bent. Even the cowmen he employed, the old hands he and Bess had both known for years, avoided him obviously, stubbornly. After the execution of the will he had built them another ranch house at a distance on the range, and there they congregated and clung. They accepted his money and obeyed his orders unquestioningly; but further than that-they were white and he was red. Howard, the one man with whom he had been friendly, had grown restless and drifted on-whither no one knew. Save for the Irish overseer and one other cowboy, the old Buffalo Butte ranch was deserted. Locally, there neither was nor had been any outward manifestation of hostility, nor even gossip. But the olden times when the hospitable ranch house of Colonel William Landor was the meeting point of ranchers within a radius of fifty miles were gone. They did not persecute the new master or his white wife; they did a subtler, crueller thing: they ignored them. To the Indian's face, when by infrequent chance they met, they were affable, obliging. His reputation had spread too far for them to appear otherwise; but, again, they were white and he was red-and between them the chasm yawned.

Thus passed the months. Winter, dead and relentless, held its sway. It was a normal winter; but ever in this unprotected land the period was one of inevitable decimation, of a weeding out of the unfit. Here and there upon the range, dark against the now background of universal white, stared forth the carcass of a weakling. Over it for a few nights the coyotes and grey wolves howled and fought; then would come a fresh layer of white, and the spot where it had been would merge once more into the universal colour scheme. Even the prairie chickens vanished, migrated to southern lands where corn was king. No more at daylight or at dusk could one hear the whistle of their passing wings, or the booming of their rallying call. Magnificent in any season, this impression of the wild was even more pronounced now. The thought of God is synonymous with immensity; and so being, Deity was here eternally manifest, ubiquitous. The human mind could not conceive a more infinite bigness than this gleaming frost-bound waste stretched to the horizon beneath the blazing winter sun. Magnificent it was beyond the power of words to describe; but lonely, lonely. Within the tiny cottage, the girl, Bess, drew the curtains tight over the single window and for days at a time did not glance without.

Then at last, for to all things there is an end, came spring. Long before it arrived the Indian knew it was coming, read incontestably its advance signs. No longer, as the mouse-coloured cayuse bore him over the range, was there the mellow crunch of snow underfoot. Instead the sound was crisp and sharp: the crackling of ice where the snow had melted and frozen again. Distinct upon the record of the bleak prairie page appeared another sign infallible. Here and there, singly and *en masse*, wherever the herds had grazed, appeared oblong brown blots the size of an animal's body. The cattle were becoming weak under the influence of prolonged winter, and lay down frequently to rest, their warm bodies branding the evidence with melted snow. The jack rabbits, ubiquitous on the ranges, that sprang daily almost from beneath the pony's feet, were changing their winter's dress, were becoming darker; almost as though soiled by a muddy hand. Here and there on the high places the sparkling white was giving way to a dull, lustreless brown. Gradually, day by day, as though they were a pestilence, they expanded, augmented until they, and not the white, became the dominant tone. The sun was high in the sky now. At noontime the man's shadow was short, scarcely extended back of his pony's feet. Mid-afternoons, in the low places when he passed through, there was a spattering of snow water collected in tiny puddles. After that there was no need of signs. Realities were everywhere. Dips in the rolling land, mere dry runs save at this season, became creeks; flushed to their capacity and beyond, sang softly all the day long. Not only the high spots, but even the north slopes lost their white blankets, surrendered to the conquering brown. Migratory life, long absent, returned to its own. Prairie kites soared far overhead on motionless wings. Meadow larks, cheeriest of heralds, practised their five-toned lay. Here and there, to the north of prairie boulders, appeared tufts of green; tufts that, like the preceding brown, grew and gr ew and grew until they dominated the whole landscape. Then at last, the climax, the *finale* of the play, came life, animal and vegetable, with a rush. Again at daylight and at dusk swarms of black dots on whistling wings floated here and there, descended to earth; and, following, indefinite as to location, weird, lonely, boomed forth in their mating songs. Transient, shallow, miniature lakes swarmed with their new-come denizens. Last of all, fina‐ assurance of a new season's advent, by day and by night, swelling, diminishing, unfailingly musical as distant chiming bells, came the sound of all most typical of prairie and of spring. From high overhead in the blue it came, often so high that the eye could not distinguish its makers; yet alway distinctive, alway hauntingly mysterious. "Honk! honk! honk!" sounded and echoed and re-echoed that heraldry over the awakened land. "Honk! honk! honk!" it repeated; and listening humans smiled and commented unnecessarily each to the other: "Spring is not coming. It is here."

Chapter XV
The Fruit of the Tree of Knowledge

A shaggy grey wolf, a baby no longer but practically full grown, swung slowly along the beaten trail connecting the house and the barn as the stranger appeared. He did not run, he did not glance behind, he made no sound. With almost human dignity he vacated the premises to the newcomer. Not until he reached his destination, the ill-lighted stable, did curiosity get the better of prudence; then, safe within the doorway, he wheeled about, and with forelegs wide apart stood staring out, his long, sensitive nose taking minutest testimony.

The newcomer, a well-proportioned, smooth-faced man in approved riding togs, halted likewise and returned the look; equally minutely, equally suspiciously. The horse he rode was one of a kind seldom seen on the ranges: a thoroughbred with slender legs and sensitive ears. The rider sat his saddle well; remarkably well for one obviously from another life. Both the horse and man were immaculately groomed. At a distance they made a pleasant picture, one fulfilling adequately the adjective "smart." Not until an observer was near, very near, could the looseness of the skin beneath the man's eyelids, incongruous with his general youth, and the abnormal nervous twitching of a muscle here and there, have been noted. For perhaps a minute he sat so, taking in every detail of the commonplace surroundings. Then, apparently satisfied, he dismounted and, tying the animal to the wheel of an old surrey drawn up in the yard, he approached the single entrance of the house and rapped.

To the doorway came Elizabeth Landor; her sleeves rolled to the elbow, a frilled apron that reached to the chin protecting a plain gingham gown. A moment they looked at each other; then the man's riding cap came off with a sweep and he held out his hand.

"Bess!" he said intimately; and for another moment that was all. Then he looked her fair between the eyes. "I came to see your husband," he exclaimed. "Is he at home?"

The girl showed no surprise, ignored the out-stretched hand.

"I was expecting you," she said. "How told me last night that you had returned."

A shade of colour stole into the man's blonde cheeks and his hand dropped; but his eyes held their place. "Yes. I only came yesterday," he returned. "I've a little business to talk over with How. That's why I'm here this morning. Is he about?"

Just perceptibly the girl smiled; but she made no answer.

"Don't you wish to be friends, Bess?" persisted the man. "Aren't we to be even neighbourly?"

"Neighbourly, certainly. I have no desire to be otherwise."

"Why don't you answer me, then?" The red shading was becoming positive now, telltale. "Tell me why, please."

"Answer?" The girl rolled down one sleeve deliberately. "Answer?" She undid its mate. "Do you really fancy, cousin by courtesy, that after I've lived the last four months I'm still such a child as that? Do you really wish me to answer, Neighbour Craig,"

For the first time the man's eyes dropped. Some silver coins in his trousers pocket jingled as he fingered them nervously. Then again he looked up.

"I beg your pardon, Bess," he said. "I saw your husband leave an hour ago. I knew he wasn't here." He looked her straight. "It was you I came to see. May I stay?"

Again the girl ignored the question.

"You admit then," she smiled, "that if How were here you wouldn't have come, that nothing you know of could have made you come? Let's understand each other in the beginning. You admit this?"

"Yes," steadily, "I admit it. May I stay?"

The smile left the girl's lips. She looked him fair in the eyes; silently, deliberately, with an intensity the other could not fathom, could not even vaguely comprehend. Then as deliberately she released him, looked away.

"Yes, you may stay," she consented, "if you wish."

"If I wish!" Craig looked at her meaningly; then with an obvious effort he checked himself "Thank you," he completed repressedly.

This time the girl did not smile. "Don't you realise yet that sort of thing is useless?" she queried unemotionally.

It was the man this time who was silent.

"If you wish to stay," went on the girl monotonously, "do so; but for once and all do away with acting. We're neither of us good, we're both living a lie; but at least we understand each other. Let's not waste energy in pretending-when there's no one to be deceived."

Just for a second the man stiffened. The histrionic was too much a part of his life to shake off instantly. Then he laughed.

"All right, Bess. I owe you another apology, I suppose. Anyway be it so. And now, that I'm to stay —" A meaning glance through the open door. "You were working, weren't you?"

"Yes."

"Go ahead, then, and I'll find something to sit on and watch. You remember another morning once before, don't you —a morning before you grew up —"

"Perfectly."

"We'll fancy we're back there again, then. Come."

"I am quite deficient in imagination."

"At least, though, dishes must be washed."

"Not necessarily-this moment at least. They have waited before."

"But, Bess, on the square, I don't wish to intrude or interfere."

"You're not interfering. I've merely chosen to rest a bit and enjoy the sun." She indicated the step. "Won't you be seated? They're clean, I know. I scrubbed them this very morning myself."

The man hesitated. Then he sat down.

"Bess," he said, "you've been pretty frank with me and I'm going to return the privilege. I don't understand you a bit-the way you are now. You've changed terribly."

"Changed? On the contrary I'm very normal. I've been precisely as I am this moment for —a lifetime."

"For-how long, Bess?"

"A lifetime, I think."

"For four months, you mean."

"Perhaps-it's all the same."

"Since you did a foolish thing?"

"I have done many such."

"Since the last, I mean."

"No." Just perceptibly the lids over the brown eyes tightened. "The last was when I asked you to sit down. I have not changed in the smallest possible manner since then."

The man inspected his boots.

"Aren't you, too, going to be seated?" he suggested at length.

"Yes, certainly. To tell the truth I thought I was." She took a place beside him. "I had forgotten."

They sat so, the man observing her narrowly, in real perplexity.

"Bess," he initiated baldly at last, "you're unhappy."

"I have not denied it," evenly.

The visitor caught his breath. He thought he was prepared for anything; but he was finding his mistake.

"This life you've-selected, is wearing on you," he added. "Frankly, I hardly recognise you, you used to be so careless and happy."

"Frankly," echoed the girl, "you, too, have altered, cousin mine. You're dissipating. Even here one grows to recognise the signs."

The man flushed. It is far easier in this world to give frank criticism than to receive it.

"I won't endeavour to justify myself, Bess," he said intimately, "nor attempt to deny it. There is a reason, however."

"I've noticed," commented his companion, "that there usually is an explanation for everything we do in this life."

"Yes. And in this instance you are the reason, Bess."

"Thank you." A pause. "I suppose I should take that as a compliment."

"You may if you wish. Leastways it's the truth."

The girl locked her fingers over her knees and leaned back against the lintel of the door. She looked very young that moment-and very old.

"And your reason?" persisted the man. "You know now my explanation for being-as I am. What is yours?"

"Do you wish a compliment, also, Clayton Craig?"

"I wish to know the reason."

"Unfortunately you know it already. Otherwise you would not be here."

"You mean it is this lonely life, this man of another race you have married?"

"No. I mean the thing that led me away from this life, and-the man you have named."

"I don't believe I understand, Bess."

"You ought to. You drank me dry once, every drop of confidence I possessed, for two weeks."

"You mean I myself am the cause," said the man low.

"I repeat you have the compliment-if you consider it such."

Again there was silence. Within the stable door, during all the time, the grey wolf had not stirred. He was observing them now, steadily, immovably. Though it was bright sunlight without, against the background of the dark interior his eyes shone as though they were afire.

"Honestly, Bess," said the man, low as before, "I'm sorry if I have made you unhappy."

"I thought we had decided to be truthful for once," answered a voice.

"You're unjust, horribly unjust!"

"No. I merely understand you-now. You're not sorry, because otherwise you wouldn't be here. You wouldn't dare to be here-even though my husband were away."

Again instinctively the man's face reddened. It was decidedly a novelty in his life to be treated as he was being treated this day. Ordinarily glib of speech, for some reason in the face of this newfound emotionless characterisation, he had nothing to say. It is difficult to appear what one is not in the blaze of one's own fireside. It was impossible under the scrutiny of this wide-eyed girl, with the recollection of events gone by.

"All right, Bess," he admitted at last, with an effort, "we've got other things more interesting than myself to discuss anyway." He looked at her openly, significantly. "Your own self, for instance."

"Yes?"

"I'm listening. Tell me everything."

"You really fancy I will after-the past?"

"Yes."

"And why, please?"

"You've already told me why."

"That's right," meditatively. "I'd forgotten. We were going to be ourselves, our natural worst selves, to-day."

"I'm still listening."

"You're patient. What do you most wish to know?"

"Most? The thing most essential, of course. Do you love your husband? You're unhappy, I know. Is that the reason?"

The girl looked out, out over the prairies, meditatively, impassively. Far in the distance, indistinguishable to an untrained eye, a black dot stood out above the horizon line. Her eyes paused upon it.

"You'll never tell anyone if I answer?" she asked suddenly.

"Never, Bess."

"You swear it?"

"I swear."

Just perceptibly the girl's lips twitched.

"Thanks. I merely wished to find out if you would still perjure yourself. To answer your question, I really don't know."

"Bess!" The man was upon his feet, his face twitching. "I'll stand a lot from you, but there's a limit —"

"Sit down, please," evenly. "It's wasted absolutely. There's not a soul but myself to see; and I'm not looking. Please be seated."

From his height the man looked down at her; at first angrily, resentfully-then with an expression wherein surprise and unbelief were mingled. He sat down.

The girl's eyes left the dot on the horizon, moved on and on.

"As I was saying," she continued, "I don't know. I'd give my soul, if I have one, to know; but I have no one with whom to make the exchange, no one who can give me light. Does that answer your question?"

Her companion stared at her, and forgot himself.

"Yes, it answers the now. But why did you marry him?"

"You really wish to know?" Again the lips were twitching.

"Yes."

"You're very hungry for compliments. You yourself are why."

No answer, only silence.

"You've seen a coursing, haven't you?" wandered on the girl. "A little tired rabbit with a great mongrel pack in pursuit? You're not plural, but nevertheless you personified that pack. You and the unknown things you represented were pressing me close. I was confused and afraid. I was a babe four months ago. I was not afraid of How, I had loved him-at least I thought I had, I'm sure of nothing now-and, as I say, I was afraid of you-then."

"And now —"

Just for a second the girl glanced at the questioner, then she looked away.

"I'm not in the least afraid of you now-or of anything."

"Not even of your husband?"

"No," unemotionally. "I leave that to you."

Again the man's face twitched, but he was silent.

"I said afraid of nothing," retracted the girl swiftly. "I made a mistake." Of a sudden her face grew old and tense. "I am afraid of something; horribly afraid. I'm as afraid, as you are of death, of this infinite eventless monotony." She bit her lip deep, unconsciously. "I sometimes think the old fear of everything were preferable, were the lesser of the two evils."

Just perceptibly the figure of the man grew alert. The loose skin under his eyes drew tight as the lids partially closed.

"You've been a bit slow about it, Bess," he said, "but I think you've gotten down to realities at last." He likewise looked away; but unseeingly. The mind of Clayton Craig was not on the landscape that spring morning. "I even fancy that at last you realise what a mess you've made of your life."

The girl showed no resentment, no surprise.

"Yes, I think I do," she said.

"You are perhaps even prepared to admit that I wasn't such a brute after all in attempting to prevent your doing as you did."

"No," monotonously. "You could have prevented it if you hadn't been a brute."

Again the man looked at her, unconscious of self.

"You mean that you did really and truly care for me, then, Bess? Cared for me myself?"

"Yes."

"And that I frightened you back here?"

"Yes."

Unconsciously the man swallowed. His throat was very dry.

"And now that you're no longer afraid of me, how about it now?"

The girl looked away in silence.

"Tell me, Bess," pleaded the man, "tell me!"

"I can't tell you. I don't know."

"Don't know?"

"No. I don't seem to be sure of anything now-a-days-anything except that I'm afraid."

"Of the future?"

"Yes-and of myself."

For once at least in his life Clayton Craig was wise. He said nothing. A long silence fell between them. It was the girl herself who broke it.

"I sometimes think a part of me is dead," she said slowly, and the voice was very weary. "I think it was buried in Boston with Uncle Landor."

"Was I to blame, Bess?"

"Yes. You were the grave digger. You covered it up."

"Then I'm the one to bring it to life again."

The girl said nothing.

"You admit," pressed Craig, "that I'm the only person who can restore the thing you have lost, the thing whose lack is making you unhappy?"

"Yes. I admit it."

The man took a deep breath, as one arousing from reverie.

"Won't you let me give it you again, Bess?" he asked low.

"You won't do it," listlessly. "You could, but you won't. You're too selfish."

"Bess!" The man's hand was upon her arm.

"Don't do that, please," said the girl quietly.

The man's face twitched; but he obeyed.

"You're maddening, Bess," he flamed. "Positively maddening!"

"Perhaps," evenly. "I warned you that if you stayed we'd be ourselves to-day. I merely told you things as they are."

Craig opened his lips to speak; but closed them again in silence. One of his hands, long fingered, white as a woman's, lay in his lap. Against his will now and then a muscle contracted nervously; and of a sudden he thrust the telltale member deep into his trousers pocket.

"But the future, Bess," he challenged, "your future. You can't go on this way indefinitely. What are you going to do?"

"I don't know."

"Haven't you ever thought of it?"

"It seems to me I've thought of nothing else-for an age."

"And you've decided nothing?"

"Absolutely nothing."

Again the man drew a long breath; but even thereafter his voice trembled.

"Let me decide for you then, Bess," he said.

"You?" The girl inspected him slowly through level eyes. "By what right should you be permitted to decide?"

The man returned her look. Of a sudden he had become calm. His eyes were steady. Deep down in his consciousness he realised that he would win, that the moment was his moment.

"The right is mine because I love you, Bess Landor," he said simply.

"Love me, after what you have done?"

"Yes. I have been mad-and done mad things. But I've discovered my fault. That's why I've come back; to tell you so-and to make amends."

Intensely, desperately intensely, the girl continued her look; but the man was master of himself now, sure of himself, so sure that he voiced a challenge.

"And you, Bess Landor, love me. In spite of the fact that you ran away, in spite of the fact that you are married, you love me!"

Into the girl's brown face there crept a trace of colour; her lips parted, but she said no word.

"You can't deny it," exulted the man. "You can't —because it is true."

A moment longer they sat so, motionless; then for a second time that day Clayton Craig did a wise thing, inspiration wise. While yet he was master of the situation, while yet the time was his, he arose.

"I'm going now, Bess," he said, "but I'll come again." He looked at her deeply, meaningly. "I've said all there is to say, for I've told you that I love you. Good-bye for now, and remember this: If I've stolen your happiness, I'll give it all back. As God is my witness, I'll give it all back with interest." Swiftly, before she could answer, he turned away and strode toward the impatient thoroughbred. Equally swiftly he undid the tie strap and mounted. Without another word, or a backward glance, he rode away; the galloping hoofs of his mount muffled in the damp spring earth.

Equally silent, the girl sat looking after him. She did not move. She did not make a sound. Not until the horse turned in at the C-C ranch house, until the buildings hid the owner from view, did her eyes leave him. Then, as if compelled by an instinct, she looked away over the prairie, away where the last time she had glanced a tiny black dot stood out against the intense blue sky. But look as she might she could not find it. It was there no more. It had been for long; but now was not. Clean as though drawn by a crayon on a freshly washed blackboard, the unbroken horizon line stretched out in a great circle before her eyes. With no watcher save the grey wolf staring forth from the stable doorway, she was alone with her thoughts.

Chapter XVI
The Reckoning

It was later than usual when How Landor returned that evening, and as he came up the path that led from the stable, he shuffled his feet as one unconsciously will when very weary. He was wearing his ready-made clothes and starched collar; but the trousers were deplorably baggy at the knees from much riding, and his linen and polished shoes were soiled with the dust of the prairie.

Supper was waiting for him, a supper hot and carefully prepared. Serving it was a young woman he had not seen for long, a young woman minus the slightest trace of listlessness, with a dash of red ribbon at belt and throat, and a reflection of the same colour burning on either cheek. A young woman, moreover, who anticipated his slightest wish, who took his hat and fetched his moccasins, and when the meal was over brought the buffalo robes and stretched them carefully on the gently sloping terrace just outside the ranch house door. Meanwhile she chatted bubblingly, continuously; with a suggestion of the light-hearted gaiety of a year before. To one less intimately acquainted with her than the man, her companion, she would have seemed again her old girlish self, returned, unchanged; but to him who knew her as himself there was now and then a note that rang false, a hint of suppressed excitement in the unwonted colour, an abnormal energy bordering on the feverish in her every motion. Not in the least deceived was this impassive, all-observing human, not in the least in doubt as to the cause of the transformation: yet through it all he gave no intimation of consciousness of the unusual, through it all he smiled, and smiled and smiled again. Never was there a more appreciative diner than he, never a more attentive, sympathetic listener. He said but little; but that was not remarkable. He had never done so except when she had not. When he looked at her there was an intensity that was almost uncanny in his gaze; but that also was not unusual. There was ever a mystery in the depths of his steady black eyes. Never more himself, never outwardly more unsuspicious was the man than on this occasion; even when, the meal complete, the girl had led him hand in hand out of doors, out into the soft spring night, out under the stars where she had stretched the two robes intimately close.

Thus, side by side, but not touching, they lay there, the soft south breeze fanning their faces, whispering wordless secrets in their ears; about them the friendly enveloping darkness, in their nostrils the subtle, indescribable fragrance of awakening earth and of growing things. But not even then could the girl be still. Far too full of this day's revelation and of anticipation of things to come was she to be silent. The mood of her merely changed. The chatter, heretofore aimless, ceased. In its place came a definite intent, a motive that prompted a definite question. She was lying stretched out like a child, her crossed arms pillowing her head, her eyes looking up into the great unknown, when she gave it voice. Even when she had done so, she did not alter her position. "I wonder," she said, "whether if one has made a mistake, it were better to go on without acknowledging it, living a lie and dying so, or to admit it and make another, who is innocent, instead of one's self, pay the penalty?" She paused for breath after the long sentence. "What do you think, How?"

In the semi-darkness the man looked at her. Against the lighter sky her face stood out distinct, clear-cut as a silhouette.

"I do not think it ever right to live a lie, Bess," he answered.

"Not even to keep another, who is innocent, from suffering?"

"No," quickly, "not even to keep another from suffering."

The girl shifted restlessly, repressedly.

"But supposing one's acknowledging the lie and living the truth makes one, according to the world, bad. Would that make any difference, How?"

The Indian did not stir, merely lay there looking at her with his steady eyes.

"There are some things one has to decide for one's self," he said. "I think this is one of them."

Again the arms beneath the girl's head shifted unconsciously.

"Others judge us after we do decide, though," she objected.

"What they think doesn't count. We're good or bad, as we're honest with ourselves or not."

"You think that, really?"

"I know it, Bess. There's no room for doubt."

Silence fell, and in it the girl's mind wandered on and on. At last, abrupt as before, abstract-edly as before, came a new thought, a new query.

"Is happiness, after all, the chief end of life, How?" she questioned.

"Happiness, Bess?" He halted. "Happiness?" repeated; but there was no irony in the voice, only, had the girl noticed, a terrible mute pain. "How should I know what is best in life, I, who have never known life at all?"

Blind in her own abstraction, the girl had not read beneath the words themselves, did not notice the thinly veiled inference.

"But you must have an idea," she pressed. "Tell me."

This time the answer was not concealed. It stood forth glaring, where the running might read.

"Yes, I have an idea-and more," he said. "Happiness, your happiness, has always been the first thing in my life."

Again silence walled them in, a longer silence than before. Step by step, gropingly, the girl was advancing on her journey. Step by step she was drawing away from her companion; yet though, wide-eyed, he watched her every motion, felt the distance separating grow wider and wider, he made no move to prevent, threw no obstacle in her path. Deliberately from his grip, from beneath his very eyes, fate, the relentless, was filching his one ewe lamb; yet he gave no sign of the knowledge, spoke no word of unkindness or of hate. Nature, the all-observing, could not but have admired her child that night.

One more advance the girl made; and that was the last. Before she had walked gropingly, as though uncertain of her pathway. Now there was no hesitation. The move was deliberate; even certain.

"I know you'll think I'm foolish, How," she began swiftly, "but I haven't much to think about, and so little things appeal to me." She paused and again her folded arms reversed beneath her head. "I've been watching 'Shaggy,' the wolf here, since he grew up; watched him become restless week by week. Last night,—you didn't notice, but I did,—I heard another wolf call away out on the prairie, and I got up to see what Shaggy would do. Somehow I seemed to understand how he'd feel, and I came out here, out where we are now, and looked down toward the barn. It was moonlight last night, and I could see everything clearly, almost as clearly as day. There hadn't been a sound while I was getting up; but all at once as I stood watching the call was repeated from somewhere away off in the distance. Before, Shaggy hadn't stirred. He was standing there, where you had chained him, just outside the door; but when that second call came, it was too much. He started to go, did go as far as he could; then the collar choked him and he realised where he was. He didn't make a sound, he didn't fight or rebel against something he couldn't help; but the way he looked, there in the moonlight, with the chain stretched across his back —" She halted abruptly, of a sudden sat up. "I know it's childish, but promise me, How, you'll let him go," she pleaded. "He's wild, and the wild was calling to him. Please promise me you'll let him go!"

Not even then did the man stir or his eyes leave her face.

"Did I ever tell you, Bess," he asked, "that it was to save Shaggy's life I brought him here? Sam Howard dug his mother out of her den and shot her, and was going to kill the cub, too, when I found him."

"No." A hesitating pause. "But anyway," swiftly, "that doesn't make any difference. He's wild, and it's a prison to him here."

Deliberately, ignoring the refutation, the man went on with the argument.

"Again, if Shaggy returns," he said, "the chances are he won't live through a year. The first cowboy who gets near enough will shoot him on sight."

"He'll have to take his chance of that, How," countered the girl. "We all have to take our chances in this life."

For the second time the Indian ignored the interruption.

"Last of all, he's a murderer, Bess. If he were free he'd kill the first animal weaker than himself he met. Have you thought of that?"

The girl looked away into the infinite abstractedly.

"Yes. But again that makes no difference. Neither you nor I made him as he is, nor Shaggy himself. He's as God meant him to be; and if he's bad, God alone is to blame." Her glance returned, met the other fair. "I wish you'd let him go, How."

The man made no answer.

"Won't you promise me you'll let him go?"

"You really wish it, Bess?"

"Yes, very much."

Still for another moment the man made no move; then of a sudden he arose.

"Come, Bess," he said.

Wondering, the girl got to her feet; wondering still more, followed his lead down the path to the stable. At the door the Indian whistled. But there was no response, no shaggy grey answering shadow. A lantern hung from a nail near at hand. In silence the man lit it and again led the way within. The mouse-coloured broncho and its darker mate were asleep, but at the interruption they awoke and looked about curiously. Otherwise there was no move. Look where one would within the building, there was no sign of another live thing. Still in silence the Indian led the way outside, made the circuit of the stable, paused at the south end where a chain hung loose from a peg driven into the wall. A moment he stood there, holding the light so the girl could see; then, impassive as before, he extinguished the blaze and returned the lantern to its place.

They were half way back to the house before the girl spoke; then, detainingly, she laid her hand upon his arm.

"You mean you've let him go already, How?" she asked.

"Yes. I didn't fasten him this evening."

They walked on so.

"You wanted him to go?"

No answer.

"Tell me, How, did you want him to leave?"

"No, Bess."

Again they advanced, until they reached the house door.

"Why did you let him go, then?" asked the girl tensely.

For the second time there was no answer.

"Tell me, How," she repeated insistently.

"I heard you get up last night, Bess," said a voice. "I thought I —understood."

For long they stood there, the girl's hand on the man's arm, but neither stirring; then with a sound perilously near a sob, the hand dropped.

"I think I'll go to bed now, How," she said.

Deliberately, instinctively, the man's arms folded across his chest. That was all.

The girl mounted the single step, paused in the doorway.

"Aren't you coming, too, How?" she queried.

"No, Bess."

A sudden suspicion came to the girl, a sudden terror.

"You aren't angry with me, are you?" she trembled.

"No, Bess," repeated.

"But still you're not coming?"

"No."

Swift as a lightning flash suspicion became certainty.

"You mean you're not going to come with me to-night?" She scarcely recognised her own voice. "You're never going to be with me again?"

"Never?" A long, long pause. "God alone knows about that, Bess." A second halt. "Not until things between us are different, at least."

"How!" Blindly, weakly, the girl threw out her hand, grasped the casing of the door. "Oh, How! How!"

No answer, not the twitching of a muscle, nor the whisper of a breath; just that dread, motionless silence. A moment the girl stood it, hoping against hope, praying for a miracle; then she could stand it no longer. Gropingly clutching at every object within reach, she made her way into the dark interior; flung herself full dressed onto the bed, her face buried desperately among the covers.

All the night which followed a sentinel paced back and forth in front of the ranch house door; back and forth like an automaton, back and forth in a motion that seemed perpetual. Within the tiny low-ceiled room, in the fulness of time, the girl sobbed herself into a fitful sleep; but not once did the sentinel pause to rest, not once in those dragging hours before day did he relax. With the coming of the first trace of light he halted, and on silent moccasined feet stole within. But again he only remained for moments, and when he returned it was merely to stride away to the stable. Within the space of minutes, before the east had fairly begun to grow red, silently as he did everything, he rode away astride the mouse-coloured cayuse into the darkness to the west.

It was broad day when the girl awoke, and then with a vague sense of depression and of impending evil. The door was open and the bright morning light flooded the room. Beyond the entrance stretched the open prairie: an endless sea of green with a tiny brown island, her own dooryard, in the foreground. With dull listlessness, the girl propped herself up in bed and sat looking about her. Absently, aimlessly, her eyes passed from one familiar object to another. Without any definite conception of why or of where, she was conscious of an impression of change in the material world about her, a change that corresponded to the mental crisis that had so recently taken place. Glad as was the sunshine without this morning, in her it aroused no answering joy. Ubiquitous as was the vivid surrounding life, its message passed her by. Like a haze enveloping, dulling all things, was a haunting memory of the past night and of what it had meant. As a traveller lost in this fog, she lay staring about, indecisive which way to move, idly waiting for light. Ordinarily action itself would have offered a solution of the problem, would have served at least as a diversion; but this morning she was strangely listless, strangely indifferent. There seemed to her no adequate reason for rising, no definite object in doing anything more than she was doing. In conformity she pulled the pillow higher and, lifting herself wearily, dropped her chin into her palm and lay with wide-open eyes staring aimlessly away.

Just how long she remained there so, she did not know. The doorway faced south, and bit by bit the bar of sunlight that had entered therein began moving to the left across the floor. Unconsciously, for the lack of anything better to do, she watched its advance. It fell upon a tiny shelf against the wall, littered with a collection of papers and magazines; and the reflected light from the white sheets glared in her eyes. It came to the supper table of the night before, the table she had not cleared, and like an accusing hand, lay directed at the evidence of her own slothfulness. On it went with the passing time, on and on; crossed a bare spot on the uncarpeted floor, and like a live thing, began climbing the wall beyond.

Deliberately, with a sort of fascination now, the girl watched its advance. Her nerves were on edge this morning, and in its relentless stealth it began to assume an element of the uncanny. Like a hostile alien thing, it seemed searching here and there in the tiny room for something definite, something it did not find. Fatuous as it may seem, the impression grew upon her, augmented until in its own turn it became a dominant influence. Her glance, heretofore absent, perfunctory, became intense. The glare was well above the floor by this time and climbing higher and higher. Answering the mythical challenge, of a sudden she sat up free in bed and, as though at a spoken injunction, looked about her fairly.

The place where she glanced, the point toward which the light was mounting, was beside her own bed and where, from rough-fashioned wooden pegs, hung the Indian's pathetically scant wardrobe. At first glance there seemed to the girl nothing unusual revealed thereon, nothing significant; and, restlessly observant, the inspection advanced. Then, ere the mental picture could vanish, ere a new impression could take its place, in a flash of tardy recollection and of understanding came realisation complete, and her eyes returned. For perhaps a minute thereafter she sat so, her great eyes unconsciously opening wider and wider, her brown skin shading paler second by second. A minute so, a minute of nerve-tense inaction; then with a little gesture of weariness and of abandon absolute, she dropped back in her place, and covered her face from sight.

Chapter XVII
Sacrifice

A week had gone by. Each day of the seven the thoroughbred with the slender legs and the tiny sensitive ears had stood in the barren dooryard before Elizabeth Landor's home. Moreover, with each repetition the arrival had been earlier, the halt longer. Though the weather was perfect, nevertheless the beast had grown impatient under the long waits, and telltale, a glaring black mound had come into being where he had pawed his displeasure. At first Craig on departing had carefully concealed the testimony of his presence beneath a sprinkling of dooryard litter; but at last he had ceased to do so, and bit by bit the mound had grown. Day had succeeded day, and no one had appeared to question the visitor's right of coming or of going. Even the wolf was no longer present to stare his disapproval. Verily, unchallenged, the king had come into his own in this realm of one; and as a monarch absolute ever rules, Clayton Craig had reigned, was reigning now.

For he no longer halted perforce at the doorstep. He had never been invited to enter, yet he had entered-and the girl had spoken no word to prevent. Not by request were his cap and riding stick hanging from a peg beside the few belongings of How Landor; yet, likewise unchallenged, they were there. Not by the girl's solicitation was he lounging intimately in the single rocker the room boasted; yet once again the bald fact remained that though it was not yet nine by the clock, he was present, his legs comfortably crossed, his eyes, beneath drooping lids, whimsically observing the girl as she went about the perfunctory labour of putting the place to rights.

"I say, Bess," he remarked casually at length, "you've dusted that unoffending table three times by actual count since I've been watching. Wouldn't it be proper to rest a bit now and entertain your company?"

The girl did not smile.

"Perhaps." She put away the cloth judicially. "I fancied you were tolerably amused as it was. However, if you prefer —" She drew another chair opposite, and, sitting down, folded her hands in her lap.

A moment longer the man sat smiling at her; then shade by shade the whimsical expression vanished, and the normal proprietary look he had grown to assume in her presence took its place.

"By the way, Bess," he commented, "isn't it about time to drop sarcasm when you and I are together? I know I've been a most reprehensible offender, but haven't I been punished enough?"

"Punished?" There was just the ghost of a smile. "Is this your idea of punishment?"

The man flushed involuntarily. His face had cleared remarkably in the past week of abstinence, and through the fair skin the colour showed plain.

"Well, perhaps punishment is a little too severe. Leastways you've held me at arm's length until I'm beginning to despair."

"Despair?" Again the ghost smiled forth. "Do you fancy I'm so dull that I don't realise what I'm doing, what you've done?"

For the second time the involuntary colour appeared; but the role that the man was playing, the role of the injured, was too effective to abandon at once.

"You can't deny that you've held me away all this last week, Bess," he objected. "You've permitted me to call and call again; but that is all. Otherwise we're not a bit nearer than we were when I first returned."

"Nearer?" This time the smile did not come. Even the ghost refused to appear. "I wonder if that's true." A pause. "At least I've gotten immeasurably farther away from another."

"Your husband you mean?"

"I mean How. There are but you and he in my life."

The pose was abandoned. It was useless now.

"Tell me, Bess," said the man intimately. "You and I mean too much to each other not to know everything there is to know."

"There's nothing to tell." The girl did not dissimulate now. The inevitable was in sight, approaching swiftly-and she herself had chosen. "He's merely given me up."

"He knows, Bess?" Blank unbelief was on the questioner's face, something else as well, something akin to exultation.

"Yes," repressedly. "He's known since that first night."

"And he hasn't objected, hasn't done anything at all?"

Just for an instant, ere came second thought, the old defiance, the old pride, broke forth.

"Do you fancy you would be here now, that you wouldn't have known before this if he objected?" she flamed.

"Bess!"

"I beg your pardon. I shouldn't have said that." Already the blaze had died, never to be rekindled. "Forget that I said that. I didn't mean to."

The man did not answer, he scarcely heard. Almost as by a miracle, the last obstacle had been removed from his way. He had counted upon blindness, the unsuspicion of perfect confidence; but a passive, conscious conformity such as this-The thing was unbelievable, providential, too unnaturally good to last. The present was a strategic moment, the time for immediate, irrevocable action, ere there came a change of heart. It had not been a part of Clayton Craig's plans to permit a meeting between himself and the Indian. As a matter of fact he

had taken elaborate, and, as it proved, unnecessary precautions to avoid such a consummation. Even now, the necessity passed, he did not alter his plans. Not that he was afraid of the red man. He had proven to himself by an incontrovertible process of reasoning that such was not the case. It was merely to avoid unpleasantness for himself and for the girl-particularly for the latter. Moreover, no possible object could be gained by such a meeting. Things were as they were and inevitable. He merely decided to hasten the move. It was the forming of this decision that had held him silent. It was under its influence that he spoke.

"When is it to be, Bess," he asked abruptly, "the final break, I mean?"

"It has already been, I tell you. It's all over."

"The new life, then," guided the man. "You can't go on this way any longer. It's intolerable for both of us."

"Yes," dully, "it's intolerable for all of us."

Craig arose and, walking to the door, looked out. In advance he had imagined that the actual move, when all was ready, would be easy. Now that the time had really arrived, he found it strangely difficult. He hardly knew how to begin.

"Bess." Of a sudden he had returned swiftly and, very erect, very dominant, stood looking down at her. "Bess," repeated, "we've avoided the obvious long enough, too long. As I said, you've succeeded in keeping me at arm's length all the last week; but I won't be denied any longer. I'm willing to take all the blame of the past, and all the responsibility of the future. I love you, Bess. I've told you that before, but I repeat it now. I want you to go away with me, away from this God-cursed land that's driving us both mad-at least leave for a time. After a while, when we both feel different, we can come back if we wish; but for the present —I can't stand this uncertainty another week, another day." He paused for breath, came a step nearer.

"Your marrying this Indian was a hideous mistake," he rushed on; "but we can't help that now. All we can do is to get away and forget it." He cleared his throat needlessly. "It's this getting away that I've arranged for since I've been here. I've not been entirely idle the last week, and every detail is complete. There are three relays of horses waiting between here and the railroad. One team is all ready at the ranch house the minute I give the signal. They'll get us to town before morning. You've only to say the word, and I'll give the sign." Again, nervously, shortly, he repeated the needless rasp, "How may, as you say, not interfere; but it's useless, to take any chances. There's been enough tragedy already between you two, without courting more. Besides, the past is dead; dead as though it had never been. My lawyer is over at the ranch house now. He'll straighten out everything after we're gone. Things here are all in your name; you can do as you please with them. There's no possible excuse for delay." He bent over her, his hands on her shoulders, his eyes looking into hers compellingly. "God knows you've been buried here long enough, girl. I'll teach you to live; to live, do you hear? We'll be very happy together, you and I, Bess; happier than you ever dreamed of being. Will you come?"

He was silent, and of a sudden the place became very still; still as the dead past the man had suggested. Wide-eyed, motionless, the girl sat looking up at him. She did not speak; she scarcely seemed to breathe. As she had chosen, so had it come to pass; yet involuntarily she delayed. Deliverance from the haunting solitude that had oppressed her like an evil dream was beckoning; yet impotent, she held back. Of a sudden, within her being, something she had fancied dormant had awakened. The instinct of convention, fundamental, inbred, more vital to a woman than life itself, intruded preventingly, fair in her path. Warning, pleading, distinct as a spoken admonition, its voice sounded a negative in her ears. She tried to silence it, tried to overwhelm it with her newborn philosophy; but it was useless. Fear of the future, as she had said, she had none. Good or bad as the man might be, she had chosen. With full knowledge of his deficiencies she had chosen. But to go away with him so, without sanction of law or of clergy; she, Bess Landor, who was a wife —.

The hands on her shoulders tightened insistently, the compelling face drew nearer.

"Answer me, Bess," demanded a tense voice; "don't keep me in suspense. Will you go?"

With the motion of a captured wild thing, the girl arose, drew back until she was free.

"Don't," she pleaded. "Don't hurry me so. Give me a little time to think." She caught her breath from the effort. "I'll go with you, yes; but to-day, now —I can't. We must see How first. He must know, must consent —"

"See How!" The man checked himself. "You must be mad," he digressed. "I can't see How, nor won't. I tell you it's between How and myself you must choose. I love you, Bess. I'm proving I love you; but I'm not insane absolutely. I ask you again: will you come?"

The girl shook her head, nervously, jerkily.

"I can't now, as things are."

"And why not?" passionately. "Haven't you said you care for me?"

For answer the red lower lip trembled. That was all.

The man came a step forward, and another.

"Tell me, Bess," he demanded. "Don't you love me?"

"I have told you," said a low voice.

Answering, coercing, swift as the swoop of a prairie hawk, as a human being in abandon, the man's arms were about her. Ere the girl could move or resist, his lips were upon her lips. "You must go then," he commanded. "I'll compel you to go." He kissed her again, hungrily, irresistibly. "I won't take no for an answer. You will go."

"Don't, please," pleaded a voice, breathless from its owner's impotent effort to be free. "You must not, we must not-yet. I'm bad, I know, but not wholly. Please let me go."

Unconscious of time, unconscious of place, oblivious to aught save the moment, the man held his ground, joying in his victory, in her effort to escape. Save that one casual glance long before, he had not looked out of doors. Had he done so, had he seen —.

But he had forgotten that a world existed without those four walls. His back was toward the door. His own great shoulders walled the girl in. Neither he nor she dreamed of a dark figure that had drifted from out the prairie swiftly into the dooryard, dreamed that that same all-knowing shadow, on soundless moccasined feet, had advanced to the doorway, stood silent, watching therein. As the first man and the first woman were alone, they fancied themselves alone. As the first man might have exulted over his mate, Clayton Craig exulted now.

"Let you go, Bess," he baited, "let you go now that I've just gotten you?" He laughed passionately. "You must think that I'm made of clay and not of flesh and blood." He drew her closer and closer, until she could no longer struggle, until she lay still in his arms. "I'll never let you go again, girl, not if God himself were to demand your release. You're mine, Bess, mine by right of capture, mine —"

The sentence halted midway; halted in a gasp and an unintelligible muttering in the throat. Of a sudden, darkening, ominous, fateful, the shadow within the entrance had silently advanced until it stood beside them, paused so with folded arms. Simultaneously the wife and the invader saw, realised. Instantly, instinctively, like similar repellent poles, they sprang apart. Enveloped in a maze of surging divergent passions, the two guilty humans stood silent so, staring at the intruder in breathless expectation, breathless fascination.

While an observer could have counted ten slowly, and repeated the count, the three remained precisely as they were. While the same mythical spectator could have counted ten more, the silence held; but inaction had ceased. While time, the relentless, checked off another measure, there was still no interruption; then of a sudden, desperately tense, desperately challenging, a voice sounded: the voice of Clayton Craig.

"Well," he queried, "why don't you do something?" He moistened his lips and shuffled his feet restlessly. "You've seen enough to understand, I guess. What are you going to do about it?"

The Indian had not been looking at him. Since that first moment when the two had sprang separate he had not even appeared conscious of his presence. Nor did he alter now. Erect as a maize plant, dressed once more in the flannels and corduroys of his station, as tall and graceful, he merely stood there with folded arms, looking down on the girl. More maddening than an execration, than physical menace itself, was that passionless, ignoring isolation to the other man. Answering, the hot blood flooded his blonde face, swelled the arteries of his throat until his collar choked him. Involuntarily his hand went to his neckband, tugged until it was free. Equally involuntarily he took a step forward menacingly.

"Curse you, How Landor," he blazed, "you've learned at last, perhaps, not to dare me to take something of yours away from you." Word by word his voice had risen until he fairly shouted. "You've lost, fool; lost, lost! Are you blind that you can't see? You've lost, I say!"

From pure inability to articulate more, the white man halted; and that instant the room became deathly still.

A second, or the fraction of a second thereof, it remained so; then, white-faced, apprehensive, the girl sprang between the two, paused so, motionless: —for of a sudden a voice, an even, passionless voice, was speaking.

"You don't know me even yet, do you, Elizabeth?" it chided. Just a step the speaker moved backward, and for the first time he recognised the white man's presence. His eyes were steady and level. His voice, unbelievably low in contrast to that of the other, when he spoke was even as before.

"I won't forgive you for what you've just done, Mr. Craig," he said. "I'll merely forget that you've done anything at all. One thing I expect, however, and that is that you'll not interrupt again. You may listen or not, as you wish. Later, I may have a word to say to you; but now there is nothing to be said." Just a moment longer the look held, a moment wherein the other man felt his tongue grow dumb; then with the old impassivity, the old isolation, the black eyes shifted until they rested on the face of the girl.

But for still another moment-he was as deliberate as nature herself, this man-he stood so, looking down. Always slender, he had grown more so these last weeks. Moreover, he had the look of one weary unto death. His black eyes were bright, mysteriously bright, and on his thin hands, folded across his chest, the veins stood out full and prominent; but look where one would on the lithe body, the muscles lay distinct beneath the close-fitting clothes, distinct to emaciation. Standing there now, very grave, very repressed, there was nevertheless no reproach in his expression, no trace of bitterness; only a haunting tenderness, infinite in its pathos. When he spoke the same incredible tolerance throbbed in the low-pitched voice.

"I've just a few things I wish to say to you, Bess," he began, "and a request to make-and that is all. I didn't come back so, unexpectedly, to be unpleasant, or to interfere with what you wish to do. I came because I fancied you were going to do an unwise thing: because I had reason to believe you were going to run away." Unconsciously, one of the folded hands loosened, passed absently over his forehead; then returned abruptly to its place. "Perhaps I was mistaken. If so I beg your pardon for the suspicion; but at least, if I can prevent, I don't want you to do so. It's this I came to tell you." Again the voice halted, and into it there came a new note: a self-conquered throb that lingered in the girl's recollection while memory lasted.

"It's useless to talk of yourself and of myself, Bess," he went on. "Things are as they are-and final. I don't judge you, I—understand. Above everything else in life, I wish you to be happy; and I realise now I can't make you so. Another perhaps can; I hope so and trust so. At least I shall not stand in your way any longer. It is that I came to tell you. It is I who shall leave and not you, Bess." Of a sudden he stepped back and lifted one hand free, preventingly. "Just a moment, please," he requested. "Don't interrupt me until I say what I came to say." His arms folded back as before, his eyes held hers compellingly.

"I said I had a request to make. This is it-that you don't leave until you are married again. You won't have to wait long if I leave. I have inquired and found out. A few days, a few weeks at the longest, and you will be free. Meanwhile stay here. Everything is yours. I never owned anything except the house, and that is yours also." For the last time he halted; then even, distinct, came the question direct. "Will you promise me this, Bess?" he asked.

Save once, when she had tried to interrupt, the girl had listened through it all without a move, without a sound. Now that he was silent, and it was her turn to speak, she still stood so, passive, waiting. Ever in times of stress his will had dominated her will; and the present was no exception. There was an infinity of things she might have said. A myriad which she should have spoken, would occur to her when he was gone. But at the present, when the opportunity was hers, there seemed nothing to offer; nothing to gainsay. She even forgot that she was expected to answer at all, that he had asked a question.

"Won't you promise me this one thing, Bess?" repeated the voice gently. "I've never made a request of you before, and I probably never shall again."

At last the girl aroused; and of a sudden she realised that her lips were very dry and hot. She moistened them with her tongue.

"Yes, How," she said dully, "I promise."

Silence fell, a silence deathly in its significance, in its finality; but the girl did not break it, said no more-and forever the moment, her moment, vanished into the past,

"Thank you, Bess," acknowledged the man monotonously. Slowly, strangely different from his usual alert certainty, he moved across the room. "There are just a few things here I'd like to take with me," he explained apologetically. "They'd only be in your way if I left them."

With a hand that fumbled a bit, he took down a battered telescope satchel from a peg on the wall and began packing. He moved about slowly here and there, his moccasined feet patting dully on the bare floor. No one offered to assist him, no one interrupted; and in dead silence, except for the sound he himself made, he went about his work. Into the satchel went a few books from the shelf on the wall: an old army greatcoat that had been Colonel William Landor's: a weather-stained cap which had been a present likewise: a handful of fossils he had gathered in one of his journeys to the Bad Lands: an inexpensive trinket here and there, that the girl herself had made for him. The satchel was small, and soon, pitifully soon, it was full. A moment thereafter he stood beside it, looking about him; then with an effort he put on the cover and began tightening the straps. The leather was old and the holes large, but he found difficulty even then in fastening the buckles. At last, though, it was done, and he straightened. Both the white man and the girl were watching him; but no one spoke. For the second time, the last time, the Indian stood so while his intense black eyes shifted from nook to nook, taking in every detail of the place that had once been his heaven, his nest, but now his no more; then of a sudden he lifted his burden and started to leave. Opposite the girl he paused and held out his hand.

"Good-bye, Bess," he said. He looked her deep in the eyes, deep into her very soul. "If I knew what religion is, I'd say God bless you, girl; but I don't, so I'll only say good-bye —and —I wish you happiness." Just a moment longer he remained so; then at something he saw, he dropped her hand and drew away swiftly, preventingly.

"Don't, Bess," he pleaded, "don't say it-as you cared for me once. Don't make things any harder-make them impossible!" Desperately, without another pause, ere she could disobey, he started for the door. Beside the entrance-for he was not watching these last minutes-stood the white man; and just for a moment at his side the Indian halted. Despite the will of Clayton Craig, their eyes met. For an instant, wherein time lapsed, they stood face to face; then swiftly as he did everything, now the Indian spoke: and, as once before in his life, those words and the look that accompanied them went with the alien to his grave.

"As for you, Mr. Craig," said the voice, "I have one thing only to say. Make Bess happy. There's nothing in the world to prevent your doing so, if you will. If you do not —" a pause of horrible ice-cold menace —"if you do not," repeated, "suicide." Just for the fraction of a second not a civilised man but a savage stared the listener in the face. "I shall know if you fail, and believe me, it were better, a thousand times better, if you do as I say."

Again, as beside the girl, there was a mute, throbbing lapse; then, similarly before there could be an answer, upon the tense silence there broke the swift pat of moccasined feet, and he was gone.

Chapter XVIII
Reward

The month was late September. The time, evening. The place, the ranch house of a rawboned Yankee named Hawkins. Upon the scene at the hour the supper table was spread appeared a traveller in an open road waggon. The vehicle was covered with dust. The team which drew it were dust-stained likewise, and in addition, on belly and legs, were covered with a white powder-like frost where the sweat had oozed to the hair tips and dried. Without announcing his arrival or deigning the formality of asking permission, the newcomer unhitched and put his team in the barn. From a convenient bin he took out a generous feed, and from a stack beside the eaves he brought them hay for the night. This done, he started for the house. A minute later, again without form of announcement or seeking permission, he opened the ranch house door and stepped inside.

Within the room, beside a table with an oilcloth cover, four men were eating. A fifth, a dark-skinned Mexican, was standing by a stove in one corner baking pancakes. All looked up as the door opened.

Then, curiosity satisfied, the eyes of all save one, the proprietor, Hawkins, returned to their plates, and the rattle of steel on heavy queensware proceeded.

"Good-evening," recognised the Yankee laconically. He hitched along his chair until a space was clear at his elbow. "Draw up and fall to, stranger. Bring the gentleman a chair, Pete."

In silence the Mexican obeyed, and in equal silence returned to his work.

Appetites are keen on the prairie, and not until the meal was complete was there further conversation. Then after, one by one, the cowmen had filed out of doors, the host produced two corn-cob pipes from a shelf on the wall and tendered one across the littered table.

"Smoke?" he again invited laconically.

The visitor fumbled in the pockets of his coat and drew out a couple of cigars.

"Better have one of these instead," he suggested.

Hawkins accepted in silence, and thereafter-for cigars were a rarity on the frontier-puffed half the length of the weed in wordless content. The Mexican went impassively about his work, cleared the table and washed the dishes methodically. The labour complete, he rolled a cigarette swiftly and, followed by a vanishing trail of blue, disappeared likewise out of doors. Then, and not until then, the visitor introduced himself.

"My name's Manning, Bob Manning," he said. "I run the store over at the Centre."

The host scrutinised his guest, deliberately, reminiscently

"I thought there was something familiar about you," he commented at last. "I haven't seen you for twenty years; but I remember you now. You're one of the bunch who was with Bill Landor that time he picked up the two kids."

It was the guest's turn to make critical inspection.

"You wouldn't remember me," explained the rancher. "I came in while you were gone, and only saw you the day you returned." The reminiscent look reappeared. "I used to know Landor pretty well when we were on the other side of the river, before the country settled up; but when we came over here we got too far apart and lost track of each other."

The visitor smoked a full minute in meditative silence. At last he glanced up.

"You knew he was dead, didn't you?"

"Yes. And the two youngsters grew up and got married and —" Hawkins laughed peculiarly —"made a fizzle of it."

"Knew them personally, did you?" queried Manning.

"No. I haven't seen the young folks for ten years, and I haven't even heard anything of them for six months now." He twirled the cigar with his fingers in the self-consciousness of unaccustomed gossip. "The girl went East with Landor's nephew, Craig, afterward, I understood."

"Yes."

Hawkins puffed at the cigar fiercely; then blew an avenue in the cloud of smoke obscuring his companion's face.

"I'm not usually so confoundedly curious," he apologised, "but, knowing the circumstances, I've often wondered how the affair ended. Did they hit it off well together?"

Manning settled farther back in his chair. One of his gnarled old hands fastened of a sudden upon the arm tightly.

"While the money lasted, yes."

"Money! Did they sell the ranch?"

"Mortgaged it, Craig did, until he couldn't get another cent."

"And then —"

"It's the old story."

"They went to pieces?"

"Craig left her-for another woman." The clawlike hands closed tighter and tighter. "He never really cared for Bess. He couldn't. It seems he was supporting the other woman all the time."

Hawkins sat chewing the stump of the cigar in silence. In a lean-to the cowboys were going to bed. Muffled by the intervening wall came the mocking sound of their intermittent laughter.

"And then what?" asked the rancher at last.

"Bess came back."

"Alone?"

Manning had sunk deeper and deeper into his seat. His face was concealed by the straggling grey beard, but beneath his shaggy brows his old eyes were blazing.

"Yes, she was alone," he said.

The cigar had gone dead in Hawkins's lips, and he lit it jerkily. The blaze of the match illumined a face that was not pleasant to look upon.

"And Craig himself," he suggested, "where is he?"

"He's back at the ranch by this time. He went through town yesterday, just before I left, with a man who wants to buy."

The rancher looked at the other meaningly.

"Back at the ranch-with the Indian?"

Equally directly Manning returned the look.

"Evidently you didn't hear all the story," he said. "The Indian is not there."

"No?" swiftly. "Where is he?"

Manning's free hand, his distorted hand, caught at the table before him.

"That's what I came to ask you," he returned equally swiftly. "He came here, to work for you, six months ago, when he left Bess. Do you mean to tell me you don't know where he is gone?"

Face to face the two men sat staring at each other. The sounds from the lean-to had ceased. In the silence they could hear each other breathing. For perhaps a minute they sat so; while bit by bit on the rancher's face incredulity merged into belief, and belief into understanding perfect.

"Know where he is? Of course I do-now." He leaned back in his chair. "To think that I never suspicioned who he was all the time he was here, or even when he left. I'm an ass, an ass!"

He did not now. "Tell me where he is, if you know."

"About twelve miles from here, unless he's changed camp in the last week." The rancher looked at the other understandingly. "He worked for me until about a month ago. Then he left and started away alone. We never got a word out of him while he was here, not even his name." Of a sudden came realisation complete, and his great bony fist crashed on the board. "I'm dull as a post, but I begin to understand at last, and I'm with you absolutely. I'll take you there to-night, it won't be a two-hour drive. I'll hitch up right now if you're ready."

For the first time in the last tense minutes Manning relaxed. The hand on the chair arm loosened its grip.

"I'm glad you know where he is," he said unemotionally. "I don't think we'll go to-night, though." He fumbled in his pocket and produced two fresh cigars. One he slid across the table to the other man and lit its mate carefully. "I don't think we'd better both go anyway. In the morning you can fit me out with a fresh team, if you will. I crowded things a bit on the way up."

For a moment the rancher sat staring at his guest blankly, unbelievingly; then for the second time came understanding.

"Perhaps after all you're right," he acquiesced. "It's only eighty miles, and there's plenty of time."

Beneath the craggy brows the blaze still glowed undimmed in the old storekeeper's deep-set eyes.

"Yes, there's plenty of time-after How Landor knows," he said.

In the midst of the prairie wilderness Providence had placed a tiny dawdling creek. At a point where the creek wandered through a spot a shade lower than the surrounding country, man, a man, had builded a dam. In the fulness of time the accumulated water had formed a fair-sized pond that glittered and shimmered in the sunlight, until from a little altitude it could be seen for miles. To this pond, for open water was very, very scarce on the prairie in September, came water fowl from near and afar; from no man knew where. As steel filings respond to a magnet, they came, and as inevitably; stragglingly, suspiciously by day, in flocks that grew to be a perfect cloud by night. A tent that had once been white, but that was now weather-stained and darkened by smoke, was pitched near at hand; but they minded it not. An evil-looking mouse-coloured cayuse grazed likewise, hard by; but for them a broncho had no terror. A rough blind, ingeniously fashioned from weeds and grasses, stood at the water's edge; yet again even of this they were unsuspicious. Now and anon, at long intervals, something happened, something startlingly sudden, bewilderingly loud; and in blind terror they would take wing and vanish temporarily, like smoke. But this something never pursued them, never repeated itself the same day, and invariably after a time they came back, to take up anew, with the confidence of children, the careless thread of their life where it had been interrupted.

Thus it had been for days past. Thus it was of a certain morning in late September. Though it was ten of the clock, they were still there: sleepy brown mallards, glossy-winged teal, long-necked shovellers, greyish speckled widgeon: these and others less common, representatives of all the native tribe. Happy as nature the common mother intended, as irresponsibly idle, they dawdled here and there, back and forth while time drifted swiftly by; and unknown to them, concealed from view within the blind, a dark-skinned man lay watching.

Since before daylight, ere they were yet awake, he had been there. On soundless moccasined feet he had come. Motionless as an inanimate thing, he had remained. Not two rods away the flock were feeding. More than once the water they carelessly spattered had fallen upon him; but he did not stir. He had no gun or weapon of any kind. Though they were within stone's throw, he had not brought even a rock. Unbelievable to an Anglo-Saxon sportsman, he merely lay there observing them. With that object he had come; for this purpose he remained. A long dark statue, he peered through the woven grasses steadily, admiringly; with an instinctive companionship, a mute forbearance, that was haunting in its revelation. Lonely as death itself were the surrounding unbroken prairies. Lonely as a desert of sand, their absolute isolation. Lonely beyond comparison, beyond the suggestion of language, was that silent human in their midst this autumn day.

How long he would have remained there so, idly watching, no one could have told; the man himself could not have told; for at last, interrupting, awakening, a new actor appeared. Answering, with a great quacking and beating of webbed feet, the flock sprang a-wing; and almost before the shower of water drops they scattered in their wake had ceased, a road waggon, with a greybearded old man on the seat, drew up beside the tent.

Then, for the first time in hours, the Indian arose and stretched himself. Still in silence he came back to where the newcomer was waiting.

They exchanged the conventionalities, and thereafter the white man sat eyeing the other peculiarly, analytically.

"Well, where's your game?" he queried at last. "There seemed to be enough around when I came."

The Indian smiled; the smile of one accustomed to being misunderstood.

"I wasn't hunting," he said. "I was merely watching."

A moment longer Manning continued the inspection; then with an effort he dismounted.

"I was over to see Hawkins yesterday on business," he digressed abruptly, "and he said you were out here somewhere, so I thought before I went back I'd look you up." The man was not accustomed to dissimulation, and the explanation halted lamely. "If you don't mind I'll go inside and smoke a bit."

In silence the Indian led the way to the tent and buttoned back the flap. There was but one chair and he indicated it impassively.

"I'm very glad to see you," he said then simply.

Manning lit a pipe clumsily with his crippled hand, and thereafter drew on it deliberately until the contents of the bowl were aglow. Even then, however, he did not speak. That which had been on his mind trembled now at the tip of his tongue. The one for whose ear the information was intended was waiting, listening; yet he delayed. With the suddenness of a revelation, in those last minutes, there had come to the old storekeeper an appreciation of the other he had never felt before. The message of the artificial pond and the harmless watcher at its edge had begun the alteration. A glimpse of the barren interior of the tent, with a pathetic little group of valueless trinkets arranged with infinite care on a tiny folding table, added its testimony. The sight of the man himself, standing erect in the doorway, gazing immovably out over the sunlit earth, looking and waiting, but asking no question, completed the impression. He had known this repressed human long and, as he fancied, well; but now of a sudden he realised that in fact he had not known him at all. Fearless unquestionably he had found him to be. That in a measure he was civilised, he had taken for granted; but more than this, that he was an individual among individuals, that beneath that emotionless exterior there lay a subtle, indescribable something inadequately termed soul, with the supercilious superiority of the white he had ignored. Before he had been merely a puppet: the play actor of an inferior, conquered race. Injustice, horrible, unforgivable injustice, with this being one of the injured, had been done in the white man's sight; and instinctively he had come to him as the agent of Providence calculated to mete out retribution. That an irresponsible, relentless savage lurked beneath the thin veneer of alien civilisation he had taken for granted, and builded thereon. Now with disconcerting finality he realised the thing he was doing. It was not a mere agent of divine punishment he was calling to action; but a fellow human being, an equal, with wh ose affairs he was arbitrarily meddling. Whatever the motive that had inspired his coming, however justifiable in itself, his interference, as a mere spectator, was under the circumstances unjustified and an impertinence. This he realised with startling suddenness; and swift in its wake came a new point of view, a readjustment absolute in his attitude. Under its influence the dissimulation of a moment ago vanished. From out of concealment he came fair into the open. What he knew he would reveal-if the other wished; but it was for the Indian to request, not him to proffer. With the decision he aroused. In the interval his pipe had gone dead and he lit it afresh suggestively.

"I lied to you a bit ago, How," he confessed abruptly. "It was not Hawkins I came to see at all, but you."

The dark statue did not turn, showed no sign of surprise.

"I thought so," it said simply.

Puff, puff went the white man's pipe, until even though it was daylight, the glow lit up his face.

"You did me a service once," he continued at last, "a big service-and I've not forgotten. I'll go now, or stay, as you wish."

Still the Indian stood in the doorway looking out into the careless, smiling infinite.

"I understand. You have something to tell me, something you think I should know."

The old man thumbed the ashes in the pipe bowl absently.

"I repeat, it is for you to choose."

Silence fell; a lapse so long that, old man as he was, Manning felt his heart beat more swiftly in anticipation. Then at last the Indian moved. Deliberately, noiselessly he turned. Equally deliberately he drew a robe opposite his visitor and, still very erect, sat down on the ground-his long fingers locked across his knees.

"I choose to listen," he said. "Tell me, please."

For the second time, because he needs must be doing something, the white man filled his pipe. The hand that held the tobacco pouch shook a bit now involuntarily, and a tiny puff of the brown flakes fell scattering outside the bowl onto his knee.

"About a month ago"—the speaker cleared his throat raspingly—"on August 16th it was, to be exact, there was a funeral in town. It started from the C-C ranch house and ended in the same lot with Mary Landor. It wasn't much of a funeral, either. Besides myself and Mrs. Burton no one was there." Again the voice halted; and following there came the sharp crackling of a match, and the quick puff, puff of an habitual smoker. "It was the funeral of a child: a child half Indian, half white."

Again the story paused; but the steady smoking continued.

"Go on, please," requested a voice.

"Early yesterday morning"—again the narrator halted perforce, to clear his throat—"just before I left three men went through town on their way to the same ranch. One was the owner, another a lawyer, the third a man who wished to buy. They were in a hurry. They only stopped to water their team and to visit Red Jennings's place. They are at the ranch house closing the bargain now."

"Yes," repeated the voice, "I'm listening."

The speaker did not respond at once. With the trick of the very aged when they relax, in the past minutes he seemed to have contracted physically, to have shrunk, as it were, within himself. The nervousness and uncertainty of a moment ago had passed now absolutely. The deep-set eyes of him were of a sudden glowing ominously as they had done when telling the same tale to Rancher Hawkins the night before; but that was all. His voluntary offering was given; more than this must come by request.

"I have nothing more to say-unless you wish," he repeated in the old formula.

For a second time silence fell; to be broken again by the crackling of a match in the white man's hand. Following, as though prompted by the sound, came a question.

"Why,"—the Indian did not stir, but his eyes had shifted until they looked immovably into those of his companion,—"why, please, was not the mother of the child at least at the funeral?"

"Because she could not come," impassively. "The baby was less than two days old."

"She had been back, though, back at the ranch, for some time?"

"Yes. Several weeks."

"She returned alone?"

"Yes."

"And to stay?"

Swifter and more swiftly came the questions. Even yet no muscle of the inquisitor's body stirred; but in the black eyes a light new to the other man, ominous in its belated appearance, was kindling.

"Yes," answered Manning.

"She, Bess, had left her husband?"

"No, Craig had left her."

Suddenly, instinctively, the impersonal had been dropped; but neither man noticed the change.

"There was a reason?"

"Yes," baldly. "Another woman."

The locked fingers across the Indian's knee were growing white; white as the sunlight without.

"And now he has returned, you say, to sell the ranch, her ranch?"

"It is her ranch no more. It is his."

"She, Bess, gave it to him after all that had happened, all that he had done? You mean to tell me this?"

Abruptly, instinctively, for the end was very close at hand, the white man got to his feet, stood so silent.

"Tell me." The Indian was likewise erect, his dark face standing clear against the white background of the tent wall. "Did Bess do this thing?"

"No," said a voice. "It came to him in another way."

"Another way!" swiftly. "Another way!" repeated. "Another way!" for the third time; and then a halt. For that moment realisation had come. "There could be but one other way!"

Swiftly, instinctively, the white man turned about, until the face opposite was hid. Hardened frontiersman as he was, prepared for the moment as he had thought himself, he could not watch longer. To do so was sacrilege unqualified. In his youth the man had been a hunter of big game. Of a sudden now, horribly distinct, he had a vision of the expression in the eyes of a great moose, mortally wounded, when at the end he himself had drawn the knife. Under its influence he halted, waiting, postponing the inevitable.

"There could be but one other way," repeated the voice slowly, repressedly. "Tell me, please. Let me know all. Am I not right?"

To hesitate longer was needless cruelty; and in infinite pity, the blow fell.

"Yes, How," said Manning gently, "Bess is dead."

Chapter XIX
In Sight of God Alone

An hour had passed. Manning had gone; and on the horizon to the east whither he had taken his way not even a dot now indicated his former presence. Even the close-fed grass whereon the wheels of the old road waggon had temporarily blazed a trail had returned normally erect. Suddenly, as a rain cloud forms over the parched earth, the storm had gathered and broken; and passed on as though it had not been. All about smiled the sunshine; sarcastic, isolate as though it had seen nothing, heard nothing. On the surface of the pond the ducks, again returned, swam and splashed and dawdled in their endless holiday. The eternal breeze of the prairie noontime, drifting leisurely by, sang its old, old song of abandon and of peace. Not in the merest detail had nature, the serene, altered; not by the minutest trifle had she deviated from her customary course. Man alone it is who changes to conform with the passing mood. Man alone it was amid this primitive setting who had altered now.

For How Landor, the Indian, was no longer idle or dreaming. Instead, his every action was that of one with a definite purpose. Yet even then he did not hurry. At first he seemed merely to be going about the ordinary routine of his life. Methodically he kindled a fire and prepared himself a generous meal. Deliberately, fair in the sunshine, he ate. Then for the first time an observer who knew him well would have detected the unusual. Contrary to all precedent the dishes were not washed or even touched. Instead, the meal complete, he went swiftly toward the tent and disappeared inside.

For minutes he remained within, moving about from place to place; and when he again returned it was to do a peculiar thing indeed. In his arms were several articles of clothing rolled into a bulky bundle. Without a halt he made his way back to the place where he had eaten. The fire which he had builded had burned low ere this; and, standing there beside it, he scraped away the ashes with the toe of his moccasined foot until the glowing embers beneath came to view. The bundle he carried had opened with the action, revealing clearly the various articles of which it was composed. Outside was an old army-blue greatcoat; within a battered felt hat and a pair of moccasins, wholly unused. A moment the Indian stood looking at them meditatively, intensely; then gently as though they were a lost child he was returning to its mother's arms he laid them fair upon the glowing coals. Wool is slow to catch ablaze and for the moment they lay there black against the brown earth; then of a sudden, like the first lifting of an Indian signal smoke, a tiny column of blue went trailing upward. Second by second it grew until with a muffled explosion the whole was ablaze. Before the man had merely stood watching; now deliberately as before, yet as unhesitatingly, he returned to the tent.

This time he was gone longer; and when he returned it was with an armful of books-and something more. The fire was crackling merrily now, and volume by volume his load disappeared. Then for the first time he hesitated. There was still something to destroy, something which he had gathered in the old felt hat from off his own head; yet he hesitated. Greedy as a hungry animal deprived of its due the fire at his feet kept sending out spurts of flame like longing tentacles toward him; yet he delayed. Like the sulky thing it was, it had at last drawn back into passive waiting, when of a sudden, without a single glance, the man laid this last sacrifice, as he had done the first, gently down. But this time he did not watch the end. Swiftly, his bare black head glistening in the sunlight, he started away toward the now expectant broncho; and back of him the pathetic little gathering of useless trinkets, bearing indelibly the mark of a woman's handiwork, a woman's trust, mingled with the ashes of the things which had gone before.

Long ere the fire had burned itself out, the wicked-looking cayuse following a bridle's length at his heels, he was back; waiting impatiently for the flame to die. No frontiersman, in a land where prairie fires spread as the breath of scandal, ever leaves fire alive when out of his sight; and to this instinct the Indian was true. Minute after minute he waited; until the flame vanished and in its stead there lay a mass of blazing coals. Then with a practical hand he banked the whole with a layer of earth until, look where one would, not a dot of red was visible. The act was the last, the culmination of preparation. At its end, with a single spoken command, the pony was alongside; his head high in the air, his tiny ears flattened back in anticipation. Well he knew what was in store, what was expected. No need was there of a second command nor the touch of a bridle rein. Almost ere the taking of the single leap that put the rider in his seat the little beast was away, his wide-spread nostrils breathing deep of the prairie air, the patter of his tiny hoofs a continuous song upon the close-cropped sod. As two human beings living side by side grow to know each other, so this dumb menial had grown to know his master. With a certainty attributed to the dog alone he had learned to recognise the mood of the hour. He did so now; and as time passed and the miles flowed monotonously beneath his galloping feet the relentless determination of the man himself was repeated in that undeviating pace.

Thus the journey southward was begun. Thus through the dragging hours of the September afternoon it continued. Many a time before the little beast had followed the trail from sun to sun. As well as the rider knew his own endurance he knew the possibilities of his mount, knew that now he would not fail. He did not attempt to quicken the pace, nor did he check it. He spoke no word. The earth was dry as tinder in the annual drouth of fall, and as time passed on the dust the pony raised collected upon the man's clothes and upon his bare head; but apparently he noticed it not. Shade by shade the mouse-coloured hair of the broncho grew darker from sweat, moistened until the man's hand on the diminutive beast's neck grew wet; but of this likewise he was unconscious. Silent as fate, as nature the immovable, he sat his place; his lithe body conforming involuntarily to the motion, to the play of muscles beneath his legs; yet as unconsciously as one breathes in sleep. Not until the sun was red in the west, until of its own accord the broncho had drawn up at the first bit of water they had met on the way —a shallow marshy pond-did he move. Then, while the pony drank and drank his fill, the man washed his face and hands, and more from instinct than volition, shook the dust from his clothing.

For a half hour thereafter the rider did not mount. Side by side the man and the beast moved ahead at a walk; but ever moved and ever southward. Darkness fell swiftly. There was no moon; but the sky was clear as it had been during the day, and the man needed no guide but the stars to show him the way. As he moved the hand of the Indian remained on the broncho's neck; and bit by bit as the time passed he felt the moist hair grow stiff and dry. Then, and not until then, came the final move, the beginning of the last relay. As when they had started, with one motion, apparently without an effort, he was once more in his seat; and again as at first, equally understandingly, equally willingly, that instant the broncho sprang into a lope. Relentlessly, silent as before, a ghostly animate shadow, the two forged ahead into the night and the solitude.

Meanwhile, for the second time within the year, the C-C ranch had changed hands. All day long Craig and the prospective buyer had driven about the place. One by one the cowboys had given testimony of the fraction of the herd intrusted to their care. At first resignedly complaisant, as the hours drifted by Craig had grown cumulatively impatient at the inevitably dragging inventory. Nothing but necessity absolute in the shape of an imminent foreclosure had brought him back to this land at all. Delay had followed delay until at last immediate action was imperative. Then, having agreed to come personally, he was in a fever of haste to have the deal complete and to be away. Since they had left the railroad and crossed the river the mood had been upon him. The team that had brought them out could not move fast enough. The preceding night, shortened by liquor as it had been, nevertheless dragged interminably. Strive as he might to combat the impression, to ignore it, this land had of a sudden become to him a land of terror. Every object which met his eye called forth a recollection. Every minute that passed whispered a menace. In a measure it had been so a half year ago ere he had tempted fate. Now, with the knowledge of what had occurred in that time staring him in the face, the impression augmented immeasurably, haunted him like a ghostly presence. Not for a minute since his return had he been alone. Not for an instant had he been without a revolver at hand.

All the previous night, despite the grumbling protest of the overseer with whom he had bunked, a lamp had burned beside the bed; yet even then he could not sleep. Whether or no he felt contrition for the past, this man, he could not have told, he never paused to consider. All he knew was that he had a deathly fear of this silent waste and of a certain human who dwelt somewhere therein. Repugnant as consideration of the return had been, it was as nothing compared with the reality. Had he realised in advance what the actual experience of his coming would mean, even the consideration of money, badly as he needed it, could not have bought his presence. Now that he was here he must needs see the transaction through; he could not well do otherwise; but as the afternoon drew to a close and the necessity of tarrying a second night became assured, the premonition of retribution, that had before lowered merely as a possibility, loomed into the proportions of certainty. Then it was that in abandon he began to drink; not at stated intervals, as had been his habit, but frequently, all but continuously, until even his tolerant companions had exchanged glances of understanding.

To all things, however, there is an end, and at last the deal was complete. Within the stuffy living-room, hazy now with tobacco smoke, by the uncertain light of a sputtering kerosene lamp Craig had accomplished a sprawling signature and received in return a check on a Chicago bank. It was already late, and very soon the new owner, with a significant look at a half-drained flask by the other's hand, and a curt "Good-night," had departed for bed. Immediately following, with a thinly veiled apology, the lawyer had likewise excused himself, and Craig and his one-time overseer were alone. For five minutes thereafter the two men sat so in silence; then, at last, despite his muddled brain, the former realised that the big Irishman was observing him with a concentration that was significant. Ever short of temper, the man's nerves were stretched to the jangling point this night, and the look irritated him. Responsive, he scowled prodigiously.

"Well," he queried impatiently, "what is it?"

No answer; only, if possible, the look became more analytic than before.

"What's on your mind?" repeated Craig. "You make me nervous staring that way. Speak up if you've got anything to say. Don't you like my selling and putting you out of a job?"

"No, it's not that," refuted the Hibernian. "There are plenty of other places I can get. I could stay right here for that matter if I wanted to-but I don't. I wouldn't live in this house any longer if my pay were doubled." As he spoke he had looked away. Now of a sudden his glance returned. "I meant to quit anyway, whether you sold or not."

"Why so?" queried Craig, and unconsciously the scowl was repeated. "You seemed glad enough to come."

"I was-then," shortly.

"And why not now? Talk up, if you've any grievance. Don't sit there like a chimpanzee, hugging it."

"You know why well enough," ignored the other. He passed a knotty hand through his shock of red whiskers absently. "I've expected the devil or worse here every night these last weeks."

Craig tried to laugh; but the effort resulted in failure.

"God," he satirised, "who'd ever imagined you were the superstitious sort! Weren't you ever in a place where anyone died before?"

"I never was where a woman and her child were murdered," deliberately.

Quick as thought Craig's red face whitened.

"Damn you, O'Reilly," he challenged, "you're free with your tongue." He checked himself. "I don't wish to quarrel with you to-night, though," he conciliated.

"Nor I with you," returned the other impassively. "I was merely telling you the truth. Besides, it's none of my affair; and even if it were, I'm thinking you'll pay for it dear enough before you're through."

Craig straightened in his seat; but not as before in attitude supercilious.

"What the deuce do you mean, O'Reilly? You keep suggesting things, but that is all. Talk plain if you know anything."

"I don't know anything," impassively; "unless it is that I wouldn't be in your shoes if I got a dollar for every cent you've made out of this cursed business."

Bit by bit Craig's face whitened. If anything the air of conciliation augmented.

"You think circumstances weren't to blame?" he queried. "That, in other words, I've brought things about as they are deliberately?"

"I don't think anything. I know what you've done-and what you've got to answer for."

Instinctively, almost with a shudder, Craig glanced about him.

The shade of the single window was up, and of a sudden he arose unsteadily and drew it over the blackness outside with a jerk.

"You're beastly hard on me," he commented, "but let that pass. It's probably the last time we'll ever see each other, and we may as well part friends." He was back in his place again with the flask before him, and with a propitiatory motion he extended the liquor toward the other man. "Come, let's forget it," he insinuated. "Have a drink with me."

"Not a drop."

"Not if I requested it?"

"Not if you got down on your knees and begged."

"All right." The hand was withdrawn with a nervous little laugh. "I'll have to spoil it all myself, then."

The Irishman watched in silence while the other gulped down swallow after swallow. The hand of the drinker trembled uncontrollably, and a tiny red stream trickled down the unshaven chin to the starched linen beneath.

"If you'll take a word of advice," commented the spectator at last, "you'll cut that-for the time being at least." He hesitated; then went on reluctantly. "I've been in your pay and I'll try to be square with you. If you've got an atom of presentiment you'll realise that this is no place for you to get into the shape you're getting." Again he halted, and again with an effort he gave the warning direct. "If I were you I wouldn't be at this ranch a second longer than it took me to leave; not as long as I had a broncho or a leg or a crutch to go on."

Slowly and more slowly came the words. Then followed silence, with the two men staring each other face to face. Breaking it, the overseer arose.

"I've said more than I intended already," he added, "and now I wash my hands of you. Do as you please. I'm going to bed."

Preventing, of a sudden sobered, Craig was likewise on his feet.

"In common decency, even if you're no friend of mine, don't go, O'Reilly," he pleaded. He had no thought of superiority now, no thought of malice; only of companionship and of protection. "I know what you mean. I'm no fool, and what you suggest is exactly what's been driving me insane these last two days. I'm going in the morning, as soon as it's daylight; the team is all ordered; but to-night, now —" instinctively he glanced at the window where recollection pictured the darkness without —"I haven't nerve to face it now. I'd go plumb mad out there alone."

The Irishman shrugged in silence and attempted to pass.

"Please don't go," repeated Craig swiftly. "I know I'm acting like a child, but this cursed country's to blame. Stay with me this last night. I couldn't sleep, and it's madness to be alone. See me through this and I swear you'll not regret it. I swear it!"

Just for a second O'Reilly paused; then of a sudden his face flamed red through his untrimmed beard.

"To hell with your money!" he blazed. "I wouldn't lift my finger for you if How Landor were to come this second." He checked himself and took a step forward meaningly. "Besides, I couldn't help you any if I would. God himself couldn't protect you now unless He performed a miracle. Out of my way. I tell you I'm done with you." Craig had not stirred. He did not now; and of a sudden the overseer turned to pass around. As he did so for the first time he faced the single window that looked north toward the second ranch house: the house which How Landor had builded to receive his bride. The curtain was still down, but to the Irishman's quick eye there rested upon it now a dull glow that was not a reflection of the light within. A second after he noticed the man halted, looking at it, speculating as to its meaning. Then of a sudden he realised; and in two steps he was across the room and simultaneously the obscuring shade shot up with a crash. Instantly following, startlingly unexpected, the red glow without sprang through the glass and filled the room.

"Fire!" announced the observer involuntarily to the sleepers above. "The other ranch house is afire!" Then, as they were slow in awakening, the cry was repeated more loudly: "Fire! Fire!"

A conflagration is the universal contagion, the one excitement that never palls. Forth into the night, forgetful of his companion, forgetful of all save the interest of the moment, rushed O'Reilly. Half dressed, hatless, working with buttons as they went, Parker, the new owner, and Mead, the lawyer, descended the rickety stairs like an avalanche and without pausing to more than look followed running in his wake. The unused ranch house was dry as cardboard and was burning fiercely. Though there was still no moon and the overseer had several minutes the start, against the light they could see his running figure distinctly. Standing in the living-room as they rushed through, white faced, hesitant, was Clayton Craig; but though he had spoken to them-they both recalled that fact afterward-neither had paused to listen or to answer. That he would not follow never occurred to them until minutes thereafter. Not until, panting, struggling for breath after the unusual effort, they had covered the intervening mile, and the heat of the already diminishing fire was on their faces, did they think of him at all. Even then it was not the first thought which occurred; for the moment they arrived O'Reilly, who was waiting, turned, facing them excitedly.

"Do you see that?" he queried, pointing to a black band that surrounded the building in a complete circle.

Parker nodded understandingly; but Mead, who was city bred, looked mystified. "What is it?" he returned.

"A firebreak," explained the Irishman. "Someone didn't want the blaze to spread and scattered earth clear around the place, with a spade." Leaning over he picked up a clod and thumbed it significantly. "It hasn't been done a half hour. The dirt isn't even dry."

Brief as the time had been, already the frail walls were settling to embers. There was nothing to do; and standing there the three men looked understandingly into each other's faces. The same thought stood clear on all; for all alike knew every detail of the story.

"The Indian, How Landor," suggested Mead adequately.

"Yes," corroborated Parker, "and I'm glad of it. I'm not squeamish, but the Lord knows I'd never have used the place myself."

Of a sudden, O'Reilly, who had turned and was staring into the blaze, faced about. That second he had remembered.

"Where's Craig?" he queried swiftly, glancing back the way they had come. "Didn't he follow?"

Until that moment none of the three had thought of the other man. Now they realised that they were alone. But even then two of the trio did not understand.

"Evidently he didn't start," said Mead. "He couldn't have missed the light if he did."

"I remember now he was standing by the door when we left," added Parker.

"Standing by the door, was he?" took up the Irishman swiftly. "As there's a Heaven and a Hell he's not standing there now, I'll wager!"

Again face to face, as when they had first caught sight of that meaning black band, the three spectators there beneath the stars stood staring at each other. It was O'Reilly again who broke the silence.

"Don't you people understand yet what this all means, what's happened?" he interrogated unbelievingly.

"It means there's been an incendiary here; I guess there's no doubt about that," said Mead.

"Yes," blurted O'Reilly, "and that incendiary's How Landor, and he's been here within the half hour; and Craig's been alone back there in the ranch house." He paused for breath. "Can't you see now? At last the Indian has found out!"

For the fraction of a minute, while understanding came home, not a man stirred. Then of a sudden Parker turned swiftly and started back into the night.

"By the Eternal," he corroborated, "I believe you're right. We can't get there a second too quick."

"Too quick!" caught up the Irishman for the last time. "We couldn't get there quick enough if we had wings. It's all over before this, take my word for it."

And it was. Though the men ran every step of the mile back they were too late. As O'Reilly had anticipated, the ranch house was empty, deserted. Similarly the stables hard by. Likewise the adjoining tool shed. Though they searched every nook, until a mouse could not have escaped detection, they found not a trace of him for whom they looked, nor a clue to his disappearance. Though they shouted his name until they were hoarse not an answer came back from the surrounding darkness. Within the ranch house itself, or upon the dooryard without, there was no sign of a struggle or of aught unusual. The living-room was precisely as it had been at that last moment when O'Reilly had left. Craig's cap and topcoat were on a chair as he had thrown them down. At the stable every horse was within its own stall: every piece of saddlery was intact. While the three men were looking, attracted by the blaze, the distant cowboys one by one began drifting in; and when they had heard the tale joined in the search. All through the night, in ever-widening circles, lanterns, like giant fireflies, played around the premises until they covered a radius of a half mile; but ever the report was the same. With the coming of morning not the home force alone but men from distant ranches appeared. The reflection of fire on the sky reaches far indeed on the prairie, and ere the sun shone again a goodly company was assembled. Then it was that the real search began and a swarm of riders scoured the country for miles and miles. And once more, from all, the testimony was as before. There was not a clue to the disappearance, nor the semblance of a clue. As out of the darkness of night surrounding, a great horned owl swoops down upon its prey, and as mysteriously disappears, so the Indian had come and gone; and satisfied at last, irresistibly awed as well into an unwonted quiet, one by one, as they had arrived, the ranchers dispersed-and the search was over.

And to this day that disappearance remains a mystery unsurmountable. One morning a week later, after Mead and O'Reilly had gone, when the new master of the ranch arose it was to find a wicked-looking mouse-coloured cayuse standing motionless by the stable door. Upon him was neither saddle nor bridle nor mark of any kind. Somewhere out on that limitless waste he had been released, and, true to an unerring homing instinct, he had returned; but from where no man could do more than speculate. He could not speak, and his rider was seen no more. Somewhere out there amid that same solitude a thing of mystery had come to pass; but what it was only Nature and Nature's God, who alone were witness, could ever know.